THE LONDON JILT

broadview editions
series editor: L.W. Conolly

THE LONDON JILT;
OR, THE POLITICK WHORE

Anonymous

edited by Charles H. Hinnant

broadview editions

Library and Archives Canada Cataloguing in Publication

The London jilt, or, The politick whore / Anonymous ; edited by Charles H. Hinnant.

(Broadview editions)
Attributed to Alexander Oldys by some sources.
Includes bibliographical references.
ISBN 978-1-55111-737-9

I. Hinnant, Charles H.   II. Oldys, Alexander.   III. Title: Politick whore.
IV. Series.

PR3291.A1L65 2007   823'.4   C2007-904890-0

Broadview Editions
The Broadview Editions series represents the ever-changing canon of literature in English by bringing together texts long regarded as classics with valuable lesser-known works.

Advisory editor for this volume: Morgan Rooney

Broadview Press is an independent, international publishing house, incorporated in 1985. Broadview believes in shared ownership, both with its employees and with the general public; since the year 2000 Broadview shares have traded publicly on the Toronto Venture Exchange under the symbol BDP.

We welcome comments and suggestions regarding any aspect of our publications—please feel free to contact us at the addresses below or at broadview@broadviewpress.com.

North America
Post Office Box 1243, Peterborough, Ontario, Canada K9J 7H5
2215 Kenmore Avenue, Buffalo, NY, USA 14207
Tel: (705) 743-8990; Fax: (705) 743-8353;
email: customerservice@broadviewpress.com

UK, Ireland, and continental Europe
NBN International, Estover Road, Plymouth PL6 7PY UK
Tel: 44 (0) 1752 202300   Fax: 44 (0) 1752 202330
email: enquiries@nbninternational.com

Australia and New Zealand
UNIREPS, University of New South Wales
Sydney, NSW, 2052 Australia
Tel: 61 2 9664 0999; Fax: 61 2 9664 5420
email: info.press@unsw.edu.au

www.broadviewpress.com

This book is printed on paper containing 100% post-consumer fibre.

Typesetting and assembly: True to Type Inc., Claremont, Canada.

PRINTED IN CANADA

Contents

Acknowledgements

I would particularly like to thank my friend and colleague, George Justice, for his enthusiasm, encouragement, and unfailingly helpful comments on all aspects of this project. Thanks also to Jim May, Kevin Berland, and Jim Chevallier for assistance on specific points. I also want to thank Ann Barker, Karen Paulik, and Kelli Hansen of Ellis Library at the University of Missouri, and Erin Gray of the Washington University Library for their practical advice and assistance. I am grateful to ProQuest Information and Learning Company of Ann Arbor, Michigan, for permission to use the complete text of *The London Jilt* from the microfilm version in the Wing Short Title Catalogue series and the digitized version in Literature Online. My thanks to the Pro-Quest Information and Learning Company for permission to use excerpts from Cervantes's *Don Quixote*, Richard Head's *The English Rogue, Volume I*, Francis Kirkman's *The English Rogue, Volume III*, the anonymous *Whore's Rhetorick*, and *Advice to the Women and Maidens of London*, Aphra Behn's *The Younger Brother* and *The Rover*, Alexander Oldys's *The Female Gallant*, and the anonymous *London Bully* in the microfilm version of the Wing Short Title Catalogue series and digitized versions of *The English Rogue, Volume I*, *The English Rogue, Volume III*, *Moll Flanders*, *The Case of Mary Carleton Considered*, *The Female Gallant*, and *The London Bully* in Literature Online. I also want to express my gratitude to Gabe Hornstein of AMS Press for permission to publish in the introduction to my edition an altered version of some parts of my essay *"Moll Flanders, Roxana,* and First-Person Female Narratives: Models and Prototypes," *The Eighteenth-Century Novel,* ed. Albert J. Rivero and George Justice, 4 (2004): 39-72. Copyright © 2005 by AMS Press. All rights reserved; reproduced and used by permission of AMS Press, Inc. New York. A part of the Introduction was published as "Forum: *The London Jilt*," in *Restoration: Studies in English Literary Culture: 1660-1700,* 29 (2005): 53-64.

Introduction

Whenever we survey the development of the novel, we are likely to take note of a tradition that is carefully divided into "major" and "minor" authors. We might trace a central line of descent in early English fiction, for example, from Aphra Behn to Eliza Haywood, Delarivier Manley, and Daniel Defoe. A short list of novels by lesser-known authors might include Richard Head's *The English Rogue, Volume I* (1666), Henry Neville's *The Isle of Pines* (1668), Dr. Walter Charleton's *The Cimmerian Matron* (1668), and William Congreve's *Incognita* (1692). What would probably be left out of consideration are the numerous contributions of writers known only as "Anon.," contributions that during the latter part of the seventeenth century included not only songs and minor lyrics; libels, lampoons, and political satires; scurrilous broadside ballads and translations of continental erotica; but also novels and romances.

The London Jilt; or, the Politick Whore belongs to this rich tradition of novels and romances by anonymous authors. A work of picaresque fiction published in two parts in 1683, it survives in only one copy, owned by the Harvard University Library. Yet there are at least two compelling reasons why it deserves to be considered alongside novels by major and minor authors. To begin with, it may very well be the finest (and by far the most entertaining) picaresque novel published in English in the late sixteenth and seventeenth centuries. It is superior in popular appeal, I would argue, to Thomas Nashe's *The Unfortunate Traveller* (1594) and Head's *The English Rogue*. Second, *The London Jilt* is the only picaresque novel produced in English in which the first-person narrator is a woman. In this regard, it may have provided a broad model for Daniel Defoe's *Moll Flanders* (1722) and *Roxana* (1724). There are a number of features of the narrative which suggest that Defoe may have had this text in mind rather than the more conventionally suggested sources when he was composing his two great novels.

The Novel's History and Significance

In spite of its anonymity, *The London Jilt* was initially well received. According to Roger Thompson, the only scholar who, so far as I know, has actually studied the novel, a second "corrected" edition appeared in 1684 and the novel, judging "by a preliminary analysis of library sales catalogues of the 1680s and 1690s, ... was second only to *The English Rogue* in popularity" during the period.[1] If the contemporary appeal of a novel can be measured by the currency of the name in its title, *The London Jilt* must have been widely known. It was incorporated into the title of a third-person criminal biography of a woman who was convicted for numerous felonies in 1684,[2] and introduced a broadside ballad entitled "The London Jilt's Lamentation, or a hue-and-cry after a lac'd smock," tentatively dated between 1685 and 1688.

Yet it is not difficult to understand why *The London Jilt*, in spite of its positive initial reception, soon fell into oblivion. It belongs to a large category of anonymous texts published in the seventeenth century that lack what Michel Foucault, in a well-known essay entitled "What is an Author," termed "the author function." By this Foucault meant the various purposes the *name* of an author might serve in relation to any given text. It was in the seventeenth and eighteenth centuries, Foucault argues, that

> literary discourse came to be accepted only when endowed with the author function. We now ask of each poetic or fictional text: From where did it come, who wrote it, when, under what circumstances, or beginning with what design? The meaning ascribed to it or value accorded it depend on the manner in which we answer these questions.[3]

Foucault's before-and-after chronology seems simplistic to many readers, but the inability of *The London Jilt* to supply answers to any of his questions helps to explain why it has virtually disappeared from literary history. In *The London Jilt*, the anonymity entailed by the improprieties of whorish speech extends as well to the implied author of the preface. It is impossible to be certain why the person who was responsible for *The London Jilt* allowed it to remain anonymous, but its transgressive style and subject

---

1 For further details concerning the novel's contemporary reception, see Thompson, "The London Jilt," *Harvard Library Bulletin*, 23 (1975): 293.

2 Anon. *The German Princess Revived or The London Jilt: Being a True Account of the Life and Death of Jenny Voss* (London: George Croom, 1684).

3 Foucault, *Aesthetics, Method and Epistemology*, ed. James D. Faubion (New York: The New Press, 1998), 213, Vol. 2 of *The Essential Works of Michel Foucault*, 3 vols. to date, 1997-.

matter offers a compelling reason why its authorship was never acknowledged.

It is significant, moreover, that *The London Jilt* appeared in aftermath of the expiration of the Licensing Act in 1679. In a study of London trade publishers between 1675 and 1750, Michael Treadwell observes that after 1679 authors were "less ready than ever before to put their names to what they issued" and detects "a rise in the number of nameless, initialed, and false imprints in the period 1679-1683."[1] These include not only novels and romances but also anonymous adaptations of continental libertine texts including *The School of Venus* (1680), *The Whore's Rhetorick* (1683), and *Tullia and Octavia* (1684). Although there have been attempts to identify the authors of many of these works, the attribution of *The London Jilt* by the early twentieth-century bibliographer, Arundell Esdaile, to an obscure poet and novelist, Alexander Oldys, is particularly unconvincing, for Esdaile's attribution was based, as Thompson noted, upon an obvious mistake. He confused the 1683 *The London Jilt* with a totally different kind of novel called *The Female Gallant or, the Female Cuckold* that Oldys published in 1692 and had as its variant title, *The London Jilt: or, the Female Cuckold.*[2]

There is at least one other novel, however, that deserves to be compared with *The London Jilt*. It is entitled *The London Bully*, a picaresque fiction that was also published anonymously in 1683. A comparison of the full titles of the two works discloses a possible family resemblance:

The London Jilt or, the Politick Whore, Shewing, All the Artifices and Stratagems which the Ladies of Pleasure make use of for the Intreaguing and Decoying of Men; Interwoven with Several Pleasant Stories of the Misses Ingenious Performances. London: Printed for Henry Rhodes, 1683.

The London Bully or the Prodigal Son, Displaying the Principal Cheats of Our Modern Debauchees; with the Secret Practices and Cabals of the Lewd Apprentices of this Town: Discovered in the Life

---

1 Treadwell, "London Trade Publishers 1675-1750," *The Library*, 6th Ser. 4.2 (June, 1982): 130.

2 Thompson, "The London Jilt," 293. Esdaile mistakenly listed *The Female Gallant* as the second edition of *The London Jilt*. See *A List of English Tales and Prose Romances Printed before 1740* (London: Bibliographical Society, 1912), 279.

& Actions of an Eminent Citizens Son. London: Printed by Hen. Clark for Tho. Malthus, 1683.

Even though a link between the two works can never be established with certainty, *The London Bully* is a lively low-life adventure narrative that bears a striking resemblance to *The London Jilt* and thus may have been intended by its author to serve as a companion piece to the latter. Selections from *The Female Gallant* and *The London Bully* are available for comparison in Appendix D. Like *The London Jilt*, *The London Bully* also survives in only one copy, located in the Bodleian Library.

The London Jilt and *The London Bully* also employ a common convention: the insertion of a preface in which an anonymous author justifies the publication of the novel in harshly moralistic terms. Defending the purpose of *The London Jilt* as an exposure of the wiles commonly employed by the whorish seductress to arouse and cheat men at the same time, the author describes his presentation of the jilt as a caution to the (male) reader:

> Shee is here set before thee as a Beacon to warn thee of the Shoales and Quick-sands, on which thou wilt of necessity Shipwrack thy All, if thou blindly and wilfully continuest and perserverest in steering that Course of Female Debauchery, which will inevitably prove at length thy utter Destruction. (41)

By publishing the whore's confession, the author aims to expose her wiles upon behalf of all men; it is a way of allowing her to reveal her whoredom, to show the truth behind her snares and artifices, the truth of her snares and artifices.

Yet it would be a mistake to assume that the subsequent whore's narrative carries out this program in any straightforward manner. What if her confession, when not represented as if governed by the moralizing purpose of the editor, were somehow quite different from what his comments might lead us to expect? What if, instead of simply disclosing a body of professional secrets, it also relates the much more sympathetic first-person account of a woman who follows the example of her mother in turning to prostitution only after her father is cheated out of his estate and they are thrust into the world without resources? In *The London Jilt*, the whore's struggles are as much economic as amorous and include her encounters with a variety of libidinous and unsatisfactory male figures. Her career is also marked by the kind of comic pranks that can be found in English fiction as late as Frances Burney's *Evelina* (1778), where a bluff naval officer, Captain Mirvan, plays a practical joke on an affected French lady, Madame Duval, and some jaded aristocrats arrange a cruel foot race between two elderly women. Crowded with adventures and escapades, *The London Jilt* contains picaresque elements like perilous flights from danger, transvestite disguises, and numerous episodes of sex, violence, and revenge.

To a degree, the appearance of *The London Jilt* also coincided with the assimilation into an indigenous English tradition of translations of Spanish picaresque fictions featuring female protagonists. A truncated version of Lòpez de Ubeda's *La Picara Justina* (1605) variously entitled *Justina, The Country Jilt,* and *The Spanish Jilt* was adapted into English by Captain John Stevens and first published in 1707, while Alonso de Castillo Solorzano's *La garduña de Sevilla* (1642) was translated by John Davies as *La Picara, or the Triumphs of Female Subtilty* (1665) and then by Roger L'Estrange and J. Ozell as *The Spanish Pole-cat.*[1] The female speaker of *The Spanish Jilt* somehow manages, through a series of witty stratagems, to preserve her maidenhead from the clutches of predatory males right up until her marriage at the close of the novel. Still, she displays the same astringent realism as other female *picaras*, as, for example, when she declares of marriage

> now a-days Love is Bought and Sold, and the fairest Bidder carries the Prize; *It is money makes the Mare to go,* and an *Ass* loaded with *Gold* is more acceptable than the Noblest Creature without that Ornament. A certain *Scholar* I remember, told me, *That in Love there were two Cases, the* Dative first, *and then follow'd the* Genitive. In short, it is *Money,* that carries all before it, *Money* covers all Defects, *Money* gives all Perfections, and without *Money* nothing is good and tollerable in this World.[2]

In contrast to Ubeda's virtuous protagonist, the anti-heroine of Solorzano's third-person whore's tale, *La garduña de Sevilla,* is an out-and-out thief who, along with a male accomplice and

---

1 *The Spanish Pole-cat; or the Adventures of Senior Rusina in Four Books,* trans. Roger L'Estrange and J. Ozell (London: E. Curll, 1717).

2 *Justina, the Country Jilt,* in *The Spanish Libertines,* trans. and adapted by Captain John Stevens (London: J. How, 1707, rpt. 1709), 61.

lover, cheats a wealthy miser out of his estate. The female pro-tagonist of *The London Jilt*, it should be noted, cannot be identi-fied with either stereotype. Occupying a mid-point between the whorish trickster and the resourceful but virtuous domestic heroine, she refuses to allow herself to be pinned down, declin-ing, at one point, "to give the Reader an Occasion to have too good, or too ill an Opinion of my Life" (134).[1]

Authorial Commentary

The positive characteristics that suggest that *The London Jilt* deserves to be compared favorably to these Spanish predecessors can be grasped from Thompson's observation that the work "has the great and rare advantage of a strong and unified narrative and a sustained attempt to develop the jilt's character through the first person."[2] In this respect, it differs from Mrs. Dorothy's nar-rative in the third part of Francis Kirkman's expansion of *The English Rogue* (1665), another whore's tale that the author of *The London Jilt* might have known. In contrast to *The London Jilt*, Kirkman's narrative, like most picaresque novels, tends to dis-solve into a string of isolated episodes and Mrs. Dorothy is not developed very fully as a character. Equally important, Mrs. Dorothy smothers two of her children at birth and later murders her maid after persuading her to serve as a virginal stand-in during Mrs. Dorothy's wedding night. As a result, she bears a closer resemblance to the female protagonists of criminal biogra-phies, dwelling in a murky world of moral depravity to which the young heroine of *The London Jilt* is never allowed to descend.

The coherence of *The London Jilt* can be seen through two of its most prominent features. The first is the careful and explicit plotting of the jilt's stages of life. At one point she observes, "I perceived that my Beauty and Youth began to perish by little and little" (146), then later that "my age was encreased, and that my Beauty was diminished" (157); near the end of her narrative, she declares, "Years have rendred me so ugly, that no Body now comes to torment me any more" (167). The sequence and variety

---

1 Her character may be contrasted with the portraits of other picaresque heroines in Appendix A.

2 Roger Thompson, *Unfit for Modest Ears: A Study of the Pornographic, Obscene, and Bawdy Works Written and Published in England in the Second Half of the Seventeenth Century* (Totowa, NJ: Rowman and Littlefield, 1979), 77.

of sexual episodes and comic escapades are thus ordered through an easily recognizable movement from youth to old age. The second is the appearance, disappearance, and belated reappearance at unexpected moments of characters who play an important part in the protagonist's life, particularly her mother and the "rope-dancer," a rogue who cheats her father out of his wealth and hastens his early death. The anonymous author's use of the reappearing character—itself a familiar plot device of romance—provides a way of linking episodes that would otherwise appear disparate and thus has nothing of gratuitous invention about it.

What contributes most to the internal unity of the novel, however, is the authorial discourse that runs through the text. Although the author of the preface claims that the text is designed to alert the reader to the ruses and artifices of women, the first person narrative has the effect of investing the protagonist with an indomitable independence and vitality. The jilt, identified in only one letter as Cornelia, has a gift for opinionated commentary that turns out to be quite disarming. In fact, we learn a great deal about Cornelia, both about her history and opinions. The author uses imagery in such a way that her character is established as much through the way she expresses herself as through what she says. However she may deceive other characters, she is always candid with the reader. At one point, she confesses, "people must not however imagine that I am too great an Enemy of the female Sex, on the contrary, I know very well that my duty engages me to bear it affection: but at present I hate all manner of dissimulation and am in love with nothing so much as plain dealing" (156). The author frequently adapts to the jilt's jaundiced view of life the homely imagery of popular sayings:

It appears sufficiently that the Common Proverb is true, *If Lasciviousness renders maidens mad, it makes Widdows devils.* (76)

Wherefore the Spanish Proverb says very patt, and to the Purpose, *Tell a Woman but once shee's handsom, and the Devil will tell it to her a thousand Times afterwards.* (109)

The warnings contained in these supposed proverbs are at one with the worldly prudential outlook of the central character. So also is the author's manipulation of the *topoi* of erotic language. Carefully avoiding the crude, scurrilous vocabulary of Restoration libels and invectives, the author fashions a discourse that is appropriate to the jilt's ambiguous status as a lady of pleasure, dwelling uneasily, as she does, in a liminal state between respectable marriage and common prostitution. She is particularly given to the type of circumlocution that attracts more attention to what she is selling than a crude bluntness might have: she refers at various points to "my garden of love," (85) "my commodity," (116) "my *Tuzzy-Muzzy*" (166). Cornelia's oblique yet erotically suggestive use of language can be seen in one of her favorite phrases; describing the seductiveness of a male suitor, she says on more than one occasion that "his Tongue was ... admirably well hung" (55).

The jilt's manner of speaking, insofar as it can be dissociated from what she says, seems quite distinctive. In her penchant for digressions, she bears an obvious resemblance to Chaucer's the Wife of Bath. The large number of parentheses in Cornelia's discourse as well as the looseness of her grammatical construction may be legitimately related to her character. At one point early in the narrative, her penchant for moralizing commentary almost makes her lose the thread of her argument: "But by these sort of extravagant Discourses I might wander too far from my Design, that I should almost forget what I have to say" (52). Later, in discoursing about cosmetics, she muses

> because there are so many several sorts of paint, and this artifice is become very common in our time, perhaps the pains I should take would be very little to the purpose; besides, I have another reason for which I am not willing to engage in this matter, which is, that I should stand in need of ten times as much Paper as is fitting for the bulk of this Book to be. (155-56)

Cornelia in this way explores, as it were, the connection between the artifice of women making up their faces and the artifice of the author making up a book. The self-consciousness of such reflections are part and parcel of her character. By giving her a lifelike individuality in this distinctive fashion, the author constructs a character who is the embodiment of worldly experience, determined freedom of thought and expression, and candid pragmatism.

The jilt's "way of writing"—which she characterizes at one point as "something bold and libertine" (168)—is not, however, merely a matter of digressions. Throughout the narrative, there is a wilful neglect or casual flouting of canons of spelling, diction, punctuation, grammar, and syntax, a self-consciously colloquial and impolite manner of presentation, an attempt, explicitly asserted, to pursue the level of spoken rather than written English:

> Do but, I beseech you, take notice of the ingratitude that all these men are guilty of: This fine Gallant had obtained of another the Favour of being brought to my House; and as soon as his Crotchets had made him fancy, that he was deeply rooted in my Heart, he would willingly have recompensed him to whom he had Obligation, by having him banished from a house that he had frequented for so long a time. (141-42)

Here and elsewhere Cornelia presents herself as a writer who has no practice in formal rhetoric, no fixed ideas about style, and, above all, no literary pretensions. She therefore opts for the only approach that is consistent with her irregular manner of life, one that disregards the niceties of composition, taking an obvious delight in colorful neologisms and ungrammatical turns of phrase. She assumes that she can carry off this idiosyncratic triumph over verbal propriety precisely because she imagines that any reader who is desirous of reading her confessions is unlikely to be a pedant or to judge her by the norms of an emergent standard of English prose.

This wandering from the norms of correct English appears unquestionably deliberate in a novel whose constant digressions are presented as the unavoidable result of the heroine's "Libertine way of Living" (161). Indeed the commentary derives part of its fascination from the wealth of observation, lore, and doctrine it incorporates into her digressions. The various topics that the author of the preface promises under the rubric of "Stratagems and Artifices" involve dress, cosmetics, feminine wiles, feminine hygiene, primitive contraceptives, and premarital sexuality, with all the detail that these subjects comprehend. To a certain extent, this material represents a point of view—often tinged with misogyny—that is diametrically opposed to the interests of the jilt. After describing the way she uses a watch to deceive a worthy merchant, she muses

> You young Sprouts, who will undoubtedly read my Life with more diligence than you have for a Godly Book, and which causes so much Grief and Charges to your Parents, and who are often the occasion of exhausting their Coffers, you may judge by these Samples what you are to expect of the Female

Sex, for I am neither the only one, nor the first, who has made use of these Artifices. (81)

At another point, she reflects upon the folly of anyone who enters into her kind of life for any other reason than dire poverty:

> But the Truth is, when I make Reflection upon the Disquiet which attends those who lead a disorderly Life, I cannot sufficiently admire [wonder] that there are Persons who commit such Sins, without being obliged thereto by Necessity: For to see a Woman abandon herself to Pleasure, for the maintaining her self in a handsome Estate and Condition; and who has not nevertheless the Conveniencies, is methinks in some manner worthy of being excused, because that Poverty is a very terrible thing; and besides it is very troublesome, nay, almost insupportable for Persons who have been well bred and born, when they are constrain'd to subject themselves to go to Service; but as for those Women who give themselves to those villanous Abominations, when Misery does not force them so to do, Methinks there is nothing in the world that merits more Blame and Chastisement. (133-34)

This kind of moralizing commentary might easily be dismissed as an example of the kind of editorial intervention promised in the preface. Yet by openly acknowledging the scandalous nature of her life, Cornelia may not be justifying it, but she is not ruling out a debate concerning the material conditions that must exist in order for women to be able to preserve their reputations and remain virtuous. This attitude, openly reflexive, is not foreshadowed in the preface; Cornelia seeks to justify not only herself but women in general. Although some women may abandon themselves to "villanous abominations," it is always possible to show how and why they were drawn into scandal. A very few may take to it all too readily, but for most women it is a matter of cruel necessity.

The term "politick whore" helps to confirm the significance of this complicated focus. While the word "whore" was theoretically interchangeable with "prostitute" in the late seventeenth century, this novel, like many plays and poems of the period, draws distinctions between exclusive whores and their more common and numerous counterparts. A lady of pleasure and a streetwalker were seen as the two ends of a spectrum. Whereas streetwalkers were associated with transient sexual encounters, often taking place outdoors, ladies of pleasure established more enduring, romantic relationships usually indoors, in discreet private quarters. Although Cornelia never ascends to the top of the social pyramid as a royal mistress at the court of Charles II, she is never answerable to a procuress and at one point laments the fate of "those poor Creatures" who "have hardly what's sufficient to satisfie their Hunger," while "Bawds and Hostesses dispose of their Money as they please, and live with these poor innocent Females just as the *Turks* do with their *Slaves*" (97). Cornelia proves willing at the beginning of the second part of the novel to abandon her life as a jilt for marriage to a man with whom she has fallen in love. James Grantham Turner has recently drawn attention to the significance of this reconceptualization of the whore for the evolution of the novel. Examining Ferrante Pallavicino's parodic rhetorical treatise, *La Retorica delle Puttane* (1642), published in an English adaptation in 1683 as *The Whore's Rhetorick*, Turner holds that it constitutes a "proto-novelistic shift" in which the courtesan, "no longer the earthy whore" of Renaissance fame, "must simulate a respectable woman swayed by genuine passion." Turner concludes that

> Pallavicino in effect *rehearses* novelistic realism by showing how to construct a new form of subjectivity, a consistent and close-woven character 'unfolded' (*piegata*) in all its particularizing 'details.' Gesture, voice, motion, interior decoration, and reading matter should form an 'authentic' model of affective individualism that the gullible client takes as a real person feeling 'all the effects of a profound and sincere love' for him and him alone.... One of the most central and enduring devices of the novel—the particularized character who develops through a wrenching crisis in the course of a 'profound and sincere' emotional relationship—appears first as a whore's trick.[1]

There can be little doubt that a similar shift seems to have taken place in *The London Jilt*. Although the prefatory author presents the jilt as an example of duplicity incarnate, Cornelia portrays

---

1 Turner, *Schooling Sex: Libertine Literature and Erotic Education in Italy, France, and England, 1534-1685* (Oxford: Oxford UP, 2003), 78-79. See also his "The Whore's Rhetorick: Narrative, Pornography, and the Origins of the Novel," *Studies in Eighteenth-Century Culture* 24 (1995): 297-306.

herself as a high-spirited individual who occupies a sexually ambiguous space quite distinct from common street prostitution.

The Narrative

In *The London Jilt*, the whorish trickery to which Turner refers is something considerably less than "affective individualism," yet it points, in a playful way, to an emotional thread that is woven into the fabric of the novel. Divided into two parts, the narrative consciously blurs the line between hypocritical duplicity and genuine feeling. In the first part, Cornelia explains her descent into whoredom as a result of her father's folly and premature death; in the second, she describes her return to the practice of accepting money for sex as a consequence of the difficulties that attend her marriage. The marriage turns out to be unsatisfactory, for her husband becomes abusive after what she terms "the Devil of Pride" (114) has led her to expenditures that exceed her allowance. Describing his brutal response, she resorts to a level of circumlocution more oblique than one finds even in the sexual episodes: "one morning when all the People were gone to Church, having called me into a Back-Room, he represented to me my Duty with such very pertinent Reasons, that I was very sensible of them for above a Week afterwards" (115). If the phrasing evokes a patriarchal discourse of domestic responsibilities, the reality casts her in the role of victim. Shifting the reader's attention from what she has done to what has been done to her, it justifies her decision to take a lover as an act of revenge, in which she seeks to punish her husband for the pain and humiliation she has suffered. Here Cornelia portrays herself not as a courtesan trickster but as a domestic heroine endowed with an authentic inner life, one whose plight is all-too-typical of women who have become victims of male oppression.

Cornelia's active response to her husband's violence results in one of several episodes in which her grievances are the driving force behind the narrative. In *The London Jilt*, the merry pranks that are a common feature of picaresque fiction mainly occur in these episodes. In contrast to the counter-cheats of the conventional picaresque novel, however, Cornelia's revenge in the first episode unfolds in three distinct stages. First comes a period of deliberation and planning: the jilt's decision to collect some form of payback from whomever she deems responsible and to search for an appropriate mode of punishment, which is presumed to be commensurate with the affront or indignity suffered. This *a priori* of resemblance, the postulate of the decision to seek revenge, leads to a rhetoric of self-justification rather than of greed, malice, or rage. Through the convention of an interpolated tale, Cornelia learns that Squire Limberham, a young man who has been assiduously courting her and whom she finds quite pleasing, is actually impotent. This prompts Cornelia to make the following comment: "when that I began to consider, that this poor *Limberham*, in case I had gone away with him, would have suffered my lower Parts to have endured Hunger after a miserable manner: I concluded that though it might have cost me Dear, I would have revenged my self for such a trick" (67). From this perspective, Limberham's deceit is censurable because it fails to acknowledge the right of women to enjoy their own bodies. Cornelia, however, hopes that the counter-trick she devises will be taken by the reader as the consequence not so much of cupidity as of careful deliberation. Her reflection seeks to vindicate her from blame even while drawing attention to her planned act of deception.

Next comes her depiction of the actual moment of revenge and subsequent escape. In recounting the event, Cornelia describes herself as torn between sympathy and a conviction that Squire Limberham, who has already had an earlier marriage annulled, deserves to be punished: "I deplored the poor Man's having had so unhappy a fate, but on the other hand I could not forbear (by reason he was so weak and helpless) to Curse his Passion for Women, since he could do nothing more than whet their Appetites, without being able to satiate them in the least" (70). The reasoning that guides this comment is presented as moral rather than mercenary. This becomes obvious when Cornelia, after having drugged Squire Limberham with an opiate and relieved him of his watch, discovers a purse of gold on his person. In spite of her avidity for "Gold," she refrains from taking all of it and instead relates, "I began to share the Gold, neither more nor less than if it had fallen to us by Inheritance, into equal Portions, without taking a Peny more than I left him" (72).

The third stage is the mechanism by which Cornelia explains the punishment and its significance to her victim after she has left the scene. Here the mechanism takes the form of a letter placed where her victim can find it. In the letter that Cornelia leaves for Limberham, she justifies the theft of his watch and gold as if it were a maintenance granted to her after she has been awarded a legal annullment of their marriage. Cornelia's letter thus constitutes a thoroughgoing rationalization of the trick she plays upon him:

A Maiden of my Age had need of something else than Bread, and since you had once been so unhappy in your Marriage, you ought to have banish'd the Female Sex wholly from your Thoughts, and no longer have applyed your Sences unto such unlucky Objects, or at least you ought to seek out one who is more stricken in Years, that your Insufficiency might not make you lose the second time, what your brave Deportment and your excellent Qualities had acquired you. Do not take it ill that I have seized upon your Watch, for in recompence I have left you all the Money in Silver, where the half did with as much Justice belong to me as that of the Gold. (72)

The primary concern of this letter is to defend her conduct while also acknowledging guilt. If Cornelia is righteously indignant about his deception, she is also restrained about a punishment that she seeks to distinguish from mere avarice. She assumes that such an act, however justified, can easily be misunderstood as a scheme proffered by money-hungry jades eager to dupe the unsuspecting. A necessary evil, revenge needs to be carefully explained by a moral agent aware of its temptations and limits.

There is also a comic aspect to the letter she leaves for Squire Limberham that is essential to the charm of a subsequent episode near the end of Part I. Here Cornelia's payback to the rope-dancer for the wrongs done to her father and family is couched in the idioms and trappings of an elaborately planned prank. Her tactics include rendering the rope-dancer comatose through drugged wine, dressing him up in worn-out women's clothes, lowering him into a coffin specially prepared with breathing holes, and thrusting into his right hand a letter explaining what has happened. The delicious irony of the situation, rather than the moral issue involved, is the primary focus of the letter's conclusion:

I would willingly make my Letter something longer, to give you some comfort in your Misfortune, but it being almost High-Water and my House as you know at a considerable distance, I have not time sufficient. Wherefore live well if you can, and know that if ever I hear you heartily pardon me this Prank, I shall then believe that you bear me as much good Will, as you have so often endeavoured to persuade me of. (104)

If the rope-dancer might have been led to expect a moment of gloating self-vindication, Cornelia's surprising insistence upon her hope for forgiveness strikes a note that is intended to leave him without any hard feelings.

In the second part of the novel, Cornelia herself becomes the target of a letter mailed to her abusive husband in which an alderman discloses that she has "Jilted" him in "all manner of ways" (131). In another episode, she is cheated out of a pair of costly pendants by an Italian trickster named Jakomo. The rope-dancer, now disguised as a woman, also reappears, seeking his own revenge, and departs only after threatening her with a knife and cruelly slitting the belly of her guard dog, Cerberus. Here the narrative reverts to a crude physicality that is central to the picaresque tradition, with an undertone of violence obviously still meant to remain comic. At other times, disgust replaces delight as the primary focus of the narrative. Cornelia's responses within the text act as a model for this kind of revulsion. In one of the final episodes, she determines to retaliate against a drunken German lord for his grotesquely boorish behavior during a sexual episode. Conforming to the pattern of his conduct, she times her revenge, which involves urine, to take place immediately after he has fallen asleep in a drunken stupor. The goal of the prefatory author has thus finally been achieved through the jilt's stratagems: the unmediated yoking of pleasure and nausea, not filtered through a third-person narrator but directly carried out by the subject herself.

What constitutes acceptable and unacceptable behavior in such situations highlights the importance of the body in *The London Jilt*, as indeed in all picaresque narratives. The female body is assumed to be a naturally given unit of significance, endowed with desires and a reproductive capacity (the latter playing only a minor role in the novel), vulnerable to disfigurement, especially from smallpox (venereal disease being mentioned only in passing), and subject to an inexorable process of decay and diminution of personal appeal. Yet even though Cornelia is acutely aware of the effect of aging on her beauty, her narrative displays a singular fascination with the body as an immutable "natural" essence. Indeed, by positing the body as an inherent site of identity, the narrative reveals the extent to which "natural" beauty is distinguished from artifice in all of its material aspects. In other words, it condemns any use of cosmetics as transgressive, if not actually deleterious, in its long-term effects. Like the technique Cornelia employs to enhance the appeal of her breasts, her account of her purchase of Spanish paper to color her cheeks red might thus be considered an integral part of the prefatory author's strategy of ironic disclosure.

In contrast to the paragraphs of graphic description that Cornelia devotes to adornment, explicit accounts of sexual scenes of the sort occasionally found in the novels of Behn, Manley, and Haywood are consistently avoided. Yet female desire sometimes effects a humorous subversion of Cornelia's mercenary motives, invariably leading to short-term humiliations and setbacks. Moreover, when she receives costly gifts from her gallants, the erotic charge is palpable; money and jewels are her aphrodisiacs. Her response to Valere's promise of financial security sounds like an erotic endearment. Why her suitors find such responses so convincing is explained in the novel by masculine sexual desire, which is taken as a natural given, a constant source of libidinal energy, even when it defies common sense or exceeds physiological capacity. Nonetheless, in spite of the fact that the narrative is structured around the amorous longings of single-minded lovers, there is little hint of masculine sexual aggression (as opposed to spousal abuse) in the novel. The most graphic depiction of physical violence occurs in a scene in which Cornelia assaults her former maid Sarah after she has publicly proclaimed that Cornelia and her mother are whores. The jilt's readiness to inflict physical harm is inseparable from her energy and resourcefulness.

Cornelia, while having only limited experience in trade, nonetheless incarnates the vitality and practical intelligence put forth as ideals for merchants and shopkeepers. In effect the vigour with which she engages in multiple liaisons, resembling the adventurous spirit of entrepreneurs, reaps benefits well beyond her immediate needs and expectations. It is thus possible that the seventeenth-century reader may have seen in Cornelia's repeated references to prostitution as a trade much more than the whore's age-old commodification of sexuality. Unlike the common street prostitute, Cornelia is not content to remain the victim of others. On the contrary, she embodies qualities antithetical to a conventional image of passive womanhood, which itself was inimical to the entrepreneurial spirit. As a result, she could easily be cited as an example of the equalizing pressures of commercial society, its threat to traditional distinctions of gender and ethnicity. In this context, she belongs to a group of women that during the Restoration included authors, poets, actresses, painters, and dramatists as well as ladies of pleasure. These were women who displayed their gifts outside the domestic sphere and who seized the unique opportunities that London afforded them to become independent and professionals worthy of respect.

A Pattern for *Moll Flanders* and *Roxana*

A traditional yet important subject of scholarly endeavour is the study of the sources of a work, not as an end in itself, but as a way of coming to an understanding of how an author adapted and possibly transformed the conventions of a particular genre. A search for the sources of Daniel Defoe's *Robinson Crusoe* (1719), for example, has yielded first-person travel narratives and spiritual autobiographies as well as contemporary accounts of marooned men by William Dampier, Edward Cooke, and Woodes Rogers. No such comparable list of sources, however, appears to exist for *Moll Flanders* or *Roxana*. Scholars have examined third-person criminal biographies and scandalous chronicles, columns of advice in contemporary periodical essays (including Defoe's own *Review*), and the lives of notorious women such as Moll King, Sally Salisbury, and Moll Cutpurse. These have proved to be useful sources of information, but, in contrast to *The London Jilt*, they have not provided instances of the actual texts Defoe might have used as models for his first-person female narratives. What makes *The London Jilt* significant in this respect is the way it affords an elegant counterpoint to the explanation offered by the anonymous editor of *Moll Flanders* concerning the circumstances in which he supposedly came to publish what he terms a "private History." The editor contends that the woman who presents her memoirs under the alias of Moll Flanders left behind her a manuscript "Written in the Year 1683,"[1] perhaps not coincidentally the same year in which *The London Jilt* was published. Without explaining how the manuscript happened to come into his hands, the editor maintains that it was too indecent in its language to be published in its original form and thus had to be altered significantly. Hence he affirms that while "the Author is here suppos'd to be writing her own History ... the original of this Story is put into new Words, and the Stile of the famous Lady we here speak of is a little alter'd, particularly she is made to tell her Tale in modester words than she told it at first" (*MF* 3). What Defoe's editor purports to be offering, then, is an expurgated

---

1 *Moll Flanders*, ed. Albert Rivero (New York: Norton, 2004), 267. Hereafter abbreviated in parenthesis as *MF*.

version of the famous lady's life, even as he preserves the basic narrative of her sexual and criminal adventures. How should this explanation be understood? It is quite possible that what Defoe's editor is offering here is a textual allegory, a disguised autobiographical version of Defoe's own practice. Indeed, the evidence strongly suggests that he is adopting as his model the earlier first-person *picara* or whore's narrative. A female variant of the rogue's narrative, as we have already seen, it can be traced back to Jean de Meun's monologue of the Duenna and Chaucer's Wife of Bath's prologue and forward, in another significant modification, to the scandalous memoirs of the middle and later eighteenth century. *The London Jilt* provides an English example of the genre, and it is at least conceivable that Defoe is transforming its conventions into something that would have been deemed acceptable by his pious readers.

It is noteworthy that Defoe eliminates not only the most blatantly erotic aspects of the picaresque narrative but also its many episodes of comic violence. The kind of practical joke that Cornelia plays on the rope-dancer is a prominent feature of *The London Jilt* but is conspicuously absent from *Moll Flanders* and *Roxana*. This would be no more than an interesting observation were it not for a second feature of Defoe's transformation of the whore's narrative: his elevation of her character. Defoe eliminates her swift descent into the realm of surreptitious prostitution, her adulteries, as well as some of the grosser cheats she plays on her would-be lovers. The chastened language of *Moll Flanders* and *Roxana* thus has a double function. If it serves to purify the novels of an objectionable vocabulary, it also enables Defoe to invest his female protagonists with a dignity not always apparent in *The London Jilt*.

It is impossible to be certain whether Defoe was acquainted with *The London Jilt* or not, but there are a number of broad resemblances between Cornelia and Moll Flanders and Roxana. Like them, Cornelia is treated more generously by merchants than by her other suitors; she reports that one merchant named Valere promises her, "if I would be faithful to him, and not abandon my self to any other Man, he would take me a Chamber, and provide me with all things I had occasion for" (77). Cornelia also shares Moll and Roxana's unabashed materialism, referring several times in the narrative to the fascination that money, especially gold, holds for her. And she resembles them in her determination to keep her material resources in reserve without telling her suitors; after Valere gives her ten pounds to buy furniture, she confesses, "I had reserved to my self about four Pounds out of the Bargain" (77). She achieves a measure of financial security by securing annuities from two different lovers, yet, like Moll and Roxana, finds herself incapable of renouncing her libertine way of life. She is similar to them in her penchant for secrecy, finding it necessary more than once to move to a new location where she is unknown. Fearing discovery by the angry spouse she has left, she declares "there were several reasons which made me think it convenient after three or four days to abandon that Room, and to take a House, where I might be something farther distant from the Eyes of my Husband" (133). Cornelia's feigned indifference to her suitors is designedly transparent but, like Moll and Roxana, she learns that she must come to know their characters before granting their wishes: "It was not my custom to be kind to any one upon running Post, I must first of all have sounded their Breasts, and penetrated their Hearts" (100). In spite of her precautions, however, Cornelia is pursued by a host of figures, including a dismissed maid named Sarah who threatens, much like Roxana's daughter, Susan, to make her secret life known to all. Meeting Cornelia and her mother in the street one day, Sarah "began immediately to ring us a Peal of injurious Languages, bawling out for a long while *Whores*" (96). In a similar manner, Roxana describes at one point how her daughter, Susan, "began to grow talktative; and as it was plain that she had told all her Head could retain of *Roxana*, and the Days of Joy which I had spent at that Part of the Town."[1]

These broad resemblances in characterization can be replicated in individual episodes. Like Moll, Cornelia and her mother both marry and find themselves in situations that lead them to become alienated from their husbands. There is nothing in *The London Jilt* comparable to Moll's shock at her discovery that she has married her brother, but Cornelia suffers at the hands of an abusive spouse and her mother from her husband's gullibility in allowing their estate to be stolen through an obvious trick. As a result, *The London Jilt* depicts marital estrangement in similar terms. As Cornelia recalls, "I would withdraw for a long time, and exchange *London* for some other Town, which proceeded from the Aversion I had conceived to my Husband, since the first time he had chastized me so severely" (119). Moll similarly states,

---

1 Daniel Defoe, *Roxana: The Fortunate Mistress*, ed. John Mullan (Oxford: Oxford UP, 1996), 283.

"indeed I mortally hated him as a Husband, and it was impossible to remove that rivited Aversion I had to him" (*MF* 80). The same pattern of resemblance occurs when Cornelia's mother and Moll both experience a revival of affection after their husbands become deathly ill. Cornelia describes how

> the pitteous condition my Mother saw him in, and his words full of Humility, had moved her something to Compassion; insomuch, that she began to melt into tears. She embraced him very affectionately, and at that time show'd him more kindness, than she had done for the space of three years. (50)

Moll similarly recalls how

> Things were now come to a lamentable height in the Family: My pity for him now began to revive that Affection which at first I really had for him, and I endeavour'd sincerely by all the kind Carriage I could to make up the Breach. (*MF* 84)

There is no question that the episode of Moll's estrangement from her husband is much more fully developed than the comparable episodes in *The London Jilt*, but both works can be seen as endeavouring to represent the gradual psychological separation of a wife from her spouse in plausible, realistic terms.

Defoe modifies the conventions of *The London Jilt* in other ways. He preserves the theme of revenge that is so central to the picaresque novel in one episode of *Moll Flanders*, for example, but relegates it to a minor character, the young lady who lives in the "House" next to Moll in London. The episode, in which the young lady, with Moll's encouragement, seeks to retaliate for an affront given to her by a suitor who angrily breaks off contact after he learns that she has made inquiries concerning his character and circumstances, retains the skeleton of the revenge tale. It has a neat plot, based on the false rumors that Moll and the young lady plant concerning his reputation. Its denouement brings about the proud suitor's expected deflation, after which he becomes "the most humble, the most modest, and the most importunate Man alive in his Courtship" (*MF* 59). But as the episode unfolds, it takes on a different character from similar events in *The London Jilt* and earlier Spanish picaresque novels. After suitable delays, the young lady agrees to marry her contrite suitor, taking care only to place "part of her Fortune ... in Trustees, without letting him know anything of it" (*MF* 60). This is an indication of the extent to which Defoe has transformed the revenge plot into something quite respectable. Moll and the young lady's conduct would be wholly admirable, were it not for the malicious gossip they circulate concerning the young gentleman's supposed doings. Yet this laughably mild stratagem becomes just one facet in a multi-sided farce that sends up the mores and ambitions of prospective suitors while also warning of the danger women face when they fail to "keep their Ground" before their would-be lovers (*MF* 61).

One stable point of reference for both *The London Jilt* and Defoe's two novels is the category of the "jilt" explored in Appendix B. This category serves as a point of comparison from which some of the broader differences between the main characters can be seen. Cornelia is a "jilt" in the sense that she manages things so that there are competitors for her favors and those to whom she consents to grant assignations (in return for generous gifts) usually imagine that they have triumphed over rivals and been granted a special privilege. But where Cornelia jilts her merchant lover Valere in the most basic sense—that is, by secretly admitting other lovers while promising fidelity—Moll Flanders jilts a bank clerk who courts her in a more nuanced way, by putting off his proposal of marriage in favor of a supposedly better offer after previously encouraging him. Roxana becomes a jilt in an even more attenuated understanding of the term when she rejects a Dutch merchant's offer of marriage after agreeing to become his mistress. Here we see the consequences of Defoe's shifting uses of the notion; it is supposed to be a simple and transparent term, belonging to a realm of obvious commonsense labels that enable us to make straightforward and unambiguous moral judgments about human character. Yet insofar as it grounds and sustains other and more complicated formulations of human behavior, it also expands to become part of their very definition. It follows that a comparison of Cornelia with Moll Flanders and Roxana should not require a reductive attention to conventional assumptions concerning the character of the "jilt." It asks rather that analysis be devoted to more complex aspects of characterization: enduring personality traits, the effects of time and circumstance on an individual's outlook, or the links between motive and action. As a consequence of this focus, the reader's attention should be guided by questions of desire and feeling rather than by how closely the character conforms to a stereotype, and Cornelia, Moll Flanders, and Roxana are more likely to come to life as we read.

The Novel's Didactic Purpose

The most important feature that *The London Jilt*, *Moll Flanders*, and *Roxana* share in common is the convention of the first-person narrative accompanied by a preface or introduction. Within this convention, the introductory matter becomes a part of the novel itself. It explains how and why the narrative is being published. The implied author of the preface to *The London Jilt*, however, defines his role differently from the editors of *Moll Flanders* and *Roxana*. Where they purport to be adapting (and sanitizing) pre-existing memoirs, he characterizes the narrative that follows as a fictional *exemplum*. Where they insist that what they are offering the reader are true histories, he nowhere suggests that he is presenting anything other than a novel. He contends that he is shaping the narrative in such a way that the reader will see "our Jilt exposed naked in all her deformities" (42). As the author of the text, he will lay bare her schemes and expose her manifest vices for all to see. By this he implies that setting the jilt "before the Eyes of Mankind" (42) (that is, allowing her to portray herself in the first person) is preferable to describing her in mere words (that is, representing her in the third person). Yet, in order to avoid "the Dulness and Gravity of a Sermon" (42), the author of the preface also informs the reader that "this Narrative of her Stratagems and Artifices will afford thee a peculiar delight and satisfaction, being agreeably interwoven with Stories of her Wiles and Juggles and in short, a perfect account of her Performances in the Art of winning others and her self" (42).

The two claims seem contradictory, for they imply that the jilt's life is being depicted in order to arouse delectation as well as disgust. They are contradictory inasmuch as we are led to expect a caustic narrative, much like Francis Kirkman's *The Counterfeit Lady Unveiled* (1673). In this criminal biography, Kirkman's jaundiced third-person commentary upon the life of Mary Carleton, the German Princess, is intended to challenge and replace Carleton's earlier first-person autobiographical narrative, *The Case of Mary Carleton* (1663), in which she speaks on her own behalf. The difference between first- and third-person narratives can be seen from a comparison of the selections from *The Case of Mary Carleton* and *The Counterfeit Lady Unveiled* in Appendix C. What we find in *The London Jilt*, as we have already seen, is another first-person narrative in which the interiorization, domestication, and characterization typical of the later novel usurp the place of Juvenalian satire. The anonymous author of the preface disappears while Cornelia, in effect, becomes a second author within the novel, establishing a point of view that is quite distinct from what is articulated in the author's preliminary remarks. To a certain extent, the difference between third- and first-person narrative corresponds to what Gotthold Ephraim Lessing envisions in chapter eight of *Laocoon* as the different ways painting and poetry treat pagan deities:

> To the artist [the gods] are personified abstractions which must always be characterized in the same way, or we fail to recognize them. In poetry, on the contrary, they are real beings, acting and working and possessing, besides their general character, qualities and passions which may upon occasion take precedence. Venus to the sculptor is simply love.... To the poet, Venus is love also, but she is the goddess of love, who has her own individuality outside of this one characteristic.[1]

In a similar manner, Cornelia is presented not only as a jilt, but also as a woman who "has her own individuality outside of this one characteristic." She reveals her individuality not only in a memoir that takes us from her earliest years as an only child to her present life as a prosperous shopkeeper in Flanders but also through the commentary, in which she seeks to maintain a direct and unmediated rapport with the reader. Her occasional references to her present circumstances are in themselves significant. They serve to reinforce her pretensions as an author who has the wisdom and experience to address her readers on a variety of topics. No longer troubled by unwanted amorous attentions, she constructs a retrospective narrative in which she can give the reader a sense of her earlier life from a certain detached vantage point. The implied reader is a person to whom she can now speak because she has aged enough to become immune to desire. If she refers to readers only in passing, their calming presence makes itself felt indirectly, by way of contrast with the impassioned ardor of her earlier gallants. By this technique, the present is introduced into a retrospective narrative; her recollections of the main events of her past life are linked to a commentary on con-

---

1 Gotthold Ephraim Lessing, *Laocoon: An Essay Upon the Limits of Painting and Poetry*, trans. Ellen Frothingham (New York: Noonday, 1961), 58-59.

temporary mores and manners without which she would not be inspired to recall these events in the first place. The commentary sometimes turns on a contrast between *then* and *now*: "Certainly I cannot forbear laughing, when I consider the Lives of those Damosels, who now have their Recourse for Livelihood to this Commerce which I was thus used to exercise in my Youth" (97). In other episodes, the opposition between past and present is simply a matter of degree. Under the convention of the first person, the author sometimes allows the child that Cornelia used to be to speak, while at the same time endowing her with the ironic and worldly perspective of the adult:

> I remember that from time to time there was some man or other laying all Night at our House, and that upon such occasions I was forced to roost with the Maid, whereas at other times I lay in my Mothers Arms, from whence I then concluded, that she must be a very Commisserating Woman, since to free people out of pain, she imported to them the half of her Bed, but she made them dearly pay for this pitty; and I could easily perceive, that the Chimney smoak'd more, and better by the half, when we had a night-Guest with us than otherwise. (51)

The resulting doubling of character constructs a persona that bears a striking resemblance to the *ingenue* of first-person satire. It is significant, moreover, that Cornelia's authorial discourse only appears full-blown after she has entered into the adult world.

Cornelia's commentary frequently encompasses the misogynistic topics promised by the author of the preface—the artifices and stratagems supposedly employed by whores to lead men to their ruin. But in her hands, they undergo a profound transmutation: located in a narrative which teaches that economic security, however compromising, trumps virtuous poverty, they become difficult to distinguish from the legitimate strategies many women are forced to adopt for survival. Thus when Cornelia insists at one point that "it is certain, when we grant all things to men, without any Resistance, their Inclination will never be of long continuance" (136), she is implicitly shifting the gendered focus of her warnings from men to women and, in the process, suggesting an ever-narrowing line between the decorum appropriate to a whore and a proper young lady. Yet the assumption that marriage can be a haven for women is also called into

question in the narrative as, for example, when Cornelia specu-
lates about

> the wretched condition of those Women who being Old and
> Ugly, abandon themselves to some young miserable Bully; for
> they are no sooner engaged together by the Bond of Marriage,
> than that these Sparks who only took this rank flesh for the
> conveniencies wherewith it is attended, begin to play the
> Master, and with the Money, which others it seems have rak'd
> up for them, they seek out Wenches who are less in years and
> have more Charms than their old toothless Spouses. (94)

This observation about the folly of widows who marry younger
men is the counterpart, on the prudential level, to the confident
perspective that Cornelia brings to her own life. She is secure
enough to acknowledge her own weaknesses, but her frank
admission of her errors leaves little room for the kind of moral
and religious reflections in which she might express remorse
about what she has done in the past. The strident self-reproaches
that have often been described as a prominent feature of
Roxana's confessions are virtually absent from Cornelia's discourse. As a consequence, she runs the risk of any woman who
appears to be relating her life-story to her own advantage, namely
that what she is affirming will carry less credence than a third-
person narrative of the same events. Cornelia does not entirely
avoid this danger but she mitigates its force by offering a candid
assessment of the scruples, risks, and errors in judgment that
attended her various adventures and misadventures. Like Moll
and Roxana, she frequently reminds the reader of mitigating circumstances and of the overwhelming temptations to which the
spectre of poverty exposed her; yet, like them, she offers us
moments of unqualified satisfaction in which these concerns sud-
denly become irrelevant.

The difficulty in establishing a secure didactic message from
The London Jilt can be seen first of all in the striking contrast
between the harshly moralistic preface and Cornelia's witty,
engaging commentary. The seductive appeal of many of her
observations is unwittingly forecast in the preface, where the
author warns the male reader of the whore's dangerously alluring
charms. Cornelia's confession, however, does not attempt to
eliminate the charms as such. Rather, it cultivates them in order
to reveal the whore's ruses more seductively. Yet the prefatory
author's triumph over female secrets is based upon doubtful

premises. He assumes that the commentary is structured in terms of a repertory of professional tricks, whereas the narrative is actually dominated by unregulated male desire. In so doing, he conveniently overlooks the extent to which the whore's snares are not only presupposed but called into existence by the very passions their exposure is intended to quell. Far from suppressing desire, their revelation may actually enhance it.

This disparity between the preface and the main text is emblematic of a central tension in the novel's narrative strategy, beginning with Cornelia's initial confession of her family's unexpected and humiliating descent into poverty. For the play between the generalizable, predictable model of marriage (the novel's ostensible norm) and the unexpected twists and turns stemming from Cornelia's adoption of a discreet mode of prostitution (the surprises entailed by her life of deception and make-believe) is a driving narratological force in the novel, even as it moves towards an unexpected conclusion in which Cornelia becomes the prosperous and defiantly unrepentant owner of a profitable lace shop in Flanders. At this point, Cornelia declares: "I am not of the rank of those who after having led a vicious Life during their Youth, and then becoming Converts, pretend to bygottism, and walk holding their right Hand upon their Heart as the truly Devout do, or, if you please, seem as modest and plain as poor Susanna is commonly painted between those two old Ruffians" (168). Within the earlier episodes, however, there is a tension, in various degrees, between the marital state and the illicit relation. Cornelia's extensive comments clearly reflect this tension, in effect raising the question of how a first-person narrative may be said to teach a universal, exemplary lesson. What is there to be learnt from a whore's confession? Does it represent how life actually is or how it ought to be? Should Cornelia's aggressively asserted observations be seen as the sign of the authority of experience or are they nothing more than a warning of the unreliability of a partial witness? The structure of the tale—comic episode joined to discursive reflection—raises a doubt about the relation between generalized comment and the particularity of a narrative. As in *Moll Flanders* and *Roxana*, where the female speaker's arguments are erected upon a constantly shifting ground of experience, so in *The London Jilt* Cornelia's moralizing reflections often seem to raise more questions than they answer.

That uncertainty, however, is balanced by the comedy of the novel, which has great fun with the precarious situations of its heroine. There are in this narrative many moments of delight, which are not necessarily distinct from the ambiguities I have indicated: a certain charm produced by the saltiness of the heroines language, for instance, and the voluptuous delicacy of her accounts of various female stratagems and unexpected reversals. Even if we complain that the characters are shadowy types rather than individuals, sketched in rather than delineated with specificity, we still remember Cornelia's mother, the rope-dancer, Squire Limberham, and the German Count. We remember these characters and the episodes in which they are involved because they are framed and interpreted within the context of the novel's most distinctive feature: the cheerful, lucid, ironic commentary of the central protagonist herself.

A Note on the Text

The copy text for this Broadview edition is the London 1683 edition held in Harvard University Library. Obvious typographical errors have been corrected but, otherwise, every effort has been made to preserve the flavor of the non-standard English of the novel. Variant and idiosyncratic spellings have been maintained, while archaisms and obsolescent forms, euphemisms and neologisms, bawdy terms and words of uncertain meaning have been noted in the footnotes. In cases of ambiguity, I have relied upon the readings given in the online *Oxford English Dictionary* and have otherwise indicated words and phrases whose meaning cannot be identified.

Bamford sc.

Courtesy of the Houghton Library, Harvard University.

THE
LONDON JILT:

OR, THE
POLITICK WHORE.

SHEWING,

All the Artifices and Stratagems which the Ladies of Pleasure make use of for the Intreaguing and Decoying of Men; Interwoven with several Pleasant Stories of the *Misses* Ingenious Performances.

LONDON,

Printed for *Hen. Rhodes*, next door to the *Bear-Tavern* near *Bride-lane* in *Fleet-street.* 1683.

TO THE READER

COURTEOUS Reader,

Notwithstanding the many Discoveries that have been made by several Authors in Pieces of this Nature, of the Subtilties and Cheats that the Misses of this Town put upon Men, yet we still dayly see that they find Cullies[1] enough to be imposed upon, to the decay and ruine-both of their Health, their Fortune and Reputation. Wherefore a Mirrour of their damned Wheadling Arts, and Cursed Devices, cannot be too often set before the Eyes of Mankind, that so the easy Fops[2] themselves may take a warning, and be diverted from falling into their Destructive Snare. For thou hast here, **Reader,** *the Jilt displayed in her true Colours, all her Wheadling and Treacherous Decoys laid open. And in short, thou hast not only the Bulcker[3] but the fine* **London Misses** *Picture drawn to the Life. Shee is here set before thee as a Beacon to warn thee of the Shoales and Quick-sands, on which thou wilt of necessity Shipwrack thy All, if thou blindly and wilfully continuest and perseverest in steering that Course of* **Female Debauchery,** *which will inevitably prove at length thy utter Destruction. This perhaps will be allowed to be no small Piece of Service, if it may be a means of dissuading, but some few from that Roving, Libertine, Lascivious Course of Life, and contribute but to the making Men be upon their Guard against all* **Female Ambuscadoes.[4]** *And indeed what greater Folly can there be than to venture one's All in such rotten Bottoms, and at length become the Horrour and Detestation of all the World, only for a Momentary Pleasure, and which in truth cannot well be termed Pleasure, considering what filthy, nasty, and stinking Carcasses, are the best and finest of our Common Whores? A Whore is but a Close-stool to Man, or a Common-shoar that receives all manner of Filth, shee's like a Barber's Chair, no sooner one's out, but t'others in, or as an other has likened 'em to* **Sampson's Foxes,** *who carry fire in their Tails to burn the standing Corn.[5] And though the danger does so vastly surpass the Delight that can be had in the Conversation and Enjoyment of the*

---

1 Men who are easily cheated or imposed upon; dupes, gulls.
2 Conceited persons, mainly male, pretending to wit; men who are foolishly attentive to and vain of their appearance.
3 A low-life person, petty thief, streetwalker, or prostitute (obsolete); may also refer to bulck, a framework projecting from the front of a shop (obsolete).
4 Forces lying in ambush (obsolete).
5 See Judges 15:4-5.

most *Charming* of 'em all, yet we see foolish silly *Men* such easy *Fops*, as to be lured by their *False Attractions* into that bitter *Trap* of theirs, which is ever followed or attended with all manner of *Diseases*, both of *Mind* and *Body*. Thus sure the *Publick* cannot blame or *Condemn* a *Man*, for drawing his *Pen* in so necessary an occasion, especially at this time, when the *Trade* of *Jilting* is grown so ripe, that *Warnings* of this kind cannot be too often repeated, nor instances of their *Devilish Pranks* and *Practices* too frequently proclaim'd, that so *Men* may be as it were teiz'd into good sence and their own security. Not that this *Piece* had the *Dulness* and *Gravity* of a *Sermon*. It shows you the *Miss* revelling in her *Culleys Arms*, it shows her displaying all her *Arts* to entice, seduce and ensnare *Mankind*, and what thou thoughtest fondness of thy *Person*, thou wilt find only a damn'd unbounded *self-interest*, and an insatiable *Avidity* of *Money*; thou wilt discover her giving every one *Entertainment* suitable to the largeness of their *Purses*, and the *Extravagances* of their *Expences*. But when the weak and *Credulous Fop* has spent his *All* upon her, thou wilt see him shee so much before *Cherish'd* and *Indulg'd* shut out of *Door*, scorn'd and despis'd by her, and treated with all manner of *Infamy* and *Contempt*. Thus all her *Carriage* that was so tender and endearing while that thou lavished thy *Stock* and *Fortune* upon her when this once begins to fail, thou wilt find her *Favours* and *Affection* decay and languish at the same time. Wherefore *Reader*, take this seasonable *Advice*, leave off in time that leud *Course* of *Life*, and be not bubled by *Detestable Creatures*, that are so little worthy of thy *Amusement* and *Application*. Avoid all their *Cursed Allurement*, and be mindful that a *Snake* lies concealed under such bewitching *Appearances*, and how beautiful and attractive soever the outside of the *Apple* may be, that it is *Rotten* and *Pestilent* at *Core*. But it is time, *Reader*, that thou seest our *Jilt* exposed naked in all her *Deformities*, that it may so create a horrour in thee for what thou before so eagerly pursuedst, and so fondly adoredst. Not but that this *Narrative* of her *Stratagems* and *Artifices* will afford thee a peculiar delight and satisfaction, being agreeably interwoven with *Pleasant Stories* of her *Wiles* and *Juggles*, and in short, a perfect account of her *Performances* in the *Art* of winning others and her self. If this undertaking prove but as beneficial in curbing the bad and unlawful *Inclinations* of *Men*, as the *Author* design'd it, the *Pains* will be sufficiently rewarded, that have been taken for thy *Good*, thy *Diversion* and *Service*.

Farewel.

The London Jilt; or, The Politick Whore

THERE is no Nation in the World, but has in all Ages, furnished Authors, who have made it their business to expose, as far as they were capable, the Frailties of the Female Sex. Some have been provoked thereunto, by their unfortunate Addresses, and by the disappointments they have met with in Love; others have undertaken that Province, without any other reason, than to show their Wit. But my Business now in Writing, is to warn Men of the danger they may run in the persuit of their Amours; for which purpose, I thought a Narrative of my Life might be of extraordinary use, since it has been a continual Series of Stratagems and Artifices for the ensnaring of Men.

London is the place of my Birth, where my Father, or at least the Man my Mother was pleased to honour with that Title, had been a Merchant until the Age of thirty two Years; but his fortune taking an other biass about that time, the good Man found himself obliged, that he might not be oppress'd with Poverty, after he had been for a while in the *Fryars*,[1] and had Compounded with his Creditors, to set up a Tipling House.[2]

Of these two Persons so full of Probity, was I the only Daughter, and for that reason, I was brought up in some sort of Libertinism; for to be an only Child, and to be rendred wanton, are two things which cannot be well separated. I was about five years old, when my Father was transformed from a Merchant into a Victualler, and I was sent to School to write and learn *French*, as also to Dance; and for that purpose, I can assure you, that my Parents strain'd their Purse, but were nevertheless well enough satisfied, since it flattered their Ambition. But it is not my Intention to stay my too Curious Reader over long, upon the childish behaviours of my Infancie, I shall onely say this, that like most young Girles I was very fond of Puppeys, tho rather of Male then Female, and my greatest pleasure consisted in dressing and kissing them. I had also a Gallant[3] at the School, and I was mightily concerned, that I was not of Age enough to marry him, for I began to imagine, that there was nothing in the World more pleasant, than to sleep

---

1   A term used familiarly for the Blackfriars, a church, precinct, and sanctuary with four gates lying between Ludgate Hill and the Thames.
2   A tavern. Tipple is obsolete for strong drink, liquor.
3   Men devoted to fashion and pleasure; men who are amorous and markedly polite and attentive to the female sex; frequently an epithet of admiration or praise.

in the Arms of a Man. I am apt to believe that I am not the only Person, who in so tender an age has harboured such like sentiments; for if all Damsells would deal as freely and as openly as I, and tell the truth, I do not doubt but that they would all with me confess, or, at least the greatest number would own as I do, that they have no sooner discovered the difference there is between the two Sexes, than they immediately are desiring to be caressed and flattered by Men, and though they often show themselves somewhat coy and disdainful, you may however firmly believe, that this is for no other reason than to try and to nourish the Lovers Passion, and augment the ardour of a young Man, by all those silly Repulses and Grimaces. But Hypocrisy, which is an inseparable property of the Female Sex, forbids them by a Fundamental Law to comport themselves in such Cases after any other manner.

When I had thus spent three years, with a Servant of the same Age as my self, my Parents took a House at *Islington*,[1] hoping there to have a better Trade than they had in the City: But to our misfortune it happened, one certain *Sunday* Morning, that my Mother accompanied by the Maid, went to Church. That day a young Man very handsome, and spruce, came to our House to drink a Pot of Purle.[2] My Father, who for the promoting of Trade, did commonly entertain himself by talking with Passengers, began immediately to fall into Discourse with this Sparke,[3] and ask'd him which way he was bent, since he had a Portmantle[4] with him, and several such like Questions, which in truth, were indifferent to him; but Hosts and Barbers must furnish Discourse, though it be of themselves. This Gentleman, who at least by his Apparel seem'd to be so, told him, as he was smoking a Pipe of Tobacco, that he came from *London*, that he was going into *Essex*,[5] that he was a Rope-dancer,[6] and that his

---

1 A rural village in the seventeenth century, covering approximately three thousand acres, north of London. Sir Walter Raleigh (1578-81) and Sir Francis Bacon (1616-28) lived there.

2 A liquor made by infusing wormword or other bitter herbs into ale or beer.

3 A young man of elegant or foppish character; one who affects smartness or display in dress or manners.

4 Variant spelling of "Portmanteau," a case or bag for carrying clothing or other necessaries when traveling.

5 A county on the eastern coast of England.

6 One who "dances" or balances on a rope suspended at some height above the ground.

Companions were all gone to *Romford*,[1] that he intended to go thither to exercise his Art, by reason that the Fair was suddainly to be there; added that he had been for a while sick at *Brandford*,[2] and therefore could not set forth jointly with his Company. This Discourse was pat to my Fathers Humour; for he was the most curious Man I ever saw in all my Life: Thus he fell immediately to talk of that Art with this Professour, saying, he could not sufficiently admire their boldness in their Tricks and Jumps, and especially their Dexterity in the plain and double Strapado,[3] and several other such like things, which my Father had, perhaps, heard the names of from one or other. As for what concerns leaping, my Dear Landlord, said the Rope-dancer, it is a thing not over easy to learn, and which requires a long time and a great deal of boldness, without reckoning the danger there is in breaking an Arm or a Leg, which is daily to be expected, but to Vault upon the High Rope is easy to learn, for there is not so much art in that, as People do imagine; provided only, continued he, that I had some body who has reasonably strong Arms, I would learn him the Strapado as well in half an hour, as if he had exercised himself in our Art for thirty years together. My Father listned to this Discourse more attentively, then he had ever done to any Sermon, though I have always known him to be a good Christian. He also desired this Hop Merchant[4] (as if by this means he could have got his Livelyhood) that he would teach him to Vault a little. The other seem'd to refuse him downright at first; but it was only (as I easily perceived afterwards) to enflame the poor Man the more upon this matter, and my Father won on him so far, at length by the promising a Free Scot,[5] that he undertook to learn him the Strapado. For that purpose they went into the Stable, which being behind our Garden, and having shut our Fore-door, that no Body might come in in the mean while, they

---

1   A town in Essex twelve miles northeast of London.
2   A town in Middlesex at the junction of the Brent and Thames, eight miles west of London.
3   Commonly understood, not as a game of skill, as it is here, but as a form of punishment or torture in which the victim was secured to a rope, usually with the hands tied behind the back, made to fall from a height almost to the ground, then stopped with a jerk.
4   A merchant who deals in hops. Hops may refer not only to beer but also to the ripened cone of the female hop-plant, used for giving a bitter flavour to malt liquors (*OED*).
5   A Scot is a payment or reckoning (obsolete).

fastned a Rope a-cross the Stable, twelve or thirteen foot high from the ground, for the Rope Dancer gave him to understand, that it must be at least so high for the better performing their business. I stood there hard by, and I was very much pleased that my Father would learn to Vault, but I knew not that his leaping would be followed with such mischiefs, as happened thereupon. Thus when all was ready, and that the Ladder was placed upon the Rope, this brave young Man put off his upper Cloaths, and then went to the Rope, where having done some Tryals of Skill, he showed my Father how he must do the Strapado. This being performed, the Rope-dancer put on his Cloaths again; and having helped his Apprentice to mount upon the Rope, he made him put his two Leggs between his Arms; after which he pull'd him by the Feet in such a manner, that my Father whose Leggs were descended somewhat too low, to turn afterwards his Bum[1] between his Arms, as the other Rope dancers do: but the Spark began to laugh at him, took away the Ladder, and the Keys out of his Pocket, and (for after the Example of his Master, he had put off his upper Cloaths that so he might be the more active and light) then went into the house, where having opened the Chests and Drawers, and Trunks, he took all that he had a mind to without making any great haste: for he knew very well, that my Father, by reason the Rope was so high from the Ground, durst not let himself fall. In the mean while the poor man cried out most lamentably, being extreamly tired with hanging in that manner; and fancying, that his Goods and Moneys were packeting up, that he became very hoarse; but because this Stable was far distant from the High-way no body could hear him. I began also to cry, and I would willingly have helped my Father, but I had not Strength sufficient to put the Ladder again in its right place: wherefore, tho I was very young, I ran out towards the Street, to call out for help from some of the Neighbours and Passengers; but I had no sooner lifted up the Latch of the Door, then that the Rope-dancer struck me, and threatned me with a naked Knife to cut my Throat, if I did not return immediately into the Stable. These Menaces were accompanied with a dozen Boxes of the Ear, which made me return back to the place swifter than I came from thence; where I was no sooner arrived, than that I saw the lamentable End of this impertinent Curiosity:[2] For my Father

---

1 Buttocks, posterior.
2 Recalls "The Story of Ill-Advised Curiosity," *Don Quixote*, I, 33-35.

being almost become mad to be robbed in this manner of all his Goods, and his Arms being no longer able to support his Body, he let go his Hold, and by a great Fall broke his left Legg, the Pain whereof made him cry out so hideously, that his Master, who quickly imagined what the matter was, came thither again, Landlord, said he to him, as soon as he saw him lying in that lamentable Condition, It is the common Fate of most of those who exercise our calling: However, I do not doubt but that you will become an expert Master; but comfort your self for having so well learnt this hard Trick. When I return, added he, bursting out alaughing, I'll teach you the double *Strapado*, and the *Balance*, and so you'll have an occasion to break your Neck after a delicate manner. Thereupon he went again into the House, and presently after away with all he could carry, pulling the Door after him. In the mean while my Father lamented, and cried out so piteously, that he forgot to order me to open the Door, and bawl out Thieves; by which means we might have recovered our Goods, whereof we have never re-got[1] the least again, tho as you will see in the Sequell of this Narrative, if you take but the pains to read so far, I made him pay dearly for his Robbery. It was about half a quarter of an hour afterwards that my Mother returned from Church with her Maid, and were much amazed to see the Door so close shut: they knocked: Whereupon I went forward, siezed with fear, by reason I imagined that the Hop-merchant was come again. As soon as I opened the Door, I leap'd upon my Mothers Neck, who seeing me in so deplorable an Estate, knew not what to think on't. She asked me what the matter was, and why I lamented so much? But for a long while I was not able to make her an Answer, by reason Sighs and Sobs hindered me from speaking. At length I related to her, that my Father had had a mind to learn to Vault, and that his Master had robbed us so piteously. Thereupon they ran to the Cupboards and Truncks, found them open, and that the best Booty was carried away: Then my Mother went to the Stable, where she saw her Husband lying upon the Ground, groaning so hideously out of Pain, that he would have moved to Compassion the hardest Heart in the World. She lamented as much as he, tho' not for his Misfortunes, but for the loss of our Goods. Whereupon she fell into such a Fury, that she swore she would let him die there, without any Help; for that by the sillyest and maddest Action in the World, he

---

1 Obtained again, gotten back.

had rendred himself unworthy of Life. I do not doubt but that she would have effected her Word, by contributing towards his Death, for very far from comforting him, or at least sending for a Chirurgeon,[1] she seized on a Fork she found in the Stable, and would have knocked out his Brains, if the Maid by good luck had not been there to prevent the Blow. I was so amazed at this terrible Enterprize, that I ran out of our House, and beseeched two or three of our Neighbours, that they would in all haste go to our House, because that my Mother would Massacre my Father. They went thither immediately, and found my Father in that lamentable Condition, and my Mother in such a Posture as the Infernal Furies are commonly seen painted: She foamed at the Mouth, and her Eyes rolled in her Head after such a ghastly dreadful manner, that I began to imagine, that she was grown distracted; and certainly this was not without reason: For I do not believe that the Devil can have a more hideous Face, than a Woman, who is extreamly in Anger.[2] In the mean while our Maid related the Business to our Neighbours, after the same manner she had heard it from me; and tho' they had before their Eyes this Tragical Spectacle, they burst out alaughing to that degree at my Father's Folly, that they were constrained to hold their Sides; which so enflamed my Mothers Anger, that she was every Minute ready to leap into the Poor Man's Face; but those good People took her aside, and sent immediately for a Chirurgeon, who having set his Leg, went to a Constable,[3] to tell him the State of the Affair, as the Custom is, and by this means, this ridiculous and lamentable Vaulting made such a Noise that same day, that there was hardly Wine and Ale enough in the House to entertain the Guests who came thither out of Curiosity.

As soon as my Father was cured of this Fall, he began to look better after his business, and app'yed himself thereto, with as much diligence and zeal, as if he had been a Ghostly Comforter, or a Preacher in a Ship; but all this did him but little good; for my Mother since the loss of her Goods, had conceived so mortal a hatred against him, that she could hardly bear the sight of him: On the otherside, my Father conjecturing at length, that with all his goodness he could not repair the fault he had committed, and that it had caused him the loss of all his Authority, began to take

---

1 Surgeon (obsolete).
2 Proverbial expression similar to the maxim, "no wild beast is as savage as a woman in her ire."
3 An officer of the peace, a policeman.

an other course, endeavouring to make his Wife be mindful of her Duty by sensible Reasons, insomuch, that sometimes the Pots and Glasses flew like Hail about the Room. They came also at length to such an extremity, that she would neither lye nor eat with him.

In the mean while our Trade began to lessen by degrees, which proceeded principally from these continual disputes and perpetual Debates, for my Mother, (as Women are not so good at dissembling and curbing their Passions as Men are) did not fear to give her Husband all manner of Affronts before their Guests, and she ratled him with so many injurious provoking words, that most commonly he was constrained to get him out of the Chamber, and to wait for a better occasion to punish her for this Affront with Interest.

This Irregular Life lasted, until I had attained the Age of eleven years old, when my Father fell into a Fit of Sickness, which I fancy, was only occasioned by his Melancholly. For since we dwelt out of the City, he was become so lean, that nothing was to be seen in all his Body, but Skin and Bone. And indeed, I had as much Commiseration for the poor Man, as a Child can have for a Father, and though I was still young, I cursed the Unnatural Cruelty of my Mother, who would hardly suffer me to speak to him, and threatned me very severely when she saw that I pittyed him, so much had hatred bastardized all Love and Humanity. The poor Man had lain about three Weeks in this condition, when upon my instant desires, we so ordered the business, that we prevailed with my Mother to see him once more, by reason he found Death approaching, and that he had still something to say to her, which imported[1] her very much. At first she would not listen to him at all; but at length, our Maid and I prevailed with her so far by our Importunities and Groans, that she came to his Bed side.

I am at present, said he, with a very feeble and languishing Voice, (as soon as she had placed her self on his Bed side) upon the brink of Death, and therefore I desire you for that I would not dye willingly with a troubled Conscience, that you would pardon me the faults that I have committed towards you. True it is that I am the cause of all our unfortunate Condition, but when you shall be pleased to consider, that I am the innocent cause thereof, and that I have been pretty severely punish'd for my impertinent Curiosity, I hope you will strip your self of all your anger, and that

---

1 Was of consequence or importance to her.

before my Death you will give me a proof of your Affection by embracing and pardoning me all the Troubles I may have given you. God knows, continued he, with tears in his eyes, that I have always loved you as tenderly as my heart, but your insuperable malice has often times brought upon you mischiefs, which I should never have thought of. However, these things are now passt and gone, and there is no way to help them. I have only one Request to make you, which is thus, You would bring up our little Daughter honourably, and give her good instructions, and encouragement to Piety, for Riches unjustly acquired do seldom profit much; and — the good Man was come so far, when a fainting fit hindred him from continuing. The pitteous condition my Mother saw him in, and his words full of Humility, had moved her something to Compassion; insomuch, that she began to melt into tears. She embraced him very affectionately, and at that time show'd him more kindness, than she had done for the space of three years. However I cannot certainly affirm that she was real in her Carriage, or whether it was only to observe the Custom, and not to refuse a dying man his Request, and indeed, methinks I have reason enough to doubt thereof, for my Father was no sooner dead, than that we could remark nothing else in all her sadness, than a gloomy look, which was put on only to deceive the World, by making it believe that she was sad for the Death of her Husband; but this the Judicious Reader will not blame the Woman for, for at present, there are so many Widdows who bewail their Husbands with one eye, and lure new Lovers with the other, that it is almost universally the Mode, and it has always been a fine thing to follow the Fashion.

My Father being thus dead, as I have said, and having been buried, my Mother remained absolute Mistress, though but of a mean stock to subsist on, and maintained the House with all that was necessary for it; though that I was still very young, I knew how to Converse with and entertain our Guests, and by telling one pleasant Story or other, I made them drink a pint or two the more, for every one took as much delight in seeing my Carriage as in hearing my reasons; thus our Trade would have undoubtedly encreased, if I had been of a riper Age, and if the Guests could have conceived the least hopes of obtaining any favour from me; but the flesh was yet too young, and wholly uncapable of being put upon the Spit.[1]

---

1   A cook's spit, used here as a euphemism for the phallus.

When we had dwelt a Year and a half longer at *Islington*, my Mother thought convenient to return to the Town, for our House was situated so far from all Conveniences, that hardly any Body came thither, unless they were necessarily obliged thereunto; especially in the Winter, for the Summer Trade indeed was pretty good: And I remember that from time to time there was some man or other lay all Night at our House, and that upon such occasions I was forced to roost with the Maid, whereas at other times I lay in my Mothers Arms, from whence I then concluded, that she must needs be a very Commiserating Woman, since to free people out of pain, she imported to them the half of her Bed, but she made them dearly pay for this pitty; and I could easily perceive, that the Chimney smoak'd more, and better by the half, when we had a night-Guest with us than otherwise. But as I deal plainly and frankly in all things, no Body must imagine that my Mother was a Woman to be made use of by all sorts of People, nothing less than that such things only happened with those who had found the art to ingratiate themselves into her favour, and who provided our Kitchin and our Bodies with all things we stood in need of. For to others, she shewed her self so inaccessible, that she would have flown in their Faces if they had but taken the boldness to kiss her. And though she had attained the Age of thirty four years when my Father dyed, yet I could not observe that there was any Body that was the less earnest to cajole her: for not being naturally ugly, and decking her self with all that is proper to please the World, there were but few, if she could in the least perceive that she might draw advantage by them, who knew how to avoid the Snares she laid them. Besides, there are many Men who have an inclination for superannuated flesh; and certainly, it is not inconvenient that there are such Fools in the World; for otherwise those poor Maidens who have lost the Flower and the best of their Youth, either for want of Gallants, or by having been too proud, would otherwise be at a terrible plunge,[1] and they must in spite of their teeths,[2] keep eternally their Maidenheads, whereas they still couple sometimes with the one or other Widdower, who is constrained to seek out a Mother for three or four

---

1   Be in a critical situation or crisis.
2   Tastes, likings (figuratively).

Worms.[1] I speak too of those who have already laid forty years aside, and who begin anew to make Love: For Men imagine that these are good Houswifes; but I assure quite the contrary often happens, and I know such of that Tribe, who without taking any notice of the Children of the first Bed, gave sufficiently to understand by their lascivious glances and impudent Caresses, that they had not kept their Maidenhead so long, but that there was no Body that Courted them in Marriage: Wretched then are those Widdowers, who are not able enough to give those old toothless Creatures their belly full, for those old Holes must be satisfyed, or else they must accustom their heads to Brow-Antlets, that their being of the Fraternity of *Acteon*,[2] may make the less noise in the World.

But by these sort of extravagant Discourses I might wander too far from my Design, that I should almost forget what I have to say: Wherefore I think it more reasonable to lay aside these old wrinckled Wenches; But let us go gently, I am mistaken, as long as they have no Husbands, no Wrinckles are discovered, because the Fore-top is so strongly fastened, that the Forehead in spite of Teeth must seem smooth; and tho' this causes a terrible pain in the Head, yet they will not complain of it: for it is much better to endure a little Pain, than to serve for a Remedy to love, by suffering a wrinckled Forehead to appear. I told you, to return to our Subject, that my Mother, to get a Trade, and subsist with Honour (for a great deal must be endured for that) she suffered her self to be often Courted; and that after the death of my Father, having dwelt about a year and a half at *Islington*, she found it more advantageous to return to Town, for to be the nearer her Customers; and not to make poor young men run so far with their troublesome Weapons. For that purpose she took a House near *Smithfield*.[3] This was a large and stately House, insomuch that we should not have been able to have furnished it in the two or three last years of my Father's Life, since that from time to time we were forced to sell some or other of our Goods to furnish the rest of the House, and the other Necessities: For then our Profit still grew less and less; but since my Mother was become a Widow, and that upon Occasion she had sometimes

---

1 Here the word is applied to children.
2 Cuckolds. In classical mythology, Acteon was a hunter who was turned into a stag after watching the Goddess Diana bathe.
3 An open space of five or six acres in extent, lying just north of the walls of London and best known as the site of Bartholomew Fair.

satisfied her Acquaintance, our Money and Goods were so visibly augmented, that we then could receive honourably a Man of Quality and Merit. However this could not in any manner be compared with what we had possessed before that this abominable Hop-merchant had learnt[1] my Father the *Strapado*; and if we could but have kept that, we might have buried the Old Man with more Honour than we did: For to speak the Truth, we had hardly then as much left as would maintain us alive for a week or two, unless we would have sold our Furniture; and if my Mother had not played with her Buttocks at that time we should have been in a poor Condition; and tho' several Men of a nice and disdainful Humor,[2] make it a Trade to criticize upon persons, who make their profit on that part of the Body; yet I do not think that herein they have any great reason: For the Fist and the Tail are made of one and the same Flesh,[3] and Sweating is as easily got by that, as by the most laborious Trade that is exercised. Thus as soon as we had brought our Moveables into our new House, we began to set all things in Order, so that in a little time we might get a good Sum of Money, and certainly something would have come of this, for our Traffick grew daily better and better, if my Mother had not happened to fall ill at the beginning of the Winter. This made me extreamly sad, tho' in the beginning I did not think that there was any Danger. But my Grief augmented in the twinckling of an Eye: when I heard our Maid say, that it was the Small Pox which began here and there to break out: For I had observed in other persons, that it is a Disease which renders People ugly, as well the young as the old; and tho' I was still young, I nevertheless observed, that one amorous Bout brought us more Profit than ten times running to the Tap. My Mother, who was void of all Comfort upon this Accident, and who was pretty well on towards her Fortieth year, wished a thousand times rather to have had the *Covent-Garden Gout*:[4] For she fancied she should be sooner freed from it than these villainous Swellings. Nevertheless they began to break out in such abundance upon her Face, that one could have hardly placed a Pins Head without touching those Devilish things, which cast the poor Woman into such a Despair, that Night and Day she did nothing else than

---

1 Taught.
2 Mental disposition, constitutional or habitual tendency.
3 Unidentified proverbial expression.
4 A slang term for venereal disease. Covent Garden was a popular location for women of ill-repute.

groan and complain. However, after nine Days the Pox began to aposthumate,[1] which render'd her Face so dreadful and hideous, that she, who before resembled a *Venus*[2] in Beauty, had then the Figure of a *Medusa*.[3] I trembled for fear every time I looked upon her: For her Nose, which in the time of her Blossom was none of the longest nor thickest, was now of a prodigious Length and Breadth, by reason of the Scabs wherewith it was so covered all over, that one would have rather taken it for a Steeple than a Nose. However, all would yet have gone well enough, if that while no body was in the Chamber, the good Woman had not leapt out of Bed, and taken a Looking Glass, which we had refused her for a long time before: She saw her Face, and observing that it was so thick, and so ugly, she gave so terrible a Shriek, that all the House rang with it. The Maid and I who were seated and chattering together, ran thither immediately; but we came not time enough to hinder a thing which has drawn Tears from her Eyes a thousand times: For she was in so desperate a Condition, that with both her Hands she scratched all her Face, insomuch that the Blood ran down her Cheeks. In the mean while we prevailed with her so far, that we brought her again somewhat to her right Sences, and put her to Bed; but she was so troubled and distracted for the Loss of her Beauty, that we had all the pains imaginable to bear with her.

Two or three Weeks being passed, she recovered her Health, and made use of all manner of Artifices, for to seem still what she had formerly been; but all in vain: For her Cheeks, when as I have said already she scratched with so much violence the Aposthumate Pox, had received such deep Wounds, that every Pit resembled a Cautery.[4] Besides, the Winter by its violent Cold, had rendred the new Skin with which her face was covered so blew that she might justly pass for a Remedy to love. Those who before valued her so highly, did now droll upon her[5] as much and laugh at her for that having spent so many years, she had not yet had the Small Pox and the Meazles. And certainly this seems somewhat ridiculous, but what remedy against an unfortunate

---

1 To fester.
2 Classical goddess of love.
3 In classical mythology, a gorgon with snakes in her hair and a gaze that turned into stone anyone who looked at her.
4 A wound made by cauterizing, that is, by burning or searing with a heated, metallic instrument.
5 Make sport or fun of her.

Destiny; But however wee should have been happy in all these adversities; if they had contented themselves with Jestings; but the most part of our giving Customers forsook the House; and if there was any one now who still frequented it, it was not for the Love of my Mother, but to caress me: For I began to become ripe, which made me have an Abomination for the Cursed Passions of certain Men, who seem to think there is no Sin in Violation and Brutality. However, I shall never be obliged to answer for so horrible a Crime: For I was so vexed to see my self Courted by those same Men, who long before had to do with my Mother, that provoked with Spite, I drove them all out of the House. In the mean while the Rumor ran abroad amongst the Lovers of Gallantry, that I was already for the Sport; which made several of them come to our House, to see if they could attain a Leap with me:[1] amongst whom there were a great Number of young Sparks, Merchants Servants, and Cash-Keepers:[2] For that Race is commonly full of Curiosity; and tho' I was tall of stature, yet I was not over discreet, and perhaps I might have been caught and tempted by those Beardless Youths, had not my Mother been watchful over my Conduct; and had she not continually preached to me, that those old Rusty blades[3] who did it only once in four and twenty hours, were the best, and gave most Money. However, we plum'd some of these young Droles[4] of their Feathers, for there was to be at least two or three dishes of Sweetmeats,[5] before they could have the honour to kiss me but once, and this difficulty rendred them so hot and eager, (because I made every one believe that it was he who enjoyed the favour of my Affection) that no means could have made them abstain from our House.

Thus while we fed every one with hopes, but granted not one any peculiar favour (for to speak the truth, I was yet something too young to do my own concern) there came to our House a certain *Surrey*[6] Gentleman, who had no sooner seen me, then that he used all manner of means to please me, which he did with much better success than he could have imagined; for he was the most beautiful man I think I ever saw in all my life; besides, his Tongue was so admirably well hung, that he had, the greatest

---

1 Copulate with me.
2 Persons who have charge of cash (treasurers, cashiers).
3 Aging gallants.
4 Variant spelling of "drolls," funny or waggish young men.
5 Sugared cakes or pastries, candied fruits or sugared nuts.
6 A southern county, lying between Middlesex and Sussex.

Capacity in the World to excite Love in the most insensible heart. My Mother quickly conjectured how Affairs went, and therefore never set foot out of the Room as long as this Spark was in our Company, Insomuch, that I had never any occasion to show him by my courtesie that I had given him my Inclinations. The good Gentleman who quickly observed that he could never bring about his Designs, as long as my Mother watch'd me so narrowly, slipt a Letter one Evening into my hand, without any one's taking notice of it, and therein he told me, *That if I would go away with him to* St. Alban's,[1] *or into some other Place, he would keep me as his Wife; that it was not possible for him to live any longer without me, and that he would not have offered me that means if he had not seen that my Mother opposed my Fortune.* With several other such like things, which pleased me to such a degree, that I resolved, by reason that from my Infancy I had had a peculiar inclination for handsom men, to grant him his Request, and take my own Passport under my heels; and methought that this was no so indecent a business, for we find so many amongst those of the highest Quality, whose insurmountable Lasciviousness has made them take this Course that our Neighbours could not be much amazed at it.

But while I was preparing all things for my flight, by reason that within two days we intended to be on the Wing, there came one time four Gentlemen to our House, whom Heaven had sent thither undoubtedly on purpose to hinder me from committing a fault which I should have so long time repented of. The Countenance of my pretty Spark, who had been seated by the side of me, for two or three hours together, became as red as Blood as soon as he saw these four Men come in, and without so much as paying the Reckoning, he went away out of our House. One of the four who had the looks of a brisk and facetious Gallant, began immediately to laugh so loud, that he was forc'd to hold his Sides. Would you believe, said he to his Company, as soon as his immoderate Laughter was something moderated, that the honest Gentleman who was seated by this Maiden was such a Man? We must own (continued he) that looks are extreamly deceitful, and that what he has done did well deserve an Exemplary Punishment. How! (said the others) is this a Robber who has merited the Gallows or some other Death? He merited much more than one Death alone (replyed he who spoke first of all) for he has suborned a young Lady, whom he was not worthy of by the thousandth part! Did he then, Sir, promise to Marry her, (asked I

---

1 A town in Hertfordshire with many inns on the road to London.

him, not being able to forbear blushing at the same time) for methought I was sufficiently concerned in the business; and that he had either broke his word, or got the person with Child? You do him too much honour, pretty Creature, said he to me who know him so well, and he might wish with all his Heart that that were true; but (continued he) not to leave you any longer in suspence, I will tell you the whole Affair just as it happen'd.

This pleasant Drole was one Squire —— is descended from one of the richest and most Considerable Families of the County of *Surrey*, and had always been esteemed for a brave and civil young Gentleman. For he had the Art to do all things with that Neatness and with so good a Grace, even before that he had yet attained to a Competent Age, that in his Countrey he pass'd for a perfect Gallant. He very rarely frequented the Company of young Men, and there was never any report of his having committed any disorder with them, insomuch, that so many fine Qualities being joyned to a vast Estate, all the young Ladies of the Countrey wish'd him for their Husband, and all Mothers for their Son in Law. As he had not thitherto given his heart to any Body, and as he seemed to love all Women equally, every Damosel[1] flattered her self with the hopes that she should be the person who should find her felicity in possessing him.

While Affairs stood in this posture a Suit at Law brought him to *London*, where he often visited a certain Widdow whom we will call *Lucinda*, who was of the same County; and his Neighbour. *Lucinda* had great famillarity with an other Lady, and her Daughter who came frequently to see her. Now our Squire was so highly extolled by *Lucinda*, and some others who had seen him, that *Celiana* the Lady and Mother of the Daughter I mentioned, conceived such an esteem for him, before she had seen him once, that from that very moment she was wishing to have him for her Son in Law, so foolish and rash are most part of Women.

These Ladies going one day to the Play together, the Squire happening to be there at the same time, had no sooner seen *Lucinda*, whom he was particularly acquainted with, surrounded with these Strangers, than that he endeavoured to Court the occasion[2] of ushering her to her Coach, which having accomplish'd, he took that opportunity to strike up a Match[3] to play

---

1 Variant spelling of "damsel"; a young, unmarried lady.
2 To take advantage of the opportunity, to show himself worthy of the occasion.
3 To set up a game.

with her and the Ladies Daughter at *Ombre*[1] the next day, not expecting that this first encounter would prove so unfortunate to him. As he had not the least design of acting the part of *Lucinda's* Lover, tho she was not much in Years, he accosted *Clara*, (this is the name of the young Lady) discourst Her,[2] and found her Conversation so charming, that he fell in Love with Her, being the first time in all his Life that e're he was enamoured. By these means growing familiarly acquainted, he quickly found the means to visit his new Mistress, and still observing more and more Charms in her Wit and Person, he made no difficulty to declare his Love to that young Widow, who immediately communicated this Piece of News to *Celiana*, *Clara's* Mother, not believing it would be unwelcome to her, and indeed *Celiana* was overjoyed at it and desired her Couzen to lend a helping Hand to this Business, after she had enquired after the Quality and Estate of our Gallant.

Lucinda who was as cunning as is necessary to be in such like Affairs, to attain to a good end, carried *Clara* into all Companies which she knew the Squire used commonly to frequent; but however to enflame him so much the more, she managed the Intrigue after such a manner, that he could not always speak to her according to his desire, even when that he once had opened his Heart to her, she represented to him the Matter something difficult, without making it seem impossible to him: She told him that *Clara* had been courted in Marriage, by many Persons of Quality, but that thitherto her Father having made choice of none, in that respect she would endeavour all she could to have him preferred before all others. This answer rendred him so much the more greedy, and made him still and still more passionately desirous to have *Clara* for a Wife, which possibly he would not have been, if he had known that he himself was courted. Yet the Truth is, that *Clara* and her Father knew nothing of all this in the beginning, and this Commerce was a long time managed by *Lucinda* and *Celiana*, but as soon as they saw that Affairs were in a good Posture, they gave an account of those secret Amours to *Cleon* that young Ladies Father who being very particularly pleased with the Person of our young Squire, and being informed

---

1 A card game, popular in the seventeenth and eighteenth centuries, played with forty cards by three people. Ombre plays a prominent part in Alexander Pope's *The Rape of the Lock* (1713), Canto 3.
2 Held discourse with her, spoke with her.

of his Estate and his Riches, was very well satisfied. At the same time, the Squire for his part declared to his own Father the Love he had for this young Lady, and he desired him to approve of this Choice: The Father, who by the report of other Persons, found that *Cleon* was able to give a Portion with his Daughter suitable to his Sons Fortune, gave his consent thereto very willingly; in case, said he to his Son, that you be assured of the Maidens Affection, and her Parents Approbation. Thereupon the Squire went immediately to *Lucinda*, related to her the Discourse he had had with his Father, and desired her to do her best endeavours that were possible in his behalf; whereupon she made him answer with a smiling Countenance, that the Affair was half done, that there was not much trouble when one had to speak for a Person so well made, and endued[1] with so many fine Qualities as himself, and assured him that if her Father asked *Clara* for him in Marriage, she would not be refused him: However you have some small Obligation to me, added she smiling, for I have spoke so many good things of you, as I believe have contributed very much towards the producing and entertaining the favourable Sentiments that her Relations have of you. The Squire gave her humble Thanks, and made her the finest Protestations imaginable, that he would never let so great a Service escape his Memory.

As soon as our Lover, (whose Heart was so deeply smitten, that he could hardly take a moments repose) had taken his leave, *Lucinda* went to discover to *Celiana* all the Discourse she had had with him touching this Marriage. *Celiana* who received an incredible Joy from this News, made known to her Husband how far Affairs were advanced, and commanded her Daughter to receive the Squire thenceforward as a Lover, who was quickly to be her Husband. *Clara* who had already had some inkling of this Commerce, was very much astonished to see that Affairs were already come so far, that it was almost impossible to hinder her Marriage any longer, had a secret Grief for that she had an other Lover, for whom her Heart had some Kindness. However, as she had Wit enough, and as she had always been obedient to her Parents, she endeavoured to surmount her Sadness, and not to make it appear either to her Relations or her Servant. In the mean while our Gallant went to visit her the day after, and made her a Declaration of Love, full of acuteness and Beauty of Wit. He protested also to her at the same time that he did not desire she should

---

1 Variant spelling of "endowed."

force her Inclinations, and he made these Complements with so many Charms of Homage and Affection, that almost in a moment he made her forget her other Lover, who had made such deep Impressions in her Heart. She declared to him thereupon that the amazement she was in at the sudden Advancement of those Affairs, did not allow her to answer after such a manner as she was willing upon the Honour she received from him, and that she did not think to have merited it, but that though she was ready to follow blindly the choice of her Parents, she should obey them with the more Courage, when she was to fall into the Arms of a Man of his Merit. As *Clara* had been satisfied with the Squire's Complements,[1] so he was no less with those she made him; for he found therein so much Prudence and Civility, that he took his leave of her more enamoured than he had ever been. However, before he went out of the House, he spoke of his Amours to *Cleon* and *Celiana*, and after having been received by them with all the Testimonies of Affection, he desired his Father again the same day to go ask *Clara* for him in Marriage, which was solemnized two days afterwards, the Damosel received him with a chearful Heart, and the Rumour of this Marriage was quickly spread about the Town.

As this Intrigue had till then been managed secretly, there were many who were much amazed at it. Those Mothers who had thought to have catch him for their Daughters were very sad: the Ladies who had given him their Inclinations were in the deepest Dispair. And those Men whom he had thought worthy of his Friendship, though there were very few of that sort, for he very seldom haunted the Company of Men, were very sensibly afflicted, because they fancied that *Clara* being the only Daughter of her Parents, that match would make him abandon the Countrey. To make short, the whole Town was in Mourning, and every one could have wished to have put a Spoke in his Wheel.[2] In the mean while, all the Relations of the Bridegroom went to congratulate the Bride, and every one by Treats and Banquets endeavouring to shew her the Joy they had for this Marriage.

All the while that these Feastings and Treats lasted, and that *Clara* had her new Lover by her Side, she quite forgot *Aleippe*, that was the Name of the Votary she abandoned, but in a while she began to think of him again, and dreaded the sight of him, by

---

1 Variant spelling of "compliments."
2 To obstruct, thwart, or impede his person or proceeding.

reason she was afraid she should still find him amiable, and she knew very well that her Love could only bring her disquiet.

But the News of this Wedding coming to *Aleippe's* Ears, and being a Friend of all the Family, he made them a Visit, that he might be perfectly assured of the Truth of the Report and as he loved this young Lady from the very bottom of his Heart, he was ᵒᵒolved to know what Measures he had to take. *Cleon* did not ᵗim long in Suspence, for after the first Complements were ᵗe related to him all that had happened in the Squires who seeing that *Aleippe* was a particular Friend of the gg'd he would honour him with his Friendship. In the ᵗle, *Aleippe* stood like a Statue, his Countenance very Moment, and he knew not what answer was best make. However he did his best to recollect himself, for should entertain some suspicions of the Truth: then the his Face began to lessen, and his Voice became bolder; when *Clara* entred the Room, the sight of her made his Face glow anew, and the Grief he had for this Marriage might easily have been taken notice of, if for the hiding of it he had not gone some Steps forward as it were to meet her, as pretending to congratulate her upon her Marriage. *Clara* for her part felt no less Emotion, and having perceived that he was informed thereof, as soon as she came into the Room, she cast her Eyes down to the Ground, for fear some Alteration should be observed in her Countenance, which was also the Cause, that she quickly found a Pretext to go out of a Room where she could not stay without feeling new Emotions. *Aleippe* in like manner did no longer delay taking leave, and went immediately to his Lodging and so to Bed, that he might not be disturbed by any Body, and that he might curse all the Female Sex upon the account of his faithless Mistress. That Night he changed his Resolution a thousand times, sometimes he resolved to challenge his Rival, then again to make his open Complaints to his Mistress, or else some other such like Design; but at length after having thought of all things, and passed all the Night without sleeping, he resolved to dissemble his resentment, seeing the Business was done, and that if he made any noise it would only tend to the banishing him the House, rather than be of any advantage to him; and as he still loved her as much as ever, he resolved to frequent her as a Friend, and not to discover any thing of all that had passed between him and her, unknown to her Parents. For he imagined that *Clara* might still love him notwithstanding her Marriage, and that the Squire in so little a time could not have won her Heart, but that she had marry'd him out of Obedience, and that perhaps he should not be so unhappy as he had represented to himself.

With these Thoughts he returned as before to *Clara's* House, and the Discourses he sometimes had with his former Mistress, made him believe that he was not deceived in his Thoughts; for whether that she loved him still, or that she was willing to hinder him from telling that she had had some Kindness for him formerly, she was always saying to him the most tender and the most touching Things imaginable, she assured him she only married the Squire out of Obedience, and made him believe that his Happiness was much greater than that of his Rival.

In the mean while *Aleippe* could not observe that Marriage had inspir'd the more Love into *Clara* for her Husband; for to say the Truth he had done nothing less than what Duty requires from a Man in such an Occasion. But however, he did not find her the less Chaste and Prudent, for though she assured him she had not banished him her Heart, and though he himself might easily read in her Eyes, that she loved him with a very violent Affection; nevertheless they endeavoured to avoid his Presence, insomuch that Virtue still more and more set at a greater Distance, what Love seem'd to be so fond of favouring.

Affairs were for above a Year in this Posture, without the amorous *Aleippe's* being able to effect any thing to his Advantage, notwithstanding all the diligence he used for that Purpose. In the mean while the Relations and Goranymphs[1] were almost dayly teazing the young Woman, if she was with Child, which Queries at length beginning to grow troublesome, she answered them after a tutchy manner, that she knew no reason she should be with Child, since she found nothing in Marriage that could render her so. Having uttered these Words she began to blush and cast down her Eyes upon the Ground, as if she would have made them believe, that it was not altogether designedly that she spoke in that manner; but only to free her self from the Importunity of those who asked her dayly the same things and such like Questions. However her Mother being present understood the thing after another manner, and having called her Daughter alone, after having ask'd her several such like Questions as are easy to be imagined, she was at length informed of the Truth, and had no longer any other Thought than to remedy the Fault she had com-

---

1 Neologism or unidentified term, perhaps an unlettered, phonetic spelling of "grownups."

mitted in precipitating the Marriage with so much Rashness.

In the mean while, the Rumour of his Insufficiency was quickly spread about the House, from the Family through all the Relations, from the Relations into the Neighbourhood, and so through all the Town. *Aleippe* was overjoyed to hear the News, and when he considered, that his Mistress having been already married for the space of a Year, was still a true Virgin, he could hardly conceal his Joy; for having pretty often observed that she loved him, and imagining that this Accident might bring about a Marriage between her and him, and that nothing was equal to her Vertue, since neither the Love she bore him, nor the Impotence of her Husband were able to move her, to suffer the least-thing that was capable of making a breach in her Honour, he received a hundred Motions of Joy, in that he had not accomplished his first Resolution; Namely, to challenge that Impotent Spark, nor to declare himself the Enemy of his Mistress, by acting against her with too much Choler.[1]

In the mean while, the Parents of this Virgins Wife, let Squire *Limberham's* Father and Friends know, that the Marriage was not accomplished, and that they who had brought him up from his Infancy, could not without doubt be ignorant of what he was; they added hereto, that, if his Son did not give and show better Signs and Testimonies of his Manhood, they would cause the Marriage to be made null: the Father, who had not seen, perhaps in twenty years, his Sons Instruments, set light by such Discourses, and would not write one word in answer to their Complaints.

In the mean while, none was more eager than Squire *Limberham* to divulge these things about, by reason that he figured to himself, that by these means he would make every one believe that there was nothing of Truth in the Matter. He also invented a Trick which was capable of blinding a thousand Persons; his Wife's Chamber-Maid was turn'd out of the House big with Child, which was well enough known in the World, but thitherto no Body could divine who was the Author of that Business. Squire *Limberham* alone knew that his Man was the Father; but as he had a great Kindness for him, and that he must have been obliged to have turned him away, if it once came to be discovered that he had got it, he had always pretended to know nothing of the Matter. Now he went to the Maid who was every moment expecting to fall in Labour, and gave her fifty Guinnies to oblige

---

1 Anger.

her to lay the Child to him, and to tell all People that he was the Father of it.

About a Week after the Chamber-Maid was brought to Bed, and she did as she was ordered, which caused such a Noise through all the Town that it became the whole Subject of Discourse, both of small and great. People began to gaze upon one another, and knew not what now to say of a Man who had so brave a Boy newly Born. Hereupon Squire *Limberham* was brought into the Spiritual Court,[1] by some that knew there would be a great deal of Money to be got, and charg'd him with having violated the Honour of his Marriage. Squire *Limberham* for his part had his Lawyers to plead the contrary with great earnestness, though he would not have been very sorry though the Cause had gone against him; for by that means his Father and Mother-in-Law would have been found to have been in the wrong, and he would have been look'd upon as a Man very proper for the Multiplication of Human kind, which was the very Hinge of the whole Business.

Now as these Affairs had been for above three Weeks or a Month in the same state, and that every one spoke diversly thereof, *Aleippe*, began to fancy that there might be some Mystery hidden in this Business, and therefore resolved to try all manner of Means to discover this Commerce. For that purpose he went to the Chamber-Maids Lodgings, whom he was very well acquainted with, believing that if Gain had obliged her to Lye, another of greater Importance would make her declare the Truth. At the very first he pretended to know the whole Affair, but the Chamber-Maid was too cunning to let her self be caught in such Snares. Afterwards, he promised much more than that vain Pretender to getting of Children, but she refused to receive his offer, fearing some Mischief might happen to her, after having too obstinately maintained such a Cheat. *Aleippe* assured her of the contrary, saying, he had Friends who were powerful enough to secure her from all Danger: These Reasons being seconded with a good Sum of Mony made her quickly yeild.[2] However she comported her self runningly[3] in this Affair: for instead of giving Evidence by Word of Mouth against Squire *Limberham* in this Affair, she gave *Aleippe* a Letter, but upon Condition he should say that

---

1 Church court, which had jurisdiction in the late seventeenth century over cases involving marriage, adultery, and fornication.
2 Obsolete spelling of "yield."
3 Rapidly, readily (obsolete).

he had found it by chance. In that Letter Squire *Limberham* writ to her, *That she should stand firm to her Instructions and Depositions, that he had got the Child, assuring her, that during all her Life she should have wherewith to live plentifully upon, provided she could make the World believe this to be a Truth.* And several other such like things. I know very well that it was a great Imprudence for a Man of Sence to confide such a thing in a Letter, and that there are many who would doubt of the Truth; but he is not the first amongst Men endued with Wit and Prudence, who has committed such a Fault.

In the mean while *Aleippe* having this Letter in his Hands, went on the Morrow Morning early to the Court, and gave Information that he had found a Letter, by which it might be evidently made appear, that the Proceedings against Squire *Limberham* were set on foot out of Malice, since he was not Father of the Child, and having delivered thereupon the Letter to the Justice, it was read publickly, which caused so excessive a Laughter in the Court that the whole Chamber rung again. Squire *Limberham's* Council having collationed[1] the Letter with those other Acts of his they had in their Hands, as if they could have justified him, found that the Writing was by the same Hand, insomuch that no Body did in the least doubt of the Truth of the Matter. However they would not wholly give up the Cause, but sent Sergeants to fetch both Squire *Limberham* and the Chamber-Maid.

Limberham not in the least suspecting how Causes went, trooped thither immediately, and arrived almost at the same time that the Chamber-Maid did. The Letter was shown him by the Court, and he ask'd if he had not written it. Whereupon poor Squire *Limberham* became so ashamed and so amazed that he could not speak. Then they asked the Chamber-Maid for what reason she accused that Gentleman of a thing whereto he had not contributed in the least, as appears by the Letter. The Chamber-Maid seeing her self pressed, confessed the Truth, saying, that he had given her fifty Guinnies and made a promise to maintain her very splendidly all her Life long if she would stand fast to her Word, and would make him loose the Cause; that he had never had any Carnal Knowledge of her, but that his Man whom he had brought out of the Countrey with him, was the Father of the Child, and that never in her Life any other Person had had to do with her.

---

1 Compared carefully.

Upon this Confession, and upon showing the Letter, the Indictment was cast out; but Squire *Limberham* was condemned for his Deceit to pay fifty Guinnies more to the Chamber-Maid, who was to be kept in the Constables Hand, until the Man who had debauched her, and who should be cited to marry her, had by that means repaired her Honour; and that thus they might afterwards by those hundred Guinnies undertake some such Employment as might help them to live honourably in the World.

This Sentence was very much commended by all People, and Squire *Limberham's* Traffick was so laught at by all People, that for a while he durst hardly appear abroad, for the Affair was so publick that the whole Town pointed at him.

In the mean while, this Adventure having more and more for-tified in *Cleon* the Opinion, that his handsome Son-in-Law was Guelt,[1] he presented a Request to Justice, by which he demanded the annullation of his Daughter's Marriage, or that his handsome Son-in-Law might be search'd by two Doctors, to know what might be the Cause of his Insufficiency, and if it was such, that according to Law the Marriage might be abolished.

The last Point was granted him, two Doctors, and one of the eldest Chyrurgions received Orders to search this honest Gentle-man, but he was wiser than that comes to, and confessed as soon as those three Men came to his House, that he had nothing at all to show them, and that since it so pleased Justice he would desist from his Wife, though he had for her the greatest Affection imag-inable. Upon this Confession the Marriage was made null within three days afterwards, and Squire *Limberham* retired into *Surrey*, for infallibly the Oyster Women[2] would have fallen upon him and scratched his Eyes out.

It is now about two Months since this happened, and *Aleippe* who was the Principal Cause of this Affair, has already made *Clara* sensible of the difference there is between him and Squire *Limberham*.

But what do you think, said that Gentleman who told us this Story, addressing himself to me, is not this a brave Spark to pretend to be thus in love with all the Women he meets with? Confess the Truth, added he, has not he made some love to you? for it is impossible for him when he is with any Woman, who has the least Beauty, to forbear Courting her. The Truth is, I was so

---

1 Obsolete form of gelt; gelded, castrated, and hence impotent.
2 Vendors of oysters, notorious for their foul, abusive language: "When damsels first renew their oyster cries," John Gay, *Trivia* (1716), I, 28.

much out of Countenance, and so full of Vexation to have been so miserably deceived by this Eunuch, that I could not utter the least Word: But my Mother who never could endure this Squire *Limberham*, for that he always sat and discourst with me, served for my Interpreter, and chattered so fast, that these Gentlemen had no small reason to laugh; for though she had hardly heard ten Words spoken by my Impotent Lover, during all the time he had haunted our House, she knew nevertheless how to relate a hundred Circumstances of our Amours so pertinently, that though this Affair did not please me in the least, I could hardly forbear Laughing my self.

In the mean while, my Thoughts were so full of this Adventure, that I could not shut my Eyes all the Night long, and when that I began to consider, that this poor *Limberham*, in case I had gone away with him, would have suffered my lower parts to have endured Hunger after a miserable manner: I concluded that though it might have cost me Dear, I would have revenged my self for such a trick; for though I had not as yet tryed if amorous Sports be diverting, or not, I could however easily judge that they could not be unpleasing; for otherwise Women would not be so silly as to suffer themselves to be dishonoured with all their Race for the pleasure of a Moment. As soon as Day was come, and that my Mother, with whom, as I said, I lay, was awake, I desired her that she would not let Squire *Limberham* know in the least that we were informed of his Insufficiency; for said I to her, I am resolved to play him a Trick, and which perhaps may be something to our Advantage. My mother ask'd me near a hundred times what my Intention was, but I would not discover it, for I knew very well that had I unfolded my Design, I should never afterwards have been able to have brought it about; and I began this Discourse in the Morning out of no other Consideration, than to hinder her from embroiling and ruining the whole Intrigue, by an unseasonable Raillery. Thus after she had promised me that she would never say a Word more of it, I prepared that same Morning, what was necessary for the accomplishing and effecting my Design.

In the Afternoon, that Favourite of *Venus* came to our House, and excused himself by a long Shoal[1] of Complements which he made my Mother, for that he the Evening before went away without paying his Reckoning. Thereupon he came to me, and after we had talked a while together, he asked me a thousand

---

1 A large number or school (usually applied to fish).

Questions full of cunning, to know also of me if I had heard something of his Business; but I was so prudent that I made not the least discovery; on the contrary, I treated him after a much more endearing manner than I had ever done before; for though I was very young, however as most young Women can, I knew how to dissemble to Perfection, so that the most cunning Man in the World would have been sufficiently puzzled to observe it: when he had strongly conceived in his Imagination, that I was ignorant of all, towards the Evening he gave me five Guinnies, for to buy what I still stood in need of for our Retreat, desiring me to meet him the next day about four a Clock in the Afternoon alone, in the Royal Exchange,[1] where he would expect me.

My Mother knew nothing of all this Enterprize, and so was not more careful to watch me, than she was used to be at other times; insomuch that it was no hard matter for me the day following to get out of the House at the time appointed. I went immediately to the Change, where I found my Servant,[2] who received me with open Arms, and put me immediately into a Coach: He put a Ring upon my Thumb, being resolved to have me pass for his Wife, that he might lye honourably with me in the Lodging he had taken for us, and which was as stately as most about Town: My Landlord and Landlady admired me strangely, Lord, Madam, said my Landlady, you were married very young, or else your Looks do make you seem younger than your Years speak you to be. I cast down my Eyes upon the Ground just as if I had been out of Countenance, but I can assure, that Shame had taken its last leave of me for above a Year before, for I had seen so much, and heard so many things in my Mothers House, that I was wholly a Stranger to growing Pale or blushing. Squire *Limberham* in the mean while was admirably well satisfied, and went the next day with me to the Change in the *Strand*,[3] to rig me anew from Top to Toe, for though the Cloaths I had were New, and in the Mode, and that I resembled rather the Daughter of a Rich Merchant, than of an Hostess, yet they did not please him, by reason they did not suit with his Cloaths, which were as Costly and Rich as if he had been a Duke.

---

1 Traditional meeting place for merchants to conduct their business, but also a resort for idlers.
2 Here, a professed lover, one who is devoted to the service of a lady.
3 A major London thoroughfare close to the strand (or shore) of the Thames in London running west from the Temple Bar to Charing Cross.

The Truth is, I was not very much dissatisfied, and though he should have bought me Diamond Rings, Pendants, and such Rarities, I believe I should not have been very much displeased.

When we had spent the Day much after this rate, he treated me with a stately Supper, and afterwards like Man and Wife we went to Bed, whereupon *Limberham*, though impotent caressed and embraced me so passionately, that he made my Mouth Water, insomuch that I would have given all I had in the World that his Gimcrack[1] had been in better Condition; for to speak the Truth, his Posture, his Looks, his Actions, and all his brave Qualities pleased me so well, that I should have infallibly had for him the greatest Passion in the World, if he had been something better provided with you know what; but when I began to think of that, all my Love vanished, and a mortal hatred came in its place to seize on my Heart. The Truth is, that I had committed something [of] a hard Action,[2] when upon the Relation of a Story, which I knew not certainly the Truth of, I durst trust a Man with my Maiden-head, who did not look like one that was Guelt: But, Courteous Reader, what shall I say thereof? Nature began to work, and it is a burdensome thing that bears the Name of a Maiden-head, and which several Damosels are obliged to keep so long for want of Servants, became every day more importunate and troublesom, insomuch that I could hardly support it any longer.

When we had thus spent an hour in Kisses and Caressing one another, and after I had made him a thousand amorous Strains in Postures the most petulant[3] imaginable, for to raise his Lust, if he had any in the least; (for my Design was, if I had found a brisk vigorous Gallant, to have stayed with him, and have left my Mother where she was) he told me that he would take a House, not far distant in the Countrey, for to dwell there together, and by reason that I was still a Maid, and very young, and that perhaps I could not endure the Torment of the first shock, without making a Noise, he would wait so long until that we were in a Place where we our selves should have Authority, without being obliged to respect any Body. Thereupon he kissed me several times and went to sleep. I said not a Word, neither do I believe could I have spoken, for Spight had so seized my Heart,

---

1 Literally, a mechanical instrument or contrivance; used here as a euphemism for the phallus.
2 A deed, a thing done.
3 Forward or immodest, wanton, lascivious (rare).

that the Tongue was become as Motionless. But as soon as this Disorder was something over, I resolved to know by Experience if he was really Guelt after the manner I had been informed. To that purpose, when his *Hogs-Norton's* Organs[1] had sufficiently assured me that he was sound asleep; I began to grope with my Hand, but I was above a Quarter of an hour before I could find it, which certainly was no very great Wonder; for first of all I was an Ignoramus in such Matters, and moreover it was so little that I knew not when I had it in my Hand, whether it was what I wanted. I deplored the poor Man's having had so unhappy a Fate, but on the other side I could not forbear (by reason he was so weak and so helpless) to Curse his Passion for Women, since he could do nothing more than whet their Appetites, without being able to satiate them in the least, I turn'd my self near a hundred times, sometimes on the one side, sometimes on the other, and tryed all ways to sleep, but all in vain; for the naked Body of the beautiful *Limberham* did so possess my Thoughts, and were too strong to suffer sleep to get the Mastery over my Sences: For when Damosels endeavour to make Men believe that they are not Lascivious, and that when they are married they will never take their Heats,[2] unless Duty forces them to render such an Obedience to their Husbands: this is the greatest Lye, I assure you, that ever could be invented; and if I had an absolute Liberty to say all that I know in this Case, I would demonstrate that there was never any Sentence pronounced with more Truth than this following, *That a Woman in a good Humour would let a Boy, a Rogue, nay a Hang-man do the Feat.*[3] But let us lay aside these Discourses, for Justice obliges me to take the Womens part, far from treading[4] them inhumanly underfoot, and exciting a great Tumult amongst that tumultuous Sex. However, I do not speak of all, but only of those who, as I was used to say, slacken their Reins too far to their irregular Lusts.

In the Morning when he awaked, I pretended to be asleep to see what he would do, and if at least he would not put his Hand,

---

1 Lungs. Hog's Norton is a humourous corruption of Hock Norton, a village in Oxfordshire. Proverbial for boorishness, Hock Norton became known as a place where pigs play on the organ.
2 Sexual passions, generally alluding to the sexual rutting of animals.
3 Unidentified proverbial expression, possibly a variant of "All women may be won."
4 Used elliptically in the participial phrase 'far from ...ing' when something is denied and the opposite is asserted (figuratively).

where he could do no good with his Gimcrack; but he was too Chaste, and could do nothing but kiss and embrace me very amorously: by reason of which I seemed to awake at length. He ask'd me how I had pass'd the Night, and if I had slept well, I told him that the Thoughts of my Mother, and of my Flight, were still so fresh and so full in my Memory, that I did not begin before Morning to sleep, and therefore I desired him that he would let me take my Rest a little longer. Squire *Limberham* did so, after having kissed me again a hundred times; and jump'd out of Bed, to go walk, as he said, in *St. James's* Park.[1]

When I had no longer this naked Statue by the side of me, and that I was thus no longer tormented by those insupportable Temptations, I fell asleep, and continued so so long, until that word was brought me that the Taylor who had my Gown and Petticoats to make, was below, and that he desired to try them on. Whereupon I got me up, and was busied in changing my old Rigging for new: When that my Valiant Lover returned home, he was so charmed with me in those Cloaths, that in the Presence of all the Company he could not forbear leaping upon my Neck. *O Heavens*! said the Landlady who was there, how fond are these young People of one another: But wait, wait, continued she, until ye have attained to my Years, and eat first seven Bushels of Salt together,[2] and then you'll see a strange Alteration. I thought to my self she would be a true Prophetess in that Affair, for I was well assured that we should not have eaten half a handful together, before we had put a Period to our Amours, and that my pretended Husband would curse the Hour he the first time saw me. The rest of the Day following being past in our Chamber in playing at Cards, and the Night being come, I put so much *Opium* into the Meat I gave Squire *Limberham* to eat (for I had got some for that Purpose, after I had heard a Druggist who was used to frequent my Mother, relate the Vertue of it) that it is proper to make a Person sleep soundly for fifteen or sixteen hours: the poor Man had it no sooner in, his Body than it began to operate, insomuch that he was constrained to go to Bed, com-

---

1 A park in London, greatly improved in 1661-62 by Charles II, of approximately sixty acres lying opposite St. James's Palace. It became noted for sexual liaisons. See Rochester's poem "A Ramble in St. James's Park."

2 Salt is here taken as a type of necessary adjunct to food and hence as a symbol of hospitality: "Trust no man unless thou hast first eaten a bushel of salt with him."

plaining that he had a great Inclination to Sleep. I went to Bed with him as the Night before, and was treated just after the same rate, only it lasted not so long this time, for in less than a quarter of an hour he was so deep a sleep, that the Roaring of a Canon could not have awaked him. When he had lain thus about two hours, and that I thought I was as safe as a Mouse, I got up softly, and taking the Candle which I had left burning for that purpose, I search'd his Pockets, where I found a Purse of Gold: I opened it with a great deal of Joy, and having counted two or three times the Money that was in it, I found about a hundred and ten broad Pieces and Guinnies. In his Pocket on the Right Hand there was about three Pound ten in Crown pieces; but a Watch which he had in his Fob did so charm my Eyes, that I found my self constrained, if I would have my Mind at rest, to carry it away with me. I found nothing more of any value, wherefore I began to share the Gold, neither more nor less than if it had fallen to us both by Inheritance, into equal Portions, without taking a Peny more than what I left him. This being done, I put the half with the Purse into the same place from whence I took it, and sat me down by a Table which was in our Room, where having found all that was necessary for Writing, I framed this Letter.

It is with Thanks that I have accepted the Honour which you have been pleased to do me during two or three Days, and therefore as it is the Duty of a Man and a Woman, in case of Separation, I have shared our Goods; for the Marriage I contracted with you is no longer pleasing to me, by reason there is something wanting, from which Joy is expected, and the Fruits of the Conjugal Estate. However, be assured, that if I had found you a better and more valiant Husband, than your former Clara did, or the Chamber-Maid you got with Child by the help of your Man, whose Reins are undoubtedly better provided than yours, I should not have withdrawn my self from you; But a Maiden of my Age had need of something else than Bread, and since you had once been so unhappy in your Marriage, you ought to have banish'd the Female Sex wholly from your Thoughts, and no longer have applyed your Sences unto such unlucky Objects, or at least you ought to seek out one who is more stricken in Years, that your Insufficiency might not make you lose the second time, what your brave Deportment and your excellent Qualities had acquired you. Do not take it ill that I have seized upon your Watch, for in recompence I have left you all the Money in Silver, whereof the half did with as much Justice belong to me as that of the Gold. In short, though at present we have made Separa-

tion of Goods, Board, and Bed, I beseech you not to pass by our House without calling to see us when you come that way, where you shall be very welcome and have a Lodging, which you know is better to take at a Friends House, than that of a Strangers: And as I have trusted you with my Virginity, and that you were the first who could prevail with me so far, you may easily believe, (for the first Amours are the strongest) that you will ever be look'd upon with a kind Eye by her, whose Heart is oppressed with Sadness, when she remembers her Disappointment, in not having found you as performing in Bed, as you were at Table.

When I had writ this Letter, I went and laid my self down by him again in Bed, but then neither could I sleep a Moment, no more than the Night before, by reason my Head was pestred with too many Thoughts, as also the fear of sleeping too long was a very great hindrance. As soon as I saw the dawn of Day, I leapt out of Bed, and put on my new Rigging, leaving the other there upon a Chair. Then as Squire *Limberham* slept as soundly as in the Night, I tyed this Letter to his Neck, after having for a long time done all that was possible to tye it to another Member, where there was not String nor hold enough. All this being so accommodated, I went down Stairs, and so out of the House, desiring my Landlady my Husband might not be disturbed in his Rest. Then taking Coach, I got overjoyed to our House, where I durst never have set my Feet, if I had followed my first Resolution of taking all my Equippage along with me, and not giving my Mother notice beforehand, that I would play Squire *Limberham* a Trick; and yet I should not have come off very well, by reason I fled away without saying a word to any Body, if the good Woman had not immediately perceived by my Garments; that I had lost nothing by this Retreat; but she was yet more satisfied, when I shewed her near three-score Pound in Gold, with the Watch which I had also taken for Company. She asked me presently how I had obtained all these fine things, whereupon I related the whole Affair, after the same manner it passed, which she laughed at soundly, but lest she would not believe all came off so happily, which obliged me to let her try it with her Finger; But having found that all was in its first Estate, we were the best Friends in the World, and presently some burnt Wine[1] was prepared, that we

---

1 Heated wine or wine from which part of the alcohol has been removed
   by burning.

might drown in the Glass the Sadness and Sorrow, which she said she suffered by my Absence.

While we were thus in Sadness, I began to ask her what would be the best course to take, in case Squire *Limberham* should Sue us upon this Business. My Dear Daughter, answered my Mother with a smiling Countenance, it will be much more prudent, than to shew to Justice for the loss of sixty or seventy Pounds, such a Letter as that thou wrotest to him at thy Departure, and wherein thou hast so shamefully reproached him with his Insufficiency; but if it should happen that he should be so mad I will immediately accuse him of having stoln thee away without my knowing the least of the Matter, so that I do not doubt but that the one Knife will keep the other in the Sheath.[1] And this proved the Truth of the Business, for Squire *Limberham* never came to seek out me, nor his Money, nor his Watch, which I was not very sorry for.

About five Months after that I had played Squire *Limberham* this Pranck, my Maiden-head was sold the first time. Be not amazed, O Reader, that I say the first time, for I have lost it several times after the manner of *Italy*, to which purpose I made use of a certain Water, which rendred me always the same; and though after the first Attack I found no pain at all in the Amorous Combate, but on the contrary an extraordinary Pleasure, nevertheless I sighed and groaned as strongly, as if I was to have given up the Ghost at the very instant, which moved so much Compassion in the poor Hunters after Maiden-heads, that they endeavoured to make me forget this feigned Grief, by the Unguent[2] of several Guinnies; but at length I was broach'd so often, that the Orifice became too large, and the Artifices were no longer of any use, so that I was constrained to let the Business take its Course, and to recreate my Gallants for a reasonable Price: I might say something thereof in this place, but because it is of no great Importance, and that we daily see such like things happen, and particularly here at *London*, I will retrench[3] upon this Point, and proceed to relate other Things of more Consideration.

Now as by these Means we saw our Goods dayly augment, & that we should in a short time have got considerable Gains, for my Flesh was reasonably well sought after, there came a Bully[4] to

---

1 Variant of the expression "one sword keeps another in the sheath."
2 An ointment or salve, here used figuratively.
3 Cut short, cut back (obsolete).
4 A blustering gallant, one who makes himself a terror to the weak.

our House in very sorry Apparel, and who however would have willingly show'd me some Inclination, if I had only received him with the least favourable Eye: but I had already learnt that Money must be had to buy Butter, and therefore not a Man received the least Testimony of Affection from me, unless I was assured I should be paid for it with ready Money, my Mother opposed it with all her might, and gave not this professed Bully ever any occasion to say one word in private to me, wherewith I was very much satisfied, for his Presence importuned me, since he had hardly the Means sufficient to spend the value of half a Pint of Wine a Day; but I knew not in the least that it was her own Interest that made her act in that manner, and I should never have thought that she could have fallen into so extravagant a Folly.

To speak more clearly, Reader, know that one certain Day, about Noon, as I was going to look [on] some things in the Chamber where we lay, I found her couch'd upon the Bed with this young Gallant, hugging one another so closely, that I was constrained to believe that they had a reciprocal Soul, or at least my Mother bore him more Affection than she ought to have done, for to see this *Joseph* thus drawn into Lasciviousness,[1] I believe that it rather happened to remedy his Poverty, and to introduce himself into some good Kitchin, than by a Passion of Love; for as I said before, since my Mother had had the Small Pox, she was become so ugly, that a Man must have been extreamly sharp set that could have drawn his Knife for such a Piece of Flesh.[2] I went out of the Chamber again, without saying so much as a Word, for my Heart was so full of vexation that the Tears gush'd out at my Eyes, but if I had that day reason to be vexed, one day after I had a hundred times more reason to be so; for my Mother went with this *Adonis*[3] to *Long-lane*,[4] where she bought him a new Suit, a Hat, Stockings, Shoes, and all other things necessary, that she might not be scoffed and pointed at for a Worm,[5] whom she was resolved to make her Husband. But

---

1 An implied contrast to the Biblical Joseph, who resisted the advances of Potiphar's wife. See Genesis 39.
2 The knife is a synonym for the penis; a piece of flesh, for a woman in her sexual capacity, or a whore.
3 In classical mythology, a young man loved by Venus because he was so handsome.
4 A street in London, mainly occupied by pawnbrokers and old-clothes dealers, running east from West Smithfield to Aldersgate.
5 Here, a human being viewed as an object of scorn or pity.

what shall I say more, it seems this Woman could not live without that Instrument, and therefore she judged it more proper to accept a poor Devil, than to remain untill'd any longer, from whence it appears sufficiently that the Common Proverb is true,

If Lasciviousness renders Maidens mad, it makes Widdows Devils. [1]

For there are never so silly Marriages, as those that are made by Widows. It seems their Flesh being too Lustful, through the remembrance of past Delights, and their Countenance too old and too ugly to charm a Man of any Fashion, obliges them to abandon themselves to those Extravagancies.

When I saw that my Mother went thus seriously to work, and that she began to spend so fast the Money for which my Buttocks had laboured so vigorously, I began to be something unruly, and swore that if she accomplish'd this so unequal Match, I would abandon her, and that she would perhaps find too late, that my Buttocks had not been hatching of Eggs full of Wind. [2] She made me answer thereupon, that I might do what I pleased, and that she was not over fond of having me stay any longer in her House: And my future Father was still less courteous; for being already Master of the House, he threatned me that he would put me in mind of my Duty, by sensible Means, if I did not pay due respect to his well-beloved.

In the mean while this fine Couple's Banes [3] were published, which rendred me so void of Comfort, that I resolved to pocket up all my things, and to vanish away without making any one acquainted whither I went.

While that I was possessed with these Thoughts, there came to our House a certain Merchant, who was one of those, whom my last Virginities had been sold to, and who for that reason had some Kindness for me, having the Fancy that he had been the first who had had to do with me. He seeing me in so doleful an Humour, and melting in Tears, asked me from whence that proceeded? I told him, that my Mother had made choice of a young and poor Bully, and that she was resolved to marry him; and that this brave Spark did already play the Master through all the House, which had obliged me to resolve to take my flight, and

1 Unidentified proverb.
2 Variant of the proverb "eggs are full of meat."
3 Obsolete spelling of "banns," the proclamation or public notice given in church of an impending marriage.

that I desired him, since I unbosomed all things to him with so open an Heart, that he would help me with his Counsel in this Occasion. This honest Man plainly perceiving by all my Reasons, that I should not easily be diverted from this Design, told me, after having considered with himself for a while, that if I would be faithful to him, and not abandon my self to any other Man, he would take me a Chamber, and provide me with all things I had occasion for; this Offer was very pleasing to me in such a Conjuncture of Affairs, and as Promises cost neither Money nor Expence, his obliged me to make him such in return, as I had not any Intention to keep. *Valere*, so was this honest Man's Name, took his leave, with a purpose to provide me with all speed with a convenient Habitation, and two days afterwards came to give me notice that he had taken a Chamber with a Dining-Room for me in *Hatton-Garden*,[1] and that therefore I was to pacquet up all my Baggage, and go take Possession of it with all Diligence. I assure you that this was not spoken to one that was Deaf, for he had no sooner given me the Key and Direction, than that I gathered up all things that I could gripe[2] and catch[3] and on the Morrow Morning, when *Mars* and *Venus* were still in Conjunction at our House, I fled to my new Lodging, where that day I was forc'd to content my self with somewhat a sober Life, by reason there was not yet any menial[4] Provision.

Valere came to see me the day following, for I had sent a Porter to let him know that I had broke up my Camp[5] with Bag and Baggage, and seeing this abode resembled in some manner a poor *Bethlem*,[6] he gave me ten Pounds to buy me Furniture and Moveables,[7] which I did with so much Care and Diligence, that within two or three Days after I could have lodged a Man of Honour, though I had reserved to my self about four Pounds out of the Bargain; for he had caused the principal Necessaries to be brought thither the very first Day, namely a Bed with all its Appurtenances; however I gave him to understand that the

---

1   Constructed on the site of the orchard and garden of Ely Place, Holborn, where a mansion had been pulled down in 1656.
2   To clutch or grasp at (obsolete).
3   To take forcible possession of (obsolete).
4   Domestic, relating to the household (obsolete).
5   Quarters (loosely).
6   The manger in Bethlehem, Judea, where Jesus was born. See Luke 2:15-16.
7   Personal property capable of being moved.

Money had been every Farthing laid out, which the poor Man did easily believe; by reason he imagined that I had bought all New in the Shops; whereas on the contrary I had ferreted and laid out most of my Money in *Long-lane*, the backside of *St. Clements*,[1] and the Pawn-Brokers, for I knew how to shew him all the Items and Articles with more Dexterity than all the Taylors in the Town, though that Race of People understand making a Bill to Perfection.

When I had lodged here about a Fortnight, I told *Valere* that I stood in great need of a Maid, by reason that I was not used to wash the House and clean it my self, nor to run to the Cooks and Shops for my Victuals. The Truth is, that it was partly for this reason, but I had another reason, which I was far from acquainting him with, and which the Reader shall be presently informed of. The good Man who really loved me from the bottom of his Heart, gave me for answer, that I might take any one I pleased. Whereupon having provided my self with as good a Maid as I could have wish'd for my Purpose, and who was necessary to me for the Messages I particularly designed to employ her in. Now when I was sufficiently acquainted with her Fidelity to me in small Matters, I sent her to the Lodgings of two or three of those Sparks, with whom I had had some small Conversation in my Mothers House, for to let them know the place of my abode, and if in such and such a time they would be pleased to honour me with their Visits; for though *Valere* allowed me sufficient, and even more than my Necessities required, yet I was not satisfied, by reason I had made a Resolution to scrape up on all sides, and by all manner of means; insomuch, that in case *Valere* came one day to abandon me, I might not have reason to bewail his loss.

In the mean while, there was not any of those Sparks, who knew in the least of one another, unless it was only *Valere*, and it was I my self who told them that he kept me; now as for the others I knew so well how to lure them, that every one imagined that he alone enjoyed my Favour and Affection, and I shared so well the times which I appointed them, that never did one meet or surprize the other, which was no hard Matter for me, by reason my Lord and Master, or at least he who made himself believe he was so, driving a great Trade in *Italy*, *Spain*, and *France*, and by

---

1 St. Clement Danes, a church in London at the east end of the Strand, was pulled down in 1680 and rebuilt by Sir Christopher Wren in 1681-82.

Consequence being taken up on Post-days,[1] left me Occasions enough to drive on my Trade as well as he, of which however he had not the least Suspicion; for I knew how to caress him so dexterously, and when he told me could only stay to such an hour, that the most cunning Gallant of all the City would thereby have been deceived. I fell a Weeping when he began to tell me of going away, and I swore that it was almost impossible for me to live one Moment without him; which the good easy credulous Man, was almost bound to believe, for my Maid, as if she had no concern therein, confirmed it by all that was Sacred, telling him, that he never left me, without my Weeping for at least an hour, whereas on the contrary I should have been much more ready to Cry, if he had staid with me but a quarter of an hour beyond the time he had appointed, for then I feared I might have lost the Money of one Gallant or other, to whom I had given a Rendezvouse at that time.

My Maid lived after this manner with my four other Lovers, for she had no sooner perceived that she had the Conveniency of speaking privately with those Sparks, to which purpose as I had two Rooms, I pretty often gave her an Opportunity, seeming to have something else to do in the other Room, when she swore worse than ever any Renegado[2] in the World did, that Love would hardly allow me to sleep, and that I loved him, (namely him she spoke to) a thousand times more than my self; and that Valere would be happy if for all his Costs and Charges, I bore him but the tenth part of such an Affection, and that there was hardly a Moment in the Day but I had his Name in my Mouth.

These Artifices brought a great Advantage to us both; for first of all my Maid, who as she had and did contribute so much to the maintaining in me a great Opinion of their brave Qualities, was to be greased in the Fist,[3] and besides my Caresses were likewise to be recompenced, if not with Money, with a piece of Plate, or a Ring, or some such like matter, that might mount to the value of two or three hundred of a Lady of Pleasures Kisses, which I purchased them with.

Now as by these Artifices I heap'd up a considerable Sum of Money, and that I plum'd[4] each of my Lovers as bravely as was possible for me, to which the Dexterity of my Maid was a sea-

1 Days on which the post or mail was due or departed.
2 Obsolete spelling of "renegade"; here, an abusive person.
3 Bribed (figurative).
4 In its literal sense, plucked, stripped them of plumes or feathers.

sonable help; there happened an Adventure which would quickly have reduced all my Affairs to Ashes, if I had not made use of Cunning to free my self out of it. *Valere* was sitting and discoursing with me, and he was necessarily at six a Clock to be at *Ratcliff*,[1] by reason there was a Sale to be there of some Merchandize which imported him very much. I knew of this three Days before, wherefore I had appointed one of my Lovers at seven a Clock, with design to dispatch him about eight, that I might divert my self with another about half an hour after that, as my custom was to catch two Flies[2] in one Evening: for if I had granted them a longer time than an hour, or an hour and a half, I could hardly have served them all four, unless it had been every other fifth or sixth day, which would have rendred my Gains much smaller by the half. But while we were thus sitting together caressing one another the Clock struck six without his hearing it, for he was too busy, or at least the time seem'd to him too short to imagine that it was already so late. However, he continued sitting until about half an hour after six, and would not perhaps have considered how the time went away, seeing he did nothing but hug and kiss me continually: I was in the greatest disquiet Imaginable, by reason that contrary to my custom, I had appointed my Gallants so shortly after his Departure, for otherwise I practised what follows. When I knew that *Valere* would leave me at four a Clock, I appointed no other before seven, that I might have at least half an hour or an hours time to counterfeit the fond Lover. I besought him a hundred times that he would be so kind as to keep me Company for one quarter of an hour longer. Yet as I did all that was possible for me to entertain him in this Opinion, that I loved him so passionately I durst not make mention of the Clock, but he thought my self of another Expedient which was much more proper for that Purpose. I had, as I said before, took a Watch from Squire Limberham, I always carryed it in my Pocket, and it went so exactly that it rarely failed a Moment; insomuch, that I was very well assured, that if *Valere* came to see it, he would immediately be gone. But it was a difficult matter to find out the Means of shewing him it, without my seeming to have had any such Design. But I bethought my self, to run my

---

1 A natural landing place in the parish of Stepney on the north bank of the Thames and hence the site of people engaged in maritime occupations.

2 Here the word refers to persons who are insignificant, or who flit from place to place.

Hand into my Pocket and break the Chrystal, after which taking it out, with the Pieces: Here, *Sarah*, said I to my Maid, carry this to Morrow when you go to Market, to a Watch-maker, and let him put in another Chrystal. Prethee, my Dear, give it me, said *Valere*, I know one that will do it well. No, my sweet Angel, said I, you'll perhaps put it to another use. But why so, replyed he: You perhaps would look on't, said I, and that must not be. Where-upon, *Valere* beginning to conjecture that it was later than perhaps he imagined, ask'd *Sarah* for the Watch, who as if she durst not disobey him, gave it him into his Hands.

He look'd upon it immediately, and seeing it was six a Clock and a half; Ha, Ha, said he, was this the reason that I might not see it: S'Death it is above half an hour too late for me to have been at the Place appointed; and thereupon taking his Cloak he pretended to go away: But I hung about his Neck, and in the mean while chid the Maid severely, calling her by all the filthy Names, and Cursing her for that she had given him the Watch: However I could not hold him so fast but that he broke out of my Arms, and ran in all haste to the Place appointed.

You young Sprouts,[1] who will undoubtedly read my Life with more diligence than you have for a Godly Book, and which causes so much Grief and Charges to your Parents, and who are often the occasion of exhausting their Coffers, you may judg by these Samples what you are to expect from the Female Sex, for I am neither the only one, nor the first, who has made use of these Artifices; I can assure you on the contrary, that there are many who put them in practice daily, and that it is as impossible dive into the Heart[2] of a Woman, as it is to run your Head, Body and all into her Fundament.

Tho that my Territory was so frequently cultivated by five Men; and that by this Reason it seem'd there could not arise any Fruit, by reason that I figured to my self, that the too great abun-dance of Humidity would be capable of stifling it in its Birth. Nevertheless, after having led this Life six Months, I began to perceive I was with Child. It is certain that I was not over-joyed; for I imagined, that this would not come out so commodiously, nor so easily as it went in; and that my Beauty, which I was pro-vided with after a reasonable passable manner, would receive

---

1 Young men (figuratively).
2 Here, the seat of secret or innermost feelings; the proverb may be a variant of the maxim, "there is no other Riddle but a Woman," Richard Ames, *The Folly of Love* (1691), 594.

great Injury thereby: But since such was the State of Affairs, and that I could not hinder the Progress but by wicked and unlawful means, I resolved to make use of it to my best Advantage; and as soon as *Valere* came to my Lodging, I let him know how things stood with me. This poor Man, really imagining that he had got the Child, was so transported with Joy, that he hardly knew what he did: He hung about my Neck, and having given me at least a thousand Kisses, he opened his Purse of Gold, and gave me Fifteen Guinneys, for me to begin with preparing Clouts[1] and Necessaries for my Child; and 'tis certain this was only a Beginning: for this Appanage[2] cost him afterwards thrice that Sum, by reason there was not a Clout but was of the finest Cloth, and besides garnished with Laces.

Besides this Sum, I did what I could to get twice as much from my other Lovers: For as the one knew nothing of the other, I found it no difficult matter to make each of them believe, that he had got at least half the Child, and by Consequence was obliged to buy something towards the Appanage of the Child. I endeavoured also to make them believe, that *Valere* could not contribute much thereto; and though they seemed not to believe me in this; yet I could easily perceive by their Looks, that they were not displeased at this Discourse. Thus are these young men so easie and credulous in point of getting Children; and it is very convenient that they can have no perfect Knowledge thereof: For otherwise several Men, who are none of the best Performers in matters of Gallantry, and whose Wives do sometimes take their Heats with the one or other Spark several, I say, would suspect their Wives of Adultery when they come to be with Child, and especially if the Children did not resemble them. But the Women have found good Remedies to this Inconveniency: For they can so easily perswade these credulous men, that commonly the Children have some Conformity with the Objects on which the Woman with Child does fix her Eyes; that they would be thought the most incredulous Hereticks, if they did not add Faith to such Suppositions; and moreover, if there be only a Neighbour-Gossip at the Labour or Christening, who swears upon the truth of a Woman, that this Child resembles the man who bears the Name of its Father, as perfectly as if he had been spit out of his Mouth: Then

---

1 Swaddling clothes (obsolete).
2 In its literal sense, the provision made by a king or prince for the maintenance of his younger children.

it is the Husband, tho' he sees the contrary plain enough, is obliged to believe it, according to the ancient Custom, and must seem to be over-joyed at the matter.

In the mean while my Belly began daily to swell so big, that it became neither more nor less than what is related of *Vitelle* the *Spanish* Colonel;[1] so that like him, I was almost constrained to have a Band fastened to my Neck, that I might with the less difficulty bear with the weight of my Belly. Now *Valere* took as much care of me as if I had been his own wife, and was absolutely against my putting my hands into cold Water, by reason he feared it might be prejudicial to my Fruit. At length the Term of *Lying in* being come, I fell into Labour one *Wednesday* Noon with such dreadful Pains, as if I had had my Entrails torn out of my Body, which made me curse the Hours and Day that I suffer'd that unruly Member to rummage[2] my Body, just as a Number of silly women do in such like Occasions.

I was in this lamentable Condition crying and groaning untill the *Saturday* following, at which time I was delivered of a dead Child; which by reason of the Compressions and Contorsions of my Body, seem'd so blew[3] and deformed, that one could hardly perceive it had the Form of a humane Figure. I lay aside its resembling *Valere*, who fancied himself the Father of it; but it very much resembled me so well in one part, except the difference there was in the Bigness and Length; but without doubt, with Time and frequent use of it, there would have been wrought great Alterations.

Valere was very sad upon the Death of his little imaginary Girle; so that he was hardly to be comforted: For my part, I pretended likewise to be very much afflicted, that I might please him, tho' indeed I was over-joyed: For I easily foresaw, that it was not very convenient for a Maiden of my Circumstances to have Children; and besides, I do not believe that there is a Miss in all this City, who will say, that I am mistaken in this Matter, by reason that this young Baggage gives so much trouble, and is attended with so many Inconveniencies, that most of our time is lost upon it; and we must abandon our own Affairs. It were to be

---

1   Probably an allusion to Lucius Vitellius (before 5 BCE-51 CE), a
    Roman general and emperor whose interests lay exclusively in eating
    and whose name became a synonym for gluttony and a large belly. I am
    indebted to Kevin Berland and Jim Chevallier for this reference.
2   Here, to ransack, to disarrange or disorder, to stir or drive about.
3   Obsolete spelling of "blue."

wished that no Children could be gotten but in Marriage: For then the young and Gentile[1] Damosels would not be so disdainful, and would not so obstinately refuse to mingle familiarly what they have with their Lovers, whereas they are often hinder'd by the fear they have such Misfortunes may happen to them, tho indeed they do but too often happen; and especially since the Artifice has been found out to prevent a womans being with Child; but there is in this also a great Inconveniency: for we lose half the Pleasure, by reason that in such Encounters we may support the Agitation, but not the Shower.

I had lain in about three weeks, when that *Valere* imagining that things were in their former Estate, gave me to understand, by his Caresses, that he wisht with all his Heart, that we might begin to sport anew; but I opposed this so powerfully, that he could not in any wise compass his Design. He made use of Prayers, Promises and Threatnings; but this was all in vain: I had besides, according to all Appearance, such an Aversion upon my having conceived and brought forth, that I would not so much as allow him to feel the place from whence that Lump of Flesh came, that had put me to so much pain. How Sir, said I to him, what will become of me at length? the truth is, pursued I, that at present I receive so many Benefits from you, that I can live very honourably on them; but if this Child had remained alive, and that it should one day have come to pass, as all men are changeable, that you should have an Aversion for, and a Contempt of my Person; or that Death had taken you out of the World, what could I have expected with this poor Lamb but Misery and Poverty? It will be much better, added I, at last for me to abandon this disorderly and criminal Life, and to labour with my Hands to gain my Livelyhood with Honour, rather than one day to be perplex'd with two or three little Children, and be reduced to Begging, or some worse thing: Thereupon I began to weep so pitiously, as Women cry for the most part when they please, I had also Tears at my Disposal, neither more nor less than if I was immediately to have gone a begging in the Streets. Honest *Valere* was so moved with Compassion by my Tears, that he embraced me with the greatest Passion imaginable, and swore that he would never abandon me, provided that I would always remain as faithful to him, as I had thitherto been; but I assure you, that if he had known that there were four more besides himself, who sometimes

---

1   Obsolete form of "gentle" or "genteel."

made use of occasion to come and cultivate my Garden of Love, he would have had other thoughts.

In the mean while, notwithstanding all his fine Promises, I let him not win me from my design, which having at length rendred him impatient, he asked me what it was I desired of him? Nothing more (said I) than that you would settle an Annuity[1] upon me for all my Life of about thirty pounds a year, insomuch, that if I should fall under that terrible misfortune to lose you, I might have something to secure me from Poverty, and if you refuse to do this (pursued I immediately) be assured, that as long as you live, you shall never touch my Naked Body. This Gentleman would in no wise grant me my Request in the beginning, and endeavoured for a long time to satisfy me with a less Sum, but at length he began to be staggered, which as soon as I perceived, I who thitherto had showed my self so presumptuous, changed my tone immediately, took him about the Neck, kissed him, caressed him so bewitchingly, (adding Tears to all this) that at length he granted me my Request; and certainly I was very happy in having so nicked my time[2] for that Affair. For this poor *Valere*, whose Memory will ever be dear to me, happened to dye suddainly, within ten or twelve days after he had delivered to me the Deed for the Annuity, of a Pleurisy,[3] to which he was very subject.

I had hardly been four days on foot[4] since my Lying in, when I was acquainted with these sad news, for I followed the example of Persons of Condition and kept State[5] for six Weeks. You may easily imagine that I was very much grieved at his Death, since that in losing him, I lost a Man from whom I received so many Benefits, that I could not have expected the like from any other Man in the World, but I comforted my self with my Annuity, and that very moment took the Resolution of leaving my Abode, and go take a larger House, for the having the conveniency of accommodating Gentlemen according to their Condition; and in pursuit of this Resolve, did I take that very Week a House near

---

1 An investment of a sum of money whereby the designated recipient becomes entitled to receive a series of equal annual payments, sometimes for a lifetime.
2 Denied my time (archaic).
3 A disease characterized by an inflammation of the membranes lining the lungs.
4 Up and about, walking (obsolete).
5 Behaved in a dignified manner, observed the pomp and ceremony befitting a high position (rare).

Moorfields,[1] and for the furnishing it with all things necessary, the money I had from time to time squeez'd from my Gallants, was a very seasonable importance.[2]

As soon as we had taken possession of the House, I began to contrive how to second Nature; for by the bringing forth of this Child, what I had, and not without very great cause, very much feared, which was that it had not embellished my Face with one good feature, on the contrary, I appeared so bleak and so morti-fied, that I could hardly endure my Image in the Looking-glass; and as of all necessity, Provision was to be made against this unlucky business, if I intended not to lose the Inclinations of my Lovers, I made use for the rendring my Cheeks red, of the fol-lowing Remedy, for want of knowing a better.

I took some *Spanish* Wool,[3] which I macerated some hours in Brandy, by the force whereof, the Tincture of the *Spanish* Wool began to lose it self, and if one wet or rubbed any place therewith, it communicated a colour, which seem'd to be altogether natural; but I perceived in a few days that this Colour did not remain firm enough to pass for really true and natural; for when I suffered my self to be kissed a little, or when the amorous exercise had occa-sioned my sweating, a Person who should have narrowly taken notice of it, would have easily perceived the Deceit; but because I never gave my Cheeks a higher colour than that they had before my Lying-in, by good luck my Gallants never suspected it in the least: However Prudence required that I should take some other Counsel in that business. Whereupon, I went to a Person who had the reputation of knowing wonderful Secrets in such like Matters, and who for that purpose was made use of by several sorts of Damosels as well honest as other, for now Maidens how Holy and Reserved soever they may seem, make use of such like means, and if their Servants should happen to see them at the very instant they rise from their Beds, they most commonly could not do it without turning their Stomach; and it is for that reason that Ladies, and Maids, when they have been marryed but a Week or two, are subject to such great Changes, and become as ugly as *Medusae's*, for as they have no longer any Body for whom they are obliged to deck themselves, they abandon that Care, and expose

---

1 A low-lying marshy area immediately north of the old city wall of London, between Bishopgate and Cripplegate.
2 Means of support (obsolete).
3 A fine wool made from Merino sheep and imported into England from Spain from the 1680s onwards.

themselves to view so careless and nasty, that we should find the Churches all full if it was the custom that People could be unmarried; for I beseech you who would not conceive an Aversion for the Female Sex, when he should see appears before his eyes a young Woman with a dirty Coife[1] upon her head, whereas but a few days before she wore none but what was clean and Gentile, and that her Principal part, namely her Face, was as fair and beautiful as Lillies, whereas now it is as dirty and nasty as the hands? But my Passion already transports me out of the Road, and if I had suffered my Pen to take its course, I should have made you strange discoveries of the Female Sex's Artifices and Imperfections. But to return to our Subject, the Person who was so good at furnishing Women with Remedies to mend Faces, sold me some Roots of ——,[2] and at the same time acquainted me after what manner I was to make use thereof; which is as follows. You must take on your Thumb and second Fingers end, a little Butter, and afterwards you draw the Root with the other hand, through the Fingers that are anointed with Butter, and by that means the Root renders of it self a very fine red, which by means of the Butter, is much firmer than the red which is drawn from the —— then you rub that upon the Cheeks with your Finger, and at length you make it dissipate so Artificially, that no Body can observe how the White divides from the Red; for if you did not diminish this Colour, which is very high, by little and little, with a Finger wet in Spittle or Water, you might easily perceive the Deceit, whereas, on the contrary, people can make no other Judgment, but that it is a Tincture which Nature has produced.

Though I found this prov'd very much to my advantage, however, I afterwards made use of another means, which I shall add here as wholly appertaining to these Drolleries. They call it *Spanish* Paper,[3] which is now much in use both with Ladies of Pleasure and others: These Papers are not all of the same bigness, nor all of the same value, whereof you must be careful when you buy them. If they are of a Grocer,[4] upon which there seems some Gold to sparkle, you will be very seldom deceived therein: Others are good, and of a firm and durable Colour; but on the contrary,

---

1 A close fitting cap, covering the top, back, and sides of the head.
2 Possibly cochineal, a plant used as a brilliant scarlet dye.
3 Cheeks were reddened by using Spanish paper, which was bought dyed red with cochineal to rub on the skin.
4 A person buying and selling in large quantities, a wholesale dealer, a merchant (*OED*). Misspelled "gorcer" in the original text.

if they are red and of a pearl or blew Colour, they are neither good, nor firm of Colour, and by too much sweating it might be easily made appear what you endeavour to keep concealed with so much Care and Precaution. It is made use of in the following manner. The Green which conceals under it a very agreeable Red, must be somewhat wet and moisted with the Tongue or Finger. Afterwards you take the Paper, and with the place that is wet, you rub two or three times upon the Cheeks, and they become almost as red as Blood, insomuch that afterwards you by little and little dissipate it with a wet Finger, after the same manner that was prescribed in the Root of —— and that Colour is so firm, that if you have good Paper, it will hold two whole days in case of need, without renewing it. Now I made use of it a long time for this reason: As for that one need not greaze ones self so much as with the above mentioned pieces of Root.

My Breasts, which before my lying in had been always reasonably hard, tho' they had been a long time pressed, had also some need of help. For they were so soft, that when I was not laced they could not continue in their place. However because that with these glandulous Globes we cannot live after the same manner as we do with the Cheeks; I could not make use of any other means, but by lacing my Body as streight underneath as I could bear it,[1] and by doing so my Breasts rose up so high, and swell'd in such a manner, that I could rest upon 'em with my Chin; and were so hard to feel to, that I should still have been taken for a real Maid. Being thus accommodated and adorned, I received my Servants in my new Abode, without using any longer the Caution I had before of never appointing more than one at a time: For if I took that Course it was only because I was afraid of babling and tatling; and that I would not willingly have given occasion to *Valere* to abandon me, being the person who furnished me with all Provisions. On the contrary. I was then engaged to no Body, as neither did I wish so to be, because I had observed several times, that for that Consideration, I had lost and let slip several fine Occasions.

Amongst all those who came to pay me Visits from time to time, there was one, whom I will for some reasons call *Philander*, as being still alive: He was about Fifty years Old: Here I made no reckoning of a young Colt, by reason I knew very well that they

---

1 Presumably lacing the bodice, an inner garment made for the upper part of the body and quilted and straitened with whalebone.

could not keep Silence, and that they have no sooner obtained any favour from a Nymph, than that incontinently they go, and boast thereof, and proclaim it every where; by which means a woman in a short time is much better known in the world than she would desire to be, and often to be put to Shame and scandalized by such like Parrots, a Maid is obliged to grant the same Favour to their Companions. These on the contrary, whose years have given more Modesty, are careful of preserving their Honour; and they set the more value upon a Nymph whom they find knows how to be silent. They are also much more free to part from their Money; so that there are several reasons why we ought to prefer Aged men before young Colts. This *Philander* had no sooner seen me, than that he conceived immediately an Inclination for my Person, which he made me acquainted with in so many several manners, that I must have been the most incredulous person in the world if I had doubted of it in the least. However I would not grant him the least Favour, and I made him find in me as much Honour and Reservedness as if there had never a Finger come therein, by which Resistance his amorous Passion was so provoked, that he hardly knew when he was seated by my side how to behave himself. Nevertheless he saw several others besides himself come to our House, and by Consequence might easily judge, considering they were all persons of Condition and Means; that they came not there to make Love to me; and this with so much the more reason, that there were some amongst 'em who had Wives living: But I knew so well how to counterfeit a person sage and discreet when he was there present, that at length he lost the Courage and Hopes of being able to obtain from me what made him visit me, and what had obliged him to make me so many Presents. When I began to perceive this (for I had only thus counterfeited the haughty, the proud and severe, that I might catch him the more cunningly; because the means which I put in practice, are infallibly the most proper for that purpose) I shewed him by little and little, more and more Kindness, and swore to him, that he was the only Man who could be pleasing to me; that I had no Esteem for all the others whom he saw daily come to my House; and that their Presence was very uneasie and troublesome to me; but that as for him, I would in time do what so many others had in vain solicited of me. Poor *Philander* hearing all those fair Discourses, was so satisfied in his mind, that the day after he sent me a Silver Dish and Ewer, that were so artificially wrought, that I should have done great Injustice to the Master, if I had not received them with all possible

Acknowledgment: Yet I feigned to be in some manner sorry and displeased, saying, that I did not use to receive such Gifts or Presents, but only for his Gracefulness, courteous Humour, and extraordinary Quality that was seen in his Person and Actions. However, Sir, added I, since by these means you have been pleased to give me Assurance of your Inclination towards me, I will keep them for your Sake; and upon Occasion will shew you I am neither ungrateful, nor void of Acknowledgment: And really he had quickly Instances of my Acknowledgment: For within a Week I suffered this Spark to gather those Flowers for which he had so often wander'd about my House; and tho there were several others, who obtained from me the same Favor for their Money; yet this Cully took the Pleasure he received from me as a mark of the greatest Passion I could show him.

After that Bout I allowed him from time to time to spend a whole Night with me; and in so doing I had no ill Reason: for my pains were admirably well paid. As I was one Night lying in his Arms, amongst other things, he told me, that he had a great Desire to have a Child by me; and that then he would make me sensible how ardent the amorous Passion was that he bore me. My dear Angel, answered I him, all that Heaven pleases; but pursued I, do only your best for that purpose, and then we shall see what will come of it. Altho I knew very well that I should not so easily be with Child as the first time (for now instead of having to do only with five, I had full three times as many daily Gallants, who lay with me in their Turns) however I took the Resolution of being once more with Child, were it only for the pleasure to see what Advantage I might get thereby. For that purpose I told him about three weeks afterwards (for I was not willing to do it immediately, for fear he should find out the Cheat) that undoubtedly I was with Child: For, added I to that, this was just the week I was to have had my Courses;[1] and yet I had them not, which however never failed me one day in my Life. *Philander* was so over-joyed to hear this News, that there was easily to be seen in his Face the Signs of Satisfaction and Delight; and he promised me Mountains of Gold, if I was so happy as to bring a Boy into the World.

When I had entertained him for about three Months in this good Opinion, my Belly began to swell by little and little, and to appear of such a roundness, as it is seen to be of the first Months that Women are with Child. As I was only with Child for my

---

1 Menstrual discharges (obsolete).

pleasure, certainly my Reader cannot well imagine, what was the Progress and Event of this Affair, and perhaps if he be still a Man without experience, he will fancy that I fastned a Cushion or some other such like thing upon my Belly, as many silly Women do who can tell Wonders of such businesses. Not at all, for those Artifices are something too innocent, and we should receive a great deal of shame and scandal thereby, if the imaginary Father should unluckily think of feeling when the Child began to live, for it is a hard matter to deny one to feel what belongs to him. Wherefore I proceeded in this manner. When I knew *Philander* was to come, I half unlaced my self, I found my Body hard under my Bosom, which made my Belly swell bravely, and rendred it so hard, by reason it was loose and free, that I could have deceived the cunningest Midwife in all the Town, that is to say, if she only felt the outside of my Belly. By this means the more straitly I joyned the Body above, the more full and stiff I made it below; insomuch, that *Philander* with all his Ingenuity knew no better, but that I went with a Child of his getting, and that he might the less suspect the Cheat, I would no longer suffer him to sport with me upon the Bed, for then he might have easily felt that my Belly was by much too limber to be capable of serving for the abode of an Infant of so many Months; I did this little by little, augmenting it according to the course of time, and the Approach of the time of my feigned and imaginary bringing forth; but as soon as honest *Philander* was gone, all my big Belly vanished, and I put my Body again into it's former Posture, for I thought not fit to play in that condition at Push-pin[1] with my other Cullies.

In the mean while *Philander* came almost every Morning to my House, for to fortify my Body, by drinking Canary[2] and Possets;[3] but *Philander* did cunningly discover the Child to stir in my Belly (namely) when I had been big in this manner about five Months, and besides, he fancied he felt a stronger motion on the right side than the left, so that he did not in the least doubt but that it would be a little Boy. Certainly when I heard him reason in this manner, I could hardly forbear laughing, because I had so certain a knowledge that there was neither Boy nor Girl in my Belly, and that I so plainly observed that this fancy made a fool of a Man of so much sence as *Philander*.

---

1 A child's game, with an innuendo of phallic thrusting, copulation.
2 A sweet wine from the Canary Islands.
3 A drink of hot milk, curdled with ale, wine, or other liquor.

Perhaps some one would now ask me, how at length I could come off with honour from this business, since I could not continue ten years with Child, as Elephants go so long with their young, and I will then tell the Reader to satisfy herein his curiosity, my design was, that when it was come to about the seventh Month, to feign some inconvenience that might have made me Miscarry, and to make up a lump of Callous[1] Blood, in the figure of a Child newly Born, and to expose it to *Philander's* sight, which would have been no difficult matter to do; for Children newly born, seem always strange, and besides *Philander* was not so well skilled in such like Affairs; for without doubt he had never been with Child, nor had helpt to hold his Neighbours Wifes leggs when they were in Labour; but this was not necessary since that four days after all the mystery was discovered, of which I had notice to my great regret by the following Letter.

Henceforward, Jilting Cornelia, *you need not take so much pains to lace your self so hard on the upper part of your Body, to make People believe by the swelling of your Execrable Belly, that you are with Child. I have discovered your Tricks, and if I had found them out something sooner, assure your self that my Money should not have rusted in your Coffer.*

Nevertheless, I hope it will not remain long there, and that at length you will be reduced to such an Extremity, that you must spend in the deepest misery, what you have got from me by most abominable Cheats. I cannot sufficiently thank Heaven that it has so timely opened my eyes, for certainly that my too great and too silly passion would have made me commit things, which I should but too late have repented of. Henceforward seek out another whom you may put upon, and never think on him who has born you too much Affection, to be rewarded in this manner.

The truth is, that when I received this Letter, I became so sad and so afflicted, that tears run down from my eyes, for though that I had not any Affection for *Philander*, yet I had a very great loss in losing him, since that during the time of my counterfeited big Belly, I had got from him near a hundred pound, and I do not doubt but that I should have obtained as much more when I had been delivered; for he was one of the best Gallants I ever had. I could easily imagine at the very first who it was that had revealed

---

1 Hardened.

to him this mystery, since no Body in the World knew the least of this Enterprize, except a Maid, who certainly had plaid me this Prank, by reason that a day or two before, I had school'd her severely upon some matters which did not please me. However I resolved not to make any noise, and to take only the first occasion that was offered to discharge her, which I did within a week after.

By all this discourse you may easily observe, that the Female Sex being once crossed, will hardly ever let slip opportunities of revenge, for I had been as kind to this *Sarah* as if she had been my own Sister. Besides that, I let her receive half the profits that arose from the sale of wine, which was four times as much to her advantage, as if she had only been Kitchin-Maid in a House of any of the richest Merchants of *London*, for I never drunk Rhenish Wine,[1] but that we made our Customers pay half a Crown the bottle, tho' in the mean while we gave but Twelve Pence, and each bottle cost us no more than ninepence, by reason that instead of a Quart, we never gave more than a pint and half, so that in each Bottle we got about eighteen pence profit.

Now while I wanted a Maid, and that I made use of a poor day labourer, until that I could find one in whom I might put some confidence, I happened to meet my Mother one day in *Newgate-Market*;[2] she was so poorly clad, so dirty and thin, that I should hardly have known her again, if she had not leapt about my Neck. My dear Daughter, said she to me, by what happyness do I come to meet thee to day? I have sought thee for above this year and half without ever having been able to get the least Tydings of thee, and I thought thee dead, poor Girl, but Heavens be prais'd that I see thee still alive and in good health.

I ask'd her immediately what was become of that Bully of a Fellow, whom she had abandoned her self to, for I could never be brought to call him Father. She made me answer, that he at length turn'd Souldier to go to the *East-Indies*, after having squandered away what she had, and had a hundred times broken her Bones with beating her. That's no wonder, said I to her, these are the fruits of those extravagant Marriages; but (persued I) how do you live now at present? for, if I be not mistaken, Poverty will

---

1 Wine produced in the Rhine region.
2 On the site of Paternoster Square, between North Street, Warwick Lane, Paternoster Row, and Ivy Lane.

quickly force you to leave the Town of your Birth, unless you be a stranger to all shame, and that you do not care after what manner you are dressed. I have for these six Months, said she, took a Cellar in *Cheap-side*,[1] and by which means I make a poor shift to get my bread. The truth is, when I heard this, my heart was moved with Compassion towards her, wherefore I told her that as her Herbs and all her Moveables, were certainly of no very great importance, she needed but to leave them all for her Rent, and that she should come along with me to my house, where I would provide her with Cloaths immediately. The good Woman was so diligent in executing what I told her, that one could not at all perceive that she was in the least troubled or afflicted for her Goods, or for her Merchandize.

It was no wonderful thing that she had sought for me so long in vain, for as I had desired all my Gallants, who came formerly to her House, never to speak a word of me, I had always avoided meeting her with so much care, that I never came within six Streets near her House, and besides, I went muffled up in my Hoods, so that I knew not if she was still in the World. Besides, it is easy to remain concealed two or three years in such a City as *London*, and especially provided you appear not too often in publick, which was not at all my Custom, by reason I had sufficient to do in my own house.

Then I observed in my Mother the wretched condition of those Women who being Old and Ugly, abandon themselves to some young miserable Bully; for they are no sooner engaged together by the Bond of Marriage, than that these Sparks who only took this rank flesh for the conveniencies wherewith it is attended, begin to play the Master, and with the Money, which others it seems have rak'd up for them, they seek out Wenches who are less in years and have more Charms than their old toothless Spouses. And truly though I am my self a Woman, I cannot blame them much, for when one is to reaccommodate[2] an old Clift, I fancy one ought to pay twice as much but enough for that! Men would imagine by my talking at this rate, that I am of their side, whereas on the contrary, I have always done what was possible to deceive them.

---

1 The chief commercial district of old London, extending from the north-west corner of St. Paul's churchyard to the Poultry.
2 Accommodate afresh or again.

Immediately I discharged my Monkey of a Maid, and began to make use of my Mother in that Quality; after having neatly rigg'd her from top to toe, which certainly was a great change, for when we lived before together, she was the Mistress, but now the Tables were turned, since that she had not a word more to say than if she had been my Chambermaid. And indeed I had trouble enough to learn her how to behave her self, insomuch that Forsooth[1] had been no longer suitable to her, for by selling of Herbs she had got so much of the *Billings-gate* breeding,[2] that I could hardly reform her so far as to make her take the manners of a Rational Person, she was also become a Soul,[3] that is, she had learnt to tope off *Brandy*, which seems to be an indespensable Propriety[4] that accompanies Poverty, and is absolutely inseparable from it, though there are those found who are considerably Rich, who can Quaff off Brandy, Anniseed,[5] and other distilled Waters, as if they had their Education at *Ratcliff*, or had been Retainers to a Strong-water-Shop; but these do it with more Address, and if their Carbunkle[6] Noses and Fiery Faces did not manifest it, it would seldom be discovered, and I assure you that Anniseed and Caraway[7] are not always employed for Ventosities[8] or Cholick, though that use is attributed to them. However I compassed in a short time all these Difficulties, though that it was not without great trouble. For when that the poor Woman began afterwards to frequent Persons of Honour, she got rid of these ill-becoming Customs, as also of drinking of Brandy, which I had ever nauseated and had in abomination.

We had not lived above five weeks together, when there happened to me a ridiculous thing, and which I cannot forbear communicating to the Reader. As I was going one *Saturday* with my Mother to the Market, *Sarah* my former Maid met me in the

---

1 Meaning uncertain here; literally, in truth, truly.
2 The breeding of a foul-mouth person, a scold. Billingsgate was a fish-market in London noted for the vituperative language of its vendors.
3 Used in relation to some attribute (obsolete): "He is a Soul, or Loves Brandy" (*Canting Dictionary*, 1700).
4 The fact of belonging to a particular person, thing, or condition (obsolete).
5 Obsolete spelling of "aniseed," the seed of the anise, used as a flavouring in drinks and candies.
6 Red spot or pimple on the nose caused by intemperance.
7 A candy or candied fruit containing caraway seeds.
8 Gases generated in the stomach or colon.

Street, and began immediately to ring us a Peal of injurious Languages, bawling out for a long while *Whores*, which without doubt proceeded from my having discharged her too soon; and that, as it is the Nature of Women, she could not disgest this without a great deal of Vexation. I was pretty sumptuously dress'd, as my Custom was; and for that Reason I thought not fit to engage or take Notice of her; but hastened on my way, neither more nor less than if I had not been at all concerned; but I could not save my self by my Silence: For the Bitch seized me by my *Manteau*,[1] and began to pull me so rudely, that she tore a great Hole in it, insomuch that you might have put your Head through. As I was not easie to suffer,[2] nor none of the weakest, I could not in any manner endure this Shame and Affront; and not seeing any other Arms more ready to revenge my self, than a kind of a Brass Peel[3] my Mother had upon her Arm: I took it by the Rim, and gave her two or three Blows upon the Head with so much Violence, that she had like to have fallen upon the Ground. However, she let not go her Hold, but tore my Gown to pieces. This made me almost mad, and with so much the more Reason, as that immediately we were surrounded with a great Number of People; and I lifted up the Peel with a Resolution to break her Head with it; but she passed the Blow stooping, and so avoided this Misfortune, but with such Imprudence that the Rim got about her Neck without doing her any Damage; which I no sooner perceived, than that I let go my Hand, and gave her so many Boxes on the Ear, while I held the Rim firm with my left Hand, that she could hardly turn her Head; and you might have seen of a suddain the Blood gush from her Nose and Mouth as from a Funnel. The Spectators seeing this so violent and bloody Combat, laughed in such a manner, that they furnished me with a fair Occasion to satisfie my Resentment at the Expence of *Sarah's* Groin; who, as strong as she was, could not rid her self of the Rim; and undoubtedly by such great Blows I gave her, I should have so mawled her, that even her Parents could not have known her again, if a Bitch of an Apple Woman, and such like People as commonly haunt the Markets, had not taken their time to free her out of my Hands; but then I also should have been paid off in my Turn: For the excessive Blood which gushed in great Lumps from *Sarah's* Nose and Mouth, moving this Scum of

---

1 A loose gown worn by women in the seventeenth and eighteenth centuries.
2 Not easily pained or injured.
3 Uncertain; perhaps a brass vessel or bracelet.

Women all at a time, both to Choler and Compassion, they came upon me like Devils, and seem'd as if they would have torn me in pieces; and according to all Appearances I should have been swing'd of, if in that extream Necessity I had not invented a piece of Cunning, which was to promise a Guinney to a Party of Butchers Men, who were in Troops amongst that Multitude, in case they would secure me from all Danger, and my Mother also. Then it was I observed the Power of this Mettal; for in the twinckling of an Eye those Heroes had cleared the Field of Battel, and afterwards conducted us into a Tavern, where I gave them with Joy the Money I had promised them, adding to the Bargain two or three Quarts of Wine, which they drank to my Health; tho to speak the Truth, I could much rather have wish'd they would have swallowed it to the happy re-establishment of my Gown: if so it be, that drinking to the Health of any one can bring him Advantage and Prosperity: For when I look'd upon it, I saw it was in a very deplorable Condition. Thus this Battel cost me very dear, tho I had the Victory on my Side, seeing my Manteau was torn to pieces, my Brass Peel was lost in the Combat, my Gold was employed in Jesting and Laughing to them Fellows; and it was six Months before I durst set my Foot in the Market again.

Between this last Inconvenience and *Christmas* there happened to me nothing else that merits the trouble of being described; for during that time I had never the occasion to do ought soever, unless it were to continue my usual way of living, that is to say, to scrape up as much, and to strip my Gallants of as much of their Money as was possible for me; and by these means I got together such a Lump, as that I purchas'd another Annuity of almost threescore pounds a year. So that now I need not be under any great fear of Poverty; for this Sum being joyned to that which poor *Valere* had given me was, pretty sufficient to live handsomly enough upon, tho not with the same Pomp and Lustre that I do at present.

Certainly I cannot forbear from laughing, when I consider the Lives of those Damosels, who now have their Recourse for Livelihood to this Commerce which I was used to exercise in my Youth: For those poor Creatures have hardly what's sufficient to satisfie their Hunger; and if there be any one among them who has one Change of Cloaths, she plays the Lady; and if there was in that sort of Life certain degrees of Dignity, such an one would undoubtedly have the Command over a Regiment of *Fleetstreet*[1] Night-walkers

---

1   Avenue extending eastwards from Temple Bar to Ludgate Circus.

or Bulkers. In the mean while, Bawds and Hostesses dispose of their Money as they please, and live with these poor innocent Females just as the *Turks* do with their Slaves; there is only this difference, that they have not over them the Right of Life and Death: For they truck, sell, and pawn 'em too for any Price they pretend, to poor innocent Creatures, who for a Gown, a Crape Manteau, or some such like thing, abandon thus their Honour and their Liberty after a most pitious manner; and must expect all that can arise from *Venus's* Occupation, in regard of Diseases and Villany. The truth is, so much the more I laugh at you, the more are you to be pitied by some other who has more Compassion; and perhaps that I should likewise fall into that silly Commiseration, if I knew not that you joyfully support the Yoke of your Servitude, were it only to have the Contentment of going dressed something more sumptuously; or at least, with something more Lustre than your Rise[1] can contribute thereunto, without considering that the Apparrel of a Gentlewoman requires other Manners than those of the Daughter of a sordid Orange Woman, or Kitchin-Stuff Wench, or of the *Billingsgate* Tribe, which is really the only cause of your Poverty: For if their Manners were such as are seen in them, whose Bodies are born to wear such like Vestments, and if your Mind knew how to make the difference between those to whom you give the Quality of being your Lovers, for only having had one time to do with you, I am sure your Hostesses would not stand in need of Love Mercuries[2] to put you in pawn, or sell you in other places; but we will cease speaking of that untill some other Occasion: For if I begin to work upon that point, I should wholly divert my self from my Designs, and perhaps I should not think at all upon my own Affairs; and that the Printer would bring me word, that there was already more Paper spoiled than we intended to make use of: For my prudent or silly Reader, be you which you please, tho I love rather to believe the latter; People now must be very careful that Books be not above Nine or Ten Sheets in Bulk, that the Haunters of Taverns and Bawdy House, may by absenting themselves from such places for an Evening or two employ their Money to the Profit of the Bookseller.

To return to my Subject, *Christmas* being come, a Bill was put upon my Door for the House to be let, not that I had any Design

---

1 Act of rising and getting dressed in the morning, or, possibly, simply coming into notice.
2 Preparation used in the treatment of venereal disease.

to go take any other; but only by reason that I endeavoured to obtain some Abatement from the Landlord. A Bill of considerable Bigness had served four or five days for a Trade to the House, when that I was one day standing at the Door, I saw passing by a Spark, who by the Sumptuousness of his Cloaths, attracted upon him the Eyes of all the Neighbourhood. Perhaps that my Face was not disagreeable to him; for he cooled me[1] at a distance; and indeed I did not forbear looking on him, untill that he had turned the Corner of the Street; for methought that his Face was not unknown to me; and I strongly imagined that I had formerly seen him somewhere else, that I was above three hours tormenting my Memory to know whom that could have been.

In the morning of the day following some body knocked at my Door: I went to open it, by reason my Mother was gone out, who had otherwise that Office. It was the same Spark who had eyed me so much the day before; and who now asked me with a peculiar Courtesie, if his seeing my House would be no trouble to me? I told him it was open for every one, and for him with so much the more reason, in that I was not used to be treated with so much Civility. Whereupon he went in, visited below, above, and all places of the House, neither more nor less than if he had designed to make his Abode there for half a dozen years. I followed him still Step by Step; or to say rather, I walked before him and shew'd him the way, without hardly ever turning for a Moment my Eyes off him: For I had the greatest Curiosity in the world to know where it was that I could have seen him. Thus when he had seen it all, he began to discourse upon one point or other; and did it with so much Ingenuity, with so charming an Air, and such smooth and rational Talk, that he was almost an hour before he took his leave of me, after having first of all beseeched me, that he might be so happy as to return to see me; which could not have been civil in me to have refused to a Gentleman of his Stamp, since that I was in hopes to receive from him in time some considerable Profit.

Three or four days afterwards, he came again to my House, and spent an whole Afternoon in my Company, without the time's proving in any manner tedious to me, for his Tongue was admirably well hung. I considered him anew with still more attention, and the more I looked upon him, the more methoughts his Physiognomy and his Meen[2] were not unknown to me,

---

1 Unidentified usage.
2 Variant spelling of "mien."

however I would not ask him downright, though I employed my mind all manner of ways to learn by some trick, from whence this knowledge could have been imprinted in my Memory; but all my Artifices were of no use to me, and perhaps to this day I should have known nothing of the matter, if by an admirable Accident he had not given me to understand it in the following manner.

He had now for a Month visited me from time to time, without my having granted him the least favour, for it was not my custom to be kind to any one upon running Post,[1] I must first of all have sounded their Breasts, and penetrated their Hearts. Thus it happened, that one certain Evening as we were together, and that we were employed in discoursing upon the Artifice of a certain Picture that hung in my Chamber, he told me that he had something about him, which though small, ought not to be less esteem'd than the rarest and the greatest Picture, and thereupon feeling in his Pocket, he took out a Box, wherein there were two Pourtaictures, whereof the one represented my Father and the other my Mother. The Poor Woman had a hundred and a hundred times bewailed the loss of this Box, though she had not had much Love for her Husband towards the end of his Life; for truly the two little Faces were drawn with so much Art, that I had seen very few that could come near their perfection. I was seized with a fright and astonishment as soon as I had it in hand, and from that moment I easily perceived who it was that was so hot to acquire the enjoyment of my Person, for those two Miniatures had been stole from us with the rest of our Goods, by that abominable Rope-Dancer, who learnt my Father the *Strapado*, as mention was made in the beginning of this Book, which perhaps proceeds from that the Box was of Silver, and that he was resolved not to leave us any thing of all that was made of that noble Mettal with which all things are brought to pass. I was for a pretty while contemplating those two Faces, that while I held my Eye firmly fixed upon them, I might remove all occasion of his perceiving the emotion and astonishment I was in, for if he had minded me in the least, he might easily have observed that there must needs have been some special and peculiar reason, which raised in me such an Emotion. Sir, (said I to him afterwards, when I returned the Box into his hand, and that I was somewhat recollected from my disorder), I must needs own that these Faces are wonderfully well

---

1 The usage is obscure; in its literal sense, a post that moves easily by mechanical means.

drawn, but if it was you that the Painter meant to represent by this Figure of a Gentleman, he has not drawn you to the Life. Pretty Lady, (answered he to me) I can in no wise impute any fault to the Workman, for the Man never saw me, but once in my Life I have seen him whom it represents, and though it be several Years ago, yet if I saw him I could easily know him again, for at that time this Picture resembled him so admirably well, that years must have made an extraordinary change in him, if he was no longer to be known by him who having his Picture before his eyes, and himself too, should confront them together. I had an extream Passion to learn more, but because I feared that my too great Curiosity might betray me, I said not a word more, and afterwards as soon as this counterfeit Gentleman had taken his leave of me, I related to my Mother the adventure I had had, and that I had found out the Rope-Dancer, or rather the Thief, for with this Trade of breaking one's Neck it was not so easy a matter to get such great gains as to spend at that rate he did, who had so miserably bereaved us of what we had, when we dwelt at *Islington*, but this Discourse had like to have reduced my whole Affairs to Ashes, for she would immediately have run to a Justice of Peace, to have informed him of this matter, that he might grant a Warrant to a Constable to seize on this Gallant, but I withheld and opposed this design of hers, by reason that it would have been of no advantage to us, and I told her that she should leave me to manage this Affair my self, without showing that she had the least knowledge of him when he returned to make me his Visits.

Though I had only set a Bill upon my Door,[1] that I might have some abatement of my Rent (for I gave to understand to all those who came to see the House, that in Hell it self it could not smoak more miserably) yet I now changed my Resolution, and in the space of three days I so ordered my business, that I found out a House to my mind, I mean that it was inhabited, and that I could enter into it as soon as I pleased, I gave notice hereof immediately to my best Gallants, that in case I came to dislodge suddainly, they might not be troubled in seeking after my Lodgings, each of them ask'd me immediately for what reason I would so unseasonably change my Quarters; but I gave them no other answer, but that they should keep themselves in repose on that side, and that they should stifle their Curiosity, until that I was disloged, and that then I would tell them the reason.

---

1 A written petition posted in a prominent public place.

In the mean while, my Rope-Dancer came to visit me once in two days, as he formerly did, and I received him with a good Eye, and even with a more favourable Meen than formerly, until that I had prepared all things necessary for the execution of my Design, and one Evening I told him with a smiling Countenance, that I desired him to send me the next Morning about eleven of the Clock a Jole of *Salmon*,[1] and that for the first time in his Life he would do me the honour to Dine with me, for he had long sollicited me to that purpose. The poor Culley was so overjoyed at this News, for that he was in hopes this favour would be accompanied with one much greater, that he hardly knew what he said or did, for in the beginning I had lived with him, just after the same manner as with those who came the first time to my House, I mean with just as many Testimonies of kindness as were requisite not to lose them.

The next Morning I had my Fish and my Guest too before ten of the Clock, so that I sate down to Dinner with my fine Gallant on my side before Eleven. In the mean while I had given order to my Mother, that she would stand behind his back and serve him with drink, and that she should mingle in the Wine every time she gave him a certain Composition which had the Power to render a Man extraordinary Drunk, and to cast him into so deep a Sleep, that it was impossible for him to open his eyes, or to wake, what noise soever was made. My piece of Cunning succeeded very well, for the Rope-Dancer had not drank off half a Dozen Glasses, then that his Eyes began to twinckle, and became so excessively Drunk, that he was hardly able to sit upon his Chair. As soon as I perceived this, I made him quaff off three Glasses more upon one another, wherein abundance of this Composition was put, and in less than a Quarter of an hour, he began to act like a Beast and tumble out of the Chair. We left him there lying for about half an hour that we might be in perfect assurance, and for that purpose I pricked him four or five times in the Thighs with a Needle. But he neither shewed motion, nor sence. Then was the time to put our design in Execution, wherein my Mother was very necessary to me, insomuch that he was quickly undrest, unto his Drawers and Waistcoat, which we did not think fit to strip him of, but first of all we felt all over to see if there was not some precious thing still concealed. This being done, I cloathed him with an old Cimarra[2] and a rotten Petticoat; and having cut

---

1 The head and shoulders of certain fish such as salmon or sturgeon.
2 Variant spelling of "simmara." An ecclesiastical garment: a soutane or fur-lined cassock with a short cape and short set sleeves.

off his Mustachoes, I put a Womans Cornet[1] upon his head, with a white Coife, insomuch, that in that Equipage, his own Mother could not have known him again no more than if she had never seen him. After we had Apparrelled him in such manner, as best pleased my Fancy, we put him into a Coffer,[2] in which I had caused three or four holes to be made, and having thrust into his right hand the following Letter, I made two Porters carry him to *Queen-Hive*,[3] with directions for *Thisselworth*,[4] for that he had endeavoured to make me believe that he was an Eminent Gentleman's Son of that Town, so that I had written the Superscription to his pretended Father. My Mother went along with the Porters, and desired the Waterman to take care of the Coffer, and not to shake it much, for that there were *Porcelain* Ware in it, and other Fragile Merchandize. The Contents of the Letter, which I put into his Hand, was as follows.

Without doubt you still remember, that some years ago, you unhappily persuaded a certain Inkeeper to learn the *Strapado*, by which means he broke his Leg, and you afterwards robbed him of so many things, that you could hardly carry them away without perhaps expecting that they should be one day demanded of you again. And indeed this Robbery would have still remained concealed, if you had not shown me those two Pictures in Miniature, for your Figure remain'd still in some manner in my Idea, but yet I should never have known without so powerful a proof that you were the Man that at the same time had the civility to make me a Present of half-a-dozen Boxes of the ear. You may easily learn by these last *words* that I am the Daughter of that Man, and by Consequence you may easily judge that I found my self constrained to repair this loss as well as was possible for me. Neither ought you to be very sad and troubled, for you come off at a much cheaper rate at present, than if I had caused you to be taken into Custody. Wherefore be pleased to reward the Civility I use towards you,

---

1 A kind of ladies' head-dress; the large white, winged hat worn by the Sisters of Charity.
2 Obsolete spelling of "coffin."
3 Queen-Hive or Queen-Hite was a quay on the north bank of the Thames adjacent to North Thames Street and a landing place for goods shipped to London from abroad.
4 Variant spelling of Thistleworth, located in West Grinstead Hundred, Sussex.

in never seeking after me; but if you are not so dispos'd you may act according to your Inclination, and assure your self that all your pains will be to no purpose, for before you can be returned from *Thisselworth*, I will be far enough from hence for you ever to find me out. In the mean while make use for some time of those Apparrel; and try if you can have as much happiness in it as I have had my self; which you ought not to despair of, since you are none of the ugliest in a white Coife, and a Womans Cornet: I would willingly make my Letter something longer, to give you some comfort in your Misfortune, but it being almost High-Water and my House as you know at a considerable distance, I have not time sufficient. Wherefore live well if you can, and know that if ever I hear you heartily pardon me this Prank, I shall then believe that you bear me as much good Will, as you have so often endeavoured to persuade me of.

Tho the River was not frozen that Winter, yet it is no hard matter to imagine he did not sweat over much in his Coffer, and I would willingly have given the fourth part of my Booty, which mounted[1] in all to the value of about forty pound, if I could have had the pleasure of seeing him awake.

That same Evening, as soon as my Mother was returned back, I went to pay my Landlord with my Rope-dancers Money. And on the morrow Morning before my Neighbours were yet up (for I was not willing any of 'em should know whither I went to lodge) we decamped, being assisted by four Porters, and went to take possession of my new Quarters, which were several Streets distant from this House; so that the Rope-dancer would have had trouble enough to have found me out; But I do not believe that he made any great Enquiry after me; or at least it never came to my Ears: For I saw him not in any place till a long time after, when that to my Misfortune I fell into his Hands; whereof I will give the Reader an Account in the following part of this present Book.

As soon as my Gallants came to visit me in my new House, and to impart to me their Money, I related to them the reason of my Dislodging,[2] and each of them seem'd to take therein a peculiar Satisfaction; tho I am however willing to believe, that this

---

1 Variant spelling of "amounted."
2 Turning out of a place of lodging.

Relation did not bring me much Profit; for by others Losses people learn to become better advised. I also presently remarked, that there were several amongst them who no longer trusted so well in me as they used to do before, wherefore I took a firm Resolution, never to make known to any one soever the least thing that concerns such Tricks and Cheats: and I also counsel all Women who trade in Flesh, never to amuse themselves, with relating to their Lovers any of those things that have happened with one or other of their Cullies; for you will rarely find that this proves to their Advantage.

I was setting Pen again to Paper, to inform the Reader how I came to take a Husband, after I had remained a year or more in my new Lodging; but that I will refer to the Second Part, wherein I will add a long List of Stories, with edifying and good Novelties; and in the mean while I shall wish my good or malicious Reader as many Blessings or Mischiefs as he can do to me my self: for I am not of that sort of People who pray for their Enemies;[1] but on the contrary I regulate my self by the Law of *Talion*,[2] or *Retribution*, whereof you may also see Examples throughout the whole Course of my Life.

FINIS.

---

1 See The Sermon on the Mount, Matthew 5:44.
2 The lex talionis, the principle of exacting compensation (an eye for an eye, a tooth for a tooth). See Exodus 21:23-24.

Courtesy of the Houghton Library, Harvard University.

THE
LONDON JILT:
OR, THE
POLITICK WHORE.

The Second and Laſt Part.

SHEWING,

All the Artifices and Stratagems which the Ladies of Plea-
ſure make uſe of for the Intreaguing and Decoying of Men;
Interwoven with ſeveral Pleaſant
Stories of the *Miſſes* Ingenious
Performances.

LONDON,

Printed for *Hen. Rhodes*, next door to the
Bear-Tavern near *Bride-lane* in
Fleet-ſtreet. 1683.

The London Jilt; or, The Politick Whore
The Second and Last Part

AFTER that I had thus deceived the *Hop Merchant,* and had removed with my Virtuous Mother into an other Lodging, a certain Sparke who for his Money enjoyed my Favours, brought an other with him, when that we had dwelt there about seven or eight Months, who was a Widdower, and drove a great Trade in Tobacco. This Man was about 23 or 24 Years old, but in a little time I observed by his Discourse, that he was a Man of great experience in things that had any Conformity with my way of living, as also in all the Circumstances, that are proper for the gaining a Woman's heart, and more Capacity could not have been expected in a Man of three times his Age; he being still so young, I was amazed that he used his Wife at that rate, as to dispatch her so soon, and I began to rally him upon the business, but he had his Answer so ready, that I might say, I had found the Man I wanted. Amongst several other Discourses that he held me, *Without doubt* (said he to me with a smiling Countenance) *after having been married only five or six Months, Death would not have deprived me of an ugly Wife, when I only Married for the sake of her Riches, than to furnish me with the Convenience of choosing another adorn'd with so many Graces and Charms as your self.* I took little notice of these Words, because I thought they proceeded more from meer Civility, than from a Heart truly sincere. However I could well enough bear with 'em coming from his Mouth, and listen to 'em, both for that he was a handsom Man and very advantageously rich, as I was assured by him that brought him to me, so that there was a Pleasure in hearing one's Praises from such a Person: and for my part I was very well satisfyed with him, which made me show him a much more Familiar and Amiable Countenance, than I was used to do to any other in a first Visit; for certainly though Women may show themselves something Disdainful and Coy, when Men exalt their Beauties in their Presence, and though they make a show of giving no ear thereto, yet I protest there is nothing they believe more easily. Wherefore the *Spanish* Proverb says very patt, and to the Purpose, *Tell a Woman but once shee's handsom, and the Devil will tell it to her a thousand times afterwards:*[1] And this is very

---

1 Variants of the proverbs: "Tell a woman she's a beauty, and the devil will tell her so ten times" and "Tell a woman she's handsome but once, the devil will tell her so fifty times."

true, for those Words run so much in their Heads, that it often breaks their Rest, and even there is not one how ugly and mishaped soever she may be, but taxes the Republick of *Venice*,[1] of having used falsification in regard of her Glass, rather than believe that she is wholly so as Nature, and the Course of Years have made her, such a strong fancy have these poor Creatures that Beauty is an inseparable Propriety of the Female Sex.

In a few days after, this Tobacco Merchant came to visit me again, and besides, that being so well made of his Person, he could not but be agreeable, he had such Pleasant Discourses, and he knew in a short-time so well to insinuate himself into my favour, that one Night I graced him with half of my Bed, with a firm Confidence that he knew how to move the rest of his Body as dextrously as his Tongue; and truly I was not at all deceived herein, for he was so great a Master in that Profession, that *Aurora*[2] sooner approach'd than I could have wish'd it, and found us lying and panting in one anothers Arms.

This caused a great Amazement in my Mother, for I had not yet received from that Lover any Benefit of any great Importance; whereas otherwise I never permitted any one should obtain the least Courtesy from me, till after having frequented me a long time, and that I had drawn from them as much Money, as I could imagine to have an Obligation to them; but one of the three Torments, which torment the Minds of Mortals,[3] now by the Flesh had so unmercifully disquieted me since the first time I saw him, that in the Night I could hardly hold my Legs still, when the Thoughts I had had in the Day-time came to renew themselves in my head, so great is the Power of a Man in the Heart of a Woman, when his Tongue is well hung and he is handsom of Person, and when they begin to maintain together a particular Conversation, and that one finds that these Parties ought not to yield to one another. I certifie to you according to the experience I have had thereof, and all Women who have so open and frank a Heart as mine, will confess as well as I do, that there is nothing under the Sun that has such powerful Attractions, and that the Load-stone cannot have more Virtue to draw Iron and Steel towards it, than those Parts have to attract one another Reciprocally.

---

1 Name of the city in north-east Italy, sometimes used to designate various articles made there, including glassware.
2 Classical goddess of the dawn.
3 The World, the Flesh, and the Devil. See The First Letter of John 1:16.

We had for about six Months spent our time in this incomparable Divertisement, without however my being in any manner obliged to abandon my other Lovers, who tickled my Toby,[1] and paid me for it sufficiently (for my Tobacco Man who had not the Civility to honour me of his own Motion, with any thing of value, and whom I never sollicited to give me any thing, because I bore him too great a Love, and was afraid of losing him) knew very well that I could not maintain my self in my Condition with wind,[2] and he did not seem to be very much disquieted upon this account, provided he might have preferably before any other, his Elbow-room with me. We had spent, I say, about so much time in this manner, when that one Morning as we were in Bed in Love and Delight, he began to relate to me how he got acquainted with his first Wife, who had been old, ugly, and rich, and with whom he had made a considerable Fortune, after having given himself to all manner of Debauches during his Youth.

This Relation having already lasted near half an hour without my comprehending what all these things tended to, he asked me after a serious manner, if I would abandon this Libertine and disorderly way of Living, and if I could live contented with one Man who loved me from the very bottom of his Heart? I made him answer in the Affirmative, and that there was nothing I aspired to with more disquiet, unless that it would please Heaven to address a good Man to me, which though I lived in that manner, was not all the same thing to me, but, that with such a Man as he, I knew how to comport my self so honourably and so virtuously, as the discreetest Woman in all the City of *London* could do.

And thereupon taking him about the Neck to kiss him, I gave him a hundred Kisses, letting at the same time many Tears trickle down my Cheeks, as if it had been for a sign of my Repentance, for the Life I had thitherto led; I knew besides, so well how to play my part, by assuring him that the first cause that had constrained me thereto, was Poverty, that his Heart began to be moved so far, as that I fancied I saw some Signs of Tears in his Eyes. I easily perceive (said he) that I run a risque to ruine my self by loving you, and that infallibly I shall fall again into my first Condition, if I do not endeavour to make speedy Provision against it, by some means which may help me, for it is absolutely impossible for me to live much longer without you. Since then I

---

1 Tickled my posterior, my buttocks (slang).
2 Here, something empty, vain, trifling or without substance; mere talk.

must of necessity make choice of one of the two Evils, methinks that it is much better to Marry together betimes, than wait till Old Age, and perhaps Poverty comes. But (added he) be careful that I never find the least Infidelity on your part, and be assured that I have padded this way long enough to know all the Turnings and Windings of it; thereupon he was going to make a considerable number of Threatnings, but I stopped his design by as many Vows, which I thought were necessary for the imprinting in him good Sentiments of my Person.

Reader, do not overmuch wonder at the Folly of him who in a short time after was my Husband, for there are so many Men who take Wives who have had to do with other Men for several Years before, that the City of *London* is able to furnish above Fifty Thousand of that sort of Sparks: And pray you, why should not those poor Devils find Men as well as others, since it is most certain, that by a long experience they have rendred themselves more capable of the business; and that besides they spare those poor Cullies the pains of employing so terrible a strength to break the Fin of an affected Maydenhead? Certainly if you are not yet Marryed, you will think with your self, that you would do your business better. And in case there be here and there a Woman who has not given her self up long to this Commerce, and who has not kept Company with many Persons, yet you are not assured that she who shall fall into your Arms, has never had to do with an other. For this is so common in the Age we live, that a certain Clerk of a Church[1] declared to me, that in the time of six Years, during which he had exercised that Charge, there had not been one Bride that had sprinkled the Chancery[2] with her Tears, which has in all times been an infallible sign of a Maydenhead; and if you have not yet lost that your self, I would yet less advise you to seek out one of that sort, for two Persons who are Novices and unexperienced in Copulation, the Children they get are commonly Fools,[3] which is a thing People ought to be more careful of than any other.

Some days after that we had held such Discourses together, we went to the Parson to have him Ask us in the Church the *Sunday* following; but it would be tedious to relate all the Particulars of those Ceremonies, some Children as well as Men in Years are

---

1 An office or position in the church.
2 The office of a chancellor; also a court of records.
3 Here, persons who are deficient or destitute of reason or intellect.

acquainted with all the Circumstances of that matter. Thus I will only tell you, that after the Publication of our Banes, we went to *Barnet*[1] and were Marryed there, because if my Dear Husband had kept his Wedding in the City, he would have seen too many Sons-in-Law.

Thus as soon as we were engaged to one another conformably to the Ceremonies, and that I had removed my goods into a new Habitation; my Husband required of me that I would take a Room for my Mother, because he would in no wise consent she should dwell with us, alledging for Pretext, that that was often an occasion of Quarrels and Trouble amongst young Marryed People, by reason that commonly young Women depend a little too much on their Parents, which hinders them from acknowledging the Soveraignty of their Husband, and from rendring themselves subject to the Laws of Obedience.

As I was very much used to my Mother's Company, I imagined at first he did me a great injury, but afterwards having taken all things into serious Consideration, I was overjoyed to find him so resolved; for tho' I had not yet any design of committing towards him any Act of Infidelity, by reason, that to speak the truth, I loved him from the bottom of my Heart, yet I knew very well that there might be such Occasions offered as might make us change our Sentiments, and that in such a case it is better to trust to Parents than to Strangers; which is beyond all Dispute.

Thus I took two Rooms for the poor Woman; but I charged her to speak but of one to my Husband, on the one side, that he might not complain of so much Money for Rent, and on the other for Reasons which you may learn in the Sequel of this Relation.

We had not been Marryed for above a Fortnight, when I took occasion to quarrel with the two Maids, who served my Husband during the time of his being a Widdower; for those Maids not being used to a Mistress, and having infallibly heard (as I could easily conjecture by their Discourse) what a Person I had been, they would in no wise submit themselves, nor suffer that an other should have rul'd over them.

In the mean while, I for my part bestirred my Jaws to such purpose, that I kept 'em under, and if my Husband was willing to be at Rest, he was no longer to defer turning away those two

---

1 A market town about twelve miles north of London on the Great North Road.

Wenches. Which nevertheless he was very loath to do, that by what I afterwards learnt from the Neighbours, he had lived a little more familiarly with them than Decency did allow of; but I was obliged to follow the Mode of Women who come to Marry with Men, that is to say, I was to turn away the Maids, that I might have no Contradictions, for that rascality finds so much to blame touching the want of experience in New Wives, that without having the greatest patience in the World they are not to be born with.

When that all things were thus setled, and in good Order, my Husband began diligently to attend his business at the Change, and to look after his Servants; while that for my part I took care of the Shop, wherein I became in a short time as skilful and as ready, as if I had been brought up to it all my Life, which certainly is no very great Subject of Admiration; for there is no great Art in weighing Tobacco and filling of Pipes.

In the mean while, all sorts of Merchants and Tradesmen came to our House, tho' with no other Design than to see and discourse with me, while they set a smoaking their Tobacco, which cannot be prohibited in such Shops; for I was dress'd like a Goddess, and you would have said that I was Queen of all the Tobacco-Sellers Wives. The truth is, that my Husband desired me several times that I would lay aside those Trappings which glittered and made too great a show, but all his Representations were in vain, that Devil of Pride had taken such deep root in my mind, that all his endeavours to destroy it were in vain. Besides I am not the only one who by such means has butter'd and nourish'd her Husband's Brow-Antlets. All Women are commonly proud, and tho' commonly they fall into a dirty sluttishness when they are Marryed, nevertheless they must have all manner of fine things, that they may not appear less than their Companions or Neighbours, without considering whether their Husband's Incomes can counterpoise that of others. They must have at home all manner of precious Moveables and Furniture, and if these poor Cullies will not consent to buy them all they have a mind to, they will never have a good Look nor a kind Word from their Spouses. Besides these difficulties there are several others which are from time to time, for if it happens to those Creatures to have their Bellies full of Pettitoes[1] they must prepare an Equipage for the little Children so rich and so pompous, that they may be an Object of Admiration to all People, and tho' they alledge for their

---

1 Literally, full of the feet of small children, that is, pregnant.

Justification, that it shall be but one time for all, however I assure you that as soon as they find themselves again in the same Circumstances, they must again make a Number of Preparations, for during that Interval all those Laces have changed the Fashion, and if the Wife does not follow the New Mode, she can never happily be delivered of the Child she goes with.

After this manner did I live with my Husband, and though I did not put him to a Hundred Pounds Charge for Clouts, by reason I imagined I should not lie in the first Year, I obliged him however to lay out so much Money for Moveables, Cloaths, Linnen, Laces, and several other such like things, that he often scratched his Head, neither more nor less, than if he had had a great many Lice, which put him to that terrible itching. To make short, I took such a course, that in a Year or two our Affairs began to go backwards like a Crab, which my Husband perceiving, and seeing clearly that I should be the cause of his Ruine, if he did not timely prevent it, kept his Purse shut and gave me nothing more than what was necessary for the Maintenance of a House; but because I still received the Money for Tobacco, it was impossible for him to hinder me from stealing from him, so much as in a little time amounted to a considerable Sum, which I gave my Mother to keep for to make use of in case I fell into a Calamitous time, and she also understood how to cheat her very dexterously. However he took notice that his Tobacco lessened and fell short, and that no Money arose from it, whereupon he ratled me the first time very sharply, but seeing that was to little purpose, he undertook to employ an other more powerful means, for one Morning when all the People were gone to Church, having called me into a Back-Room, he represented to me my Duty with such very pertinent Reasons, that I was very sensible of them for above a Week afterwards.

I could not easily digest this Affront, and tho' after his Anger was appeased, he besought me several times, that I would think no more thereof, protesting that he would never treat me after that manner, provided I would have comported myself as I ought to do, nevertheless, I would not suffer him to touch me for above a Fortnight, and I not only plagued him in that respect, but I also took an irrevocable Resolution of planting two Horns upon his Front, that in no wise should yield to those of *Acteon*, and exercise my Body in Labour as strongly as ever did *Lais*, or *Messalina* the Wife of the Emperour *Claudius*.[1]

---

1 Common examples, drawn from classical antiquity, of female vice and profligacy.

I wanted not an occasion to effect all this, for though above two years time, I had not done the Feat with any Body, nor had I given any one hopes of doing it, my Old *Inamorato's*[1] fail'd not still of coming in Crowds to the Door, and even those too who had had all their Lives long an Aversion for Tobacco, had tortur'd themselves with smoking since that they might have a familiar Conversation, and an honourable access to my House: True it is that they were to be careful how they employed then their time, because that my Husband, who knew very well that I was none of the Chastest, by little and little became very jealous, and for that reason did not look upon any of those with a good Eye in his House, who had in any wise approached me before. This Resolution having been thus taken, I showed my self oftner in the Street, than I had thitherto done, and deckt my self so spruce and so fine, that I drew the Eyes of all upon me. Moreover I dispatched my Mother to two or three of my old Gallants, alledging for pretext that she had something to tell them. These went to her Chamber without delay, where she stayed them so long with Impertinent Tatlings of one thing or other, until I had notice thereof by a Wench that lived in that House in Quality of a Maid. I went thither finely adorn'd to see again my ancient Servants, but as if it had been by chance that I met with any one of them there, that I might set the better value upon my Commodity, I showed my self too Coy and Disdainful to amuse my self in things of that Nature, insomuch, that one would have thought it had never been toucht with a Finger, and because Desires augment by Denyal, I rendred them so hot that they would have given half their Estates, to have enjoyed my Favours, which they were so much the more passionate upon, as that they saw me engaged in Marriage; for that Cursed Folly seems to be naturally imprinted in the Minds of Men, that they love much rather to Commit Adulteries, than to Divert themselves with Whores, which proceeds undoubtedly from that they imagine, that Marryed Women grant them the Enjoyment of their Bodies out of pure Inclination, though it be however most certain that there are several amongst them who prostitute themselves much more than those innocent Creatures who out of necessity are obliged to gain their Livelyhood in Bawdy Houses. And you may be assured you simple Young or Old Lovers, that when a Woman Exposes her self thus by abandoning her self to Strangers, she either does it to

---

1 Lovers.

get Money or to satisfy her Lascivious Temper; if it be for the first Reason, why should she not endeavour to receive it from an other Person as well as you? And if it be to content her Lust and Lasciviousness, you may firmly believe, that not one Man nor six, are sufficient to extinguish her Flame, and by Consequence you cannot be the only Person that possesses her Favour. In short, after we had thus agreed upon the Bargain for this New Maydenhead, which was not done, until a good quantity of Silver had first of all softned the Humour for it was particularly for my interest that I played at *Hugh Gaffer-Cookes*,[1] tho' I was also something provoked to it by the tickling of my own Nature we retired then into the Back-Room for I had taken two Chambers for my Mother as I told you before, though my Husband had knowledge but of one, and we there did our Work as Gentilely and as Pleasantly as we used to do in former times.

Nevertheless this Life could not last very long, tho' there had never been any dabling in our Water-Pots,[2] without my Husband's knowing it, he who had padded the same way often in his Youth, yet he took no notice of it, but I easily observed by the coldness of his Carriage to me afterwards, and by all his Behaviour, that he had an Inckling of it; and if he did not tell his mind upon the business, it was for no other reason which obliged him to act in that manner, than to catch me in the Fact, if it was possible for him; but I knew how to manage my Affairs with so much Circumspection, that for a long time it was impossible for him to bring his design about, though the Occasion did often happen, and if he had known my Mother's Lodgings consisted in two Rooms, there would certainly have been a great deal of Bustle amongst us, for I have heard him several times in the Fore-Room, when he came to seek me, while I was taking my Heats in the same moment in the Back-Room, with one Gallant or other, and he had also once demanded of the Taylor who dwelt underneath, who it was that had that Chamber, but I had already provided against that inconveniency, and I had so well won upon that Fellow by two Silver Salts which I gave him, that he made him answer, that he kept it himself for his own use, insomuch, that my poor Innocent Culley could not discover where it was I took my Pleasure.

---

1 Reference unknown.
2 Variant of mustard-pots or honey-pots; the vaginas of prostitutes (slang).

In the mean while, this occasioned our leading a very Pleasant Life at our Home, for though he let nothing appear of such a Conduct, yet he took occasion to quarrel at all things, and often swinged me off, after so rude a manner, as if he had been to have beaten Stock-fish[1] to have render'd it supple, which made me conceive such an Aversion against him, that I could hardly any longer bear the sight of him.

But after that this sorry course had lasted about seven or eight Months, my Mother who was my only Comfort and only Refuge, fell sick and was reduced to that extremity, that she dyed at the Weeks end, which my Husband was as joyful for as I was sad, because he hoped that when this Block was removed, I should become much the better Wife. He immediately caused all the Moveables to be brought to our House that were in the Fore-Room, tho' they were but of very small Importance; for as for the other that I had pinched from him from time to time, and which my Servants had given me for the use of my Body, I locked them up in the other Chamber, which I kept still for some time after the Death of my Mother, without my Husband's knowing the least of the matter. He caused also the Corps of the Deceased to be brought into our House, and for his own Honour, made a very great Funeral, for without that consideration, he would have rather chosen to have flung it to the Dogs.

In the mean while, as I dayly inquired after some place to exercise my Calling in Repose and Liberty (for I durst not venture it in the Chamber I kept; because that other Persons very reserved had taken Possession of the Fore-Room, and whom I feared might go and inform my Patron if they perceived that Men came Crowding to me there, to which, my Husband had me often dogged[2] by others, knowing that I had nothing more to do there) I was carried one Evening into *Drury-lane*[3] to a Widdows House, by one of my Gallants, whom I met with by chance. The Widdow kept a Mayd, of eighteen or nineteen years of Age, to whom she gave leave to get Money by the sweat of her Body, that she might appear in an honourable Posture, and for that purpose she imparted her Talent to some Gentlemen advanced in Years, and of a calm Humour, of whom every one had his particular day

---

1 The name for cod; here, an allusion to having beaten a cod before cooking.
2 Followed like a dog, usually with hostile intent.
3 Once a fashionable street, Drury Lane acquired a reputation as a haunt of vice and prostitution during the Restoration.

assigned him alone, that the others might not be taken notice of. Besides this Mayd, there came also sometimes when occasion required it, some marryed Woman or other whose Husband and she could not agree together as they ought to do, and who for that reason transported her self into that place, that she might live with another in Peace and Diversion, so that this Old Woman kept a Bawdy-House of Citizens Wives; but after that I began to frequent it, the others had not much Practice there, for so rich and stately Apparel as I usually wore, tho' it had not been accompanied with a Beautiful Face, might easily attract the Admiration of a Troop of men, and especially they all have something of the Nature of *Germans*, who had rather have to do with an ugly nasty Quean in fine Cloaths, than a Beautiful Mayd in a Plain Dress.

This House of my Landladys pleased me extreamly, and I could willingly have continued longer than my Frequentation (for Money came rolling in a-pace) if an unhappy Accident had not brought the business almost all to nothing. My Husband told me one Morning that he was to go settle some accounts, and for that purpose within a Week or eight days, he was to take a Journey to *Northampton*[1] and some other places thereabouts, as indeed, after having made great Preparations for his Journey, he took his leave of me at the time he spoke of, with Testimonies of Affection, much greater than ordinary. You may very well think, that I was not very sad at his Departure, for I promised my self that during that time, I should have Elbow-room, and might heap up a Sum of Money; which I had so much the more reason to do, as that I was to make my escape, when I had provided my self with the Profits that I had honourably gained by the Labour of my Body, as also all that I could scrape up in the management of our Trade and House-Keeping, that then I would withdraw for a long time, and Exchange *London* for some other Town, which proceeded from the Aversion I had conceived to my Husband, since the first time he had chastised me so severely. This Aversion was encreased to that degree, that I had all the Pains imaginable to bear the sight of him, wherein I resembled most Women who are commonly blind in all their Passions, and are so violently passionate in their hatred or their Love, even most commonly without any Cause, that they exceed all Bounds.

Three or four days after that my Husband was gone, I went to my Widdow's House, and gave her to understand, that I should

---

1 A town sixty-five miles north-west of London.

have henceforward the occasion to be employed in the Service of an honest Man without running any Risque; and certainly I was not long without putting in Practice so laudable an Exercise, and there presently after a Man came in who approached me, and who having an ugly Wife, diverted himself sometimes with those of other Mens, though perhaps he would have done no less, if he had had a fair one; for even the most dainty Meats cause at length Disgust, if you eat them continually. It seems as if Nature for the Mortification of Honest Women, has so deeply imprinted this abominable desire in the Hearts of Men, that they cannot get rid of it. And methinks they would be in this Case in less manner excusable, if they sought after Women, tho' none of the greatest Beauties, yet who ought not to yield that advantage to the others, that belong to them; but O! the Prodigiousness of disorderly Love: We see Husbands who have Wives as beautiful as Angels, who nevertheless run after Wenches, who are more deformed and ugly than if they were Devils; but if those Women did as I was used to do, I am sure that those Gallants would find themselves much more assiduous at their own Homes, for fear that during their absence, their Wives should dishonour them in making them bear the Arms and Crown of the Cornutors:[1] And why should our Freedom be less than that of the Men, in what concerns the violation of the Conjugal Oath? Perhaps I shall be answered as to that point, that this is the cause that Families are bastardized; but where can one find a Medium in this Affair, and if all those who fall into such extravagancies, govern themselves after the same manner that I did, let 'em take my word it would be a great Prodigy if ever they come to Bastardize a Family for the *Field produces abundance of Herbs, but the High-way has not this advantage;*[2] from whence comes then this disorder, unless it be that Men have established Laws; and when once the Women shall have in their hands the Helm of the Government, things will have another Byass? But not to Moralize too long upon this Point, and not to suffer my self to be transported in this manner by the fervency of my Zeal, I may once more return into the way I ought to keep, and pass over such things as are the least necessary to my Subject; for will it not be better in imitation of the Shoe-maker, I hold exactly to the form of the Last, since besides, my Wit is not

---

1 Those who cornute, cuckold-makers.
2 A variant of the proverb, "grass grows not upon the Highway," an observation concerning the supposed barrenness of whores.

strong enough to make such like Sallys, and that tho' they should be done pat and to the purpose, I shall only lose my time in employing my Leisure therein?

Wherefore to return to my Subject, I will tell the *Reader*, that three days after that my Husband was departed, that fore-mentioned Widdow came to my House, and besought me, since too I had no Body to be afraid of, that I would come and spend one Night in her House, protesting to me, that I should have to do with a Man, that she would be Surety that I should be well paid by. I ask't her what sort of Man it was, and if I had never had his Company before. Thereupon she answered me in the Negative, and that he was of an Humour not to be known by any Body. I remained a long time wavering if I should conclude or no this Bargain: For to pass a whole Night out of my House, methought too difficult a matter to effect, without my Servants having some knowledge thereof or some ill suspicion; and as for worldly benefits I would not have hazarded my self so far; for these Creatures are often filled with Malice, and when they have once discovered that you have committed any such fault, you are always afterwards under their Protection, without it's being possible for you to shake off this Yoke in any manner, and there is danger that their blabbing and long Tongues may make you lose your honour, or at least your good reputation. Now as for your honour it is to be supposed absolutely lost, when those Queans of Maids have once began to observe your Actions and Criticise your Conduct.

Nevertheless, as the Power of Money has ever had an absolute Dominion over my Mind, and as I was in hopes to behave my self so well in my Affairs, that no Body should know any thing thereof, I promised to come to her accordingly, upon Condition that it should be after eleven of the Clock, and that I should stay no longer than five of the Clock in the Morning; for it was in *Autumn*, which is a Season dark enough to come back to one's House without being taken notice of by the Neighbours. I protest to you, Dearest Madam (said the Widdow, as soon as I had given her my Word) that I shall be obliged to you all the rest of my Life: For that Gentleman told me this morning, that he has been so transported with Love for you these two or three days last past that he has seen you, that he promised me three Guineys, in case that by my means he could bring about his Design: From whence you may conjecture, added she, how great the Recompence will be that you are to expect. These Reasons were the Cause that I made my self very fine, and I intended to make him pay dear enough for my Commodity. But Affairs have not always that

Success that People do imagine to themselves; and we often find our selves very villainously mistaken when that we have not any Suspicion of Deceit and Treachery.

As soon as it was Ten a Clock our Shop was shut up, as was customary, and our Maids were gone to Bed before Eleven, at which time I was to be at the Rendezvouz appointed; so that I had no reason to fear, because they lay in a Room so far towards the Backside of our House, that tho' they had been awake, it would have been impossible they should have heard me open and shut the Door, tho' I had done it less gently. Whereupon I set out, after having decked my selfe to some purpose; and having taken a Coach at some distance from our House, I came to the Widows about half an hour after Eleven: I ask'd her immediately if the Gentleman was yet come? She made me Answer, that he had waited for me above an hour and an half; but that he would not that any one should see him, and that he had given her in Charge, that she should only put me to Bed, and that he would come to me in the dark. I was not over-well pleased with this new Freak[1] of his; and from the Beginning I seemed to have some Repugnance thereto: But forasmuch as that I did not much care so I got but Money, whether it was with handsom or ugly Men: And besides, as I knew, that there are several who have this Maggot in their Heads[2] of not being willing to be seen, imagining they shall not be known again, I was prevailed with at length, and was put to Bed in a Chamber where I had done that Feat several other times, according as Occasions were offered; and there I waited for my Spark whom I intended to fleece to some purpose.

Presently after, the same Widow conducted this Cavalier to my Bed side, by favour of the Darkness; and he having immediately embraced and kissed me several times, put off his Cloaths and lay softly down by my Side, without uttering one word, but by way of Whispers, and through his Teeth, insomuch that I could never judge by that kind of murmur of his voice if I had had any Acquaintance with him before. Thus after we had pass'd our time in wantoning and toying, till half an hour after Twelve, he pretended that he would go Sleep; but I could easily hear that he cast out some Sighs by Intervals, which proceeded from the Bottom of his Heart. I was so much amazed at this, that I took the Resolution of going to seek for Light, as soon as I could perceive he

---

1 A capricious notion, humour, or whimsy.
2 A whimsical, eccentric, strange, and perverse notion (archaic).

was fast asleep, to see if I knew this languishing Lover. A little after I thought that Heaven or Hell (it was certainly one of the two) would favour my Undertaking; whereof there was no other cause, as I imagine, than his Weariness which proceeded from his voluptuous Combat: For we had been very brisk, and heated our selves to some purpose in our amorous Conflict. Whereupon I got up softly from him, and having put on my Petticoat, I went below, where I found the Woman of the House fast asleep, with the Maid, who was one of *Venus's* Nuns. Having taken the Lamp which hung still lighted in the Chimney, I went up above again bare footed, with out making any Noise: For I thought it not convenient to awake them: But who can express the Fright and Consternation I was in, when I found that he with whom I had had so great an Assault was my own Husband, who without doubt came thither to convict me of my whoring, after having for a long while had Suspition thereof. I swear to you, that I was so terrified, that the Lamp had like to have fallen out of my Hand. Nevertheless, as I have always been endowed with a wonderful presence of Wit, I somewhat recollected my Sences, and considering the greatness of the Danger I should be in if he saw me there, I took all my Cloaths under my Arms, and went immediately down Stairs, and flung my self straight into the Widows Bed, who I had all the reason imaginable to suspect had played me this Pranck. The Truth is, that I told her, as soon as I had awaked her, that I could not have believed that she would have committed so cursed an Infidelity towards me as to —— How, said the poor Woman, interrupting my Discourse, have I done any thing to you that is contrary to the Duty of Civility, Honesty and Friendship. As we had not time to use many words, I ask'd her immediately who had brought that Gentleman to her House? And having conjectured by her Answer, that she was innocent in this Encounter, as this might easily be true: For before that time she had never seen my Husband, nor set Foot in our House, but only when she brought me this Message. I related to her how all went, begging her Advice at the same time, what was the best Course for me to take in this Occasion. The poor Woman was so troubled and concerned that she could hardly utter one word. I lay apart the Counsel she would have given me. In the mean while, there came a thing into my Fancy, which I thought the most suitable in the world to free me out of that Disquiet. I gave this woman the three Guinneys my Husband had promised her, and engaged to give her as many more in case she would be faithful to me, and declare she had never any Acquaintance with me; then I gave the

Damosel who dwelt in the House a Guinney, upon condition she would go lie in my place; and that when my *Husband* should come to wake, she should by one means or other give him to understand, that during all the Night long he had lain with no other Person than her self. This Damosel, who perhaps had not got so much money in a Fortnight, was easily prevailed upon by such Pathetick Arguments, and the Landlady led her to the Bed in the Dark. This was done with so much Cunning that my Husband had not the least Inckling thereof. When I had disposed all things in due manner, I went out of the House about Three of the Clock in the Night, told the Watch I met with, that I had been at a Womans Labour, without making known to the Widow, that I had a Design to return thither once again, as I thought I was obliged to do for the better securing my Honour. I only told her, that she should dissemble her ever having seen me, not only to my Husband, but also to all others who had been in my Company.

But when I had pass'd through two Streets by the Watch in this manner in the Dark, I ask'd one of the Watch if he would guard me home to my House; which I did for a reason I am going to inform my Reader of immediately. This Fellow took immediately his Lanthorn,[1] and without making any further Enquiry while we were going along, and were both talking of several Adventures, I ask'd him if he would do me a piece of Service, assuring him, that I would honestly reward him. I added, that he would have nothing more to do, than to come about Five a Clock to the House I would show him, and tell the person who should open him the Door, that he must of necessity speak to me in private. He promised me he would not fail upon Condition I would pay him well for his Pains.

Then I opened the Door as gently as was possible for me to do; where after having in great haste put all things into good Order, I went to Bed with neither more nor less Concern than if I had lain there all the Night long. No sooner had it struck Five, than that the aforesaid Watchman came knocking to some purpose at our Door, without the poor man's knowing of any other Message he had to do there; for I made no other Declaration to him of the Business; but that he was to speak to me in private, and that he was to do it without any Body's being by. I had a Bell hanging by my Bed-side, which I rang so long, until

---

1 Variant spelling of "lantern."

that one of the Maids got up, and asked me what I wanted? I told her, that I heard a strange knocking at the Door, and that she was to go, and see who it was that made such a Noise. *Betty*, so was the Maid called, came back presently to my Chamber, and told me, that there was one of the Watch at the Door, who said, that he had something of Moment to acquaint me with; but that as it was still very dark she durst not open the Door. What a Fool you are, said I to her, what hurt is there to fear from Persons who are set on purpose to hinder others from committing any mischief. Open the Door, added I, you frightful Fool you, and let us hear what this man has to say. Whereupon the Watchman was let into the House, and then into my Room, where, according to the Order he had, he would not utter a word until I had put the Maid out. When I thought he had been there long enough to have told a Message of some Business of Importance, I gave him some Money to drink; and all undrest as I was in my Night-Gown, I led him out of the Door. Ah Heavens! cried I, as soon as ever he was gone, wringing my hands, and letting abundance of Tears trickle down my Cheeks, Is it possible, is it possible, said I again, that such Actions should remain unpunished! It is a Prodigy, added I, that the Earth does not open to swallow up all alive those who commit such Abominations: And thereupon pouring forth again a Torrent of Tears, I made my Looks seem such that it might have been, painted for the Face of Sadness it self. In the mean while *Betty* considered me as a distracted Person, not knowing what to think of so suddain an Affliction. The Noise I made obliged the other Maid to come running to me, and seeing her Mistress in so lamentable a pickle she began at first to ask what the matter was; what it was that rendred me so sad and so void of Comfort: But I let her ask the same thing ten times over, before I made her any Answer: Howling in the meanwhile after such a Rate, as if I had been in the greatest Affliction imaginable. My dear Girles, said I to them at length, do not wonder to see me grieve at this rate: I have word just now brought me, that my *Husband*, whom we thought gone to *Northampton*, is in Bed with a Strumpet; and in the mean while he daily blames and scolds at me, that we gain nothing by our Trade. Ah! Madam, said *Betty*, you must not lay all things thus to heart: Perhaps that some of your Enemies have set on foot this Rumor only to grieve and vex you: I would not believe it, continued she, unless I had seen it with mine own Eyes: There is probability enough of it's being so, replied I, for I am told the very place, insomuch that we cannot be mistaken: Let us but go thither immediately; for it is impossible for me to live any longer in the Uncertainty of this Business: Thereupon I bid *Betty* dress her, as I did my self, and thus at Break of Day we went together to *Drury Lane*.

As soon as the Landlady had opened the Door, I gave her a wink, which served for a Signal, that she should not contradict her self; and at the same time turning towards my Maid, I ask'd her if we had hit the right place, and if there was any need of enquiring any farther? The Landlady looked fixedly upon me, just like a Ninny-hammer,[1] not knowing what to think of my Proceedings. In the mean time up Stairs we went, where my brave Spark was asleep with a Damosel lying by his Side. What do you think, *Betty*, said I to my Maid, and am I now in the wrong? And could you ever have believed that this Rogue should so violate the Oath of Fidelity; and dost thou not see that by his disorderly Life I shall at length be reduced to Poverty and Begging? Ah, pursued I, how wretched are women when they have such *Husbands*! Ah, how great is their Folly, and their Error, when they believe the Protestations of these deceitful men, who exalt above the Clouds that pretended Affection wherewith they flatter the poor Sex! These words were still accompanied with many other Lamentations, and made such a noise that they awaked my *Husband*; who with his Eyes half open, and seeing me as one drest, and by his Bed Side with my Maid; and seeing also another Woman lying by him, was in such a Maze, that he could hardly utter a word. He look'd upon her incessantly, and lifted up his Eyes towards Heaven, as it were to have Compassion of his miserable Condition. Well Spark, well Gallant, said I to him, seizing him by the Sleeve, there needed not much time to finish your Journey, since the places are no farther distant than our House. But, added I, we shall take care henceforward, with the good Pleasure of God, I shall prevent this Damosels possessing my place, though, pursued I, the best course would be that I troubled my self no farther, but absent my self from you. By that means I shall avoid the Danger there is of being infected with some filthy contagious Disease, which such a Life as you lead must infallibly plunge you into sooner or later. In the mean while my Husband leap'd out of Bed, and called the Maid aside, whom he ask'd where I had lain that Night, while I pretended to scold with the Wench and Landlady, who were no less frighted than if the Sky had fallen upon their heads.

---

1 A blockhead, fool, or braggart.

That poor silly Maid, who was not over well acquainted with my Tricks, protested to him upon her Conscience, that I had been all the Night long in Bed at our House, and began to relate to him after what manner we had had Notice of this Affair. He was a long while without uttering so much as a word, holding his Eyes fixed upon the Floor; but at length he lifted them up to look upon me after a terrible manner. I am, said he then, I am deceived on the one side or other; however, I do really fancy, that I heard your Voice more than once this Night; but, added he at length, I ought to have considered on your Bitchery before I married you; But you may well fear the Effects of my just Anger, if ever I catch you in a Fault; and for your parts, said he, turning towards the Landlady and the Whore, who had lain with him, you shall know in a short time, that I have practised[1] the world too well not to be jilted and laugh'd at with Impunity. Thereupon he put on his Sword, and went out of the Bawdy-house, without giving Ear to a word more, which I was not very sorry for, because I was still in the greatest Disquiet imaginable, fearing the Widow or Whore would come to contradict themselves; and for my part, that I might no longer be exposed, I thought convenient to follow my Husband's Example, insomuch that I left those two women in so great an Amazement, that I do not believe, that they ever were in such a Condition.

Being returned home, I found my Husband in the Shop, leaning upon one of his Arms, and full of so many Thoughts, that he took Notice neither of me nor the Maid; but a Volley of injurious Language and Curses which I flung in his Teeth, quickly awaked him out of his Dumps; yet as he had reason enough to take another Course (for as I have already told you, he had heard me rail against him more than once) he held his Peace, and went behind the Counter: But his Looks made me sufficiently observe, that he had not an over firm Belief, that I had passed that Night in our House. I afterwards took incredible Pains to learn who it was that had carried my Husband into that Place; But I could not discover it till a long time after, when that by chance I found a Letter that cleared the Business, and which the Reader shall be acquainted with in the Sequel of this History. After this Adventure we were about three weeks without setting our Horses together:[2] But to confess the Truth, it was not that I was afraid of

---

1 Here, frequented: "The court he practiced, not the courtier's art" (John Dryden, *Absalom and Achitophel* [1681], 825).

2 Without coming to an agreement, uniting, getting on with one another.

any Venereal Infection, My only Disquiet, was, that one Night or other he would play me some Prank, which I should keep the Remembrance of all the rest of my Life. However we terminated at length our Quarrel, and the two Parties were again reconciled to one another: But the first Night of our Re-union was not so well solemnized as my *Husband* had done when we lay together at another Lodging in *Drury Lane*, tho' I infallibly believe there was no other Cause that obliged him to make then so great an Effort, than to hinder me from having any Suspicion, and to reward me afterwards to some Purpose for those willing and vigorous Repartees.[1]

Perhaps that some innocent Creature will imagine, that the Constitution of his Thing,[2] and his way of Performing should have made me sensible with whom I had to do: most of those silly Maidens may be pleased to know, that there are so many of those Instruments which resemble one another in Length and Bigness, that there is no great Reliance to be had thereupon; and that you may not be obliged to believe me alone, enquire of all those brave Women, who abandon themselves sometimes to others than their *Husbands*, they will undoubtedly affirm the same thing, unless they are desirous to disown what they are and what they do. Since that dear Night with which far from gaining me a considerable Sum of Money, as I had been made to hope for, had made me disburse sufficient to have purchased those two above mentioned Women, I durst not set my Foot again into that house; and I had very seldom the opportunity to go into other Places, by reason my *Husband* seldom let me go out without having some body to keep me Company. This way of Living, was very tedious and troublesome to my humor; and yet I was constrained to submit to it if I intended to make my *Husband* believe that I played him no foul play. In the mean while my Lovers were continually poaching[3] about our house, which was the greatest Punishment to me in the World: For besides my knowing how to make my Markets with them,[4] there were some of 'em whose Embraces pleas'd me much more than those of my own *Husband*, who daily

---

1 Slang term for copulation; in its literal sense, ready, witty or smart replies; quick and clever retorts.
2 A person's private parts, usually proceeded by a possessive pronoun (slang).
3 Encroaching or trespassing in order to steal game.
4 To have dealings (occasionally sexual intercourse) with them, to profit from an illicit action with them (figuratively).

became more and more insupportable to me: Yet at length I had an Opportunity to have an amorous Ticket delivered to two of them, from whom in a little time I had gained by my Service a passable Sum of money. Whereupon I wrote to him, that the day following between eleven and twelve, I would meet him at a certain Tavern in *Covent Garden*,[1] which had the Reputation of a Civil House, and was so indeed to Ladies, and a great Nursery of Gallantry.

I had several times been in this Tavern with that Gentleman, to whom I was well assured they would not refuse him any Conveniencies, by reason they could not in any wise tax him of being stingy and avaricious. Besides, the appointment of this Rendezvouz, I set down to him the manner after which he was to comport himself in this Juncture of Affairs, adding to him, that I expected no Answer from him, that so we might not be hinder'd in the Prosecution of the Design I had.

The day after I pretended going to the Market, and my Husband having sent one of the Maids with me, according to his Custom; we walked very modestly along, till we came just before the Tavern, where I was sure my honest Spark had taken all the necessary Orders; as we also found in the twinckling of an Eye: For a Drawer[2] and one of the Maids were before the Door, where they made a Shew of tickling one another; but another Drawer in the Balcony, pretending as if he did it to spoil their Sport, powred upon us a Chamber-Pot full of Water, insomuch that it ran from our Heads to our Toes. I turned my self immediately, and tho' I had given order for this in my Letter, yet I made so horrible a Clamour, that in a Moment there were above Fifty persons before the Door.

In the mean while the Landlady came out to me, and desired me with the most Civil words imaginable, that I would do her the Honour to go into her House, saying, that she was extreamly sorry that the Drawer, by a piece of insolence, which nevertheless he should pay dear for, had brought that Mischance upon my Head. At first I seem'd wholly averse to make use of her offer; but at length my Cloaths were so wet, that I made a Shew of finding my self forced to accept of it. I went into the House, and so into a little Room, where Faggots were immediately lighted. Presently

---

1 Located north of the Strand, Covent Garden became a resort for loose women during the Restoration.
2 One who draws liquor for customers in a tavern.

after I sent my Maid home, tho' she was little drier than my self, that she might go fetch me other Apparel; which she could not do, nor put on fresh Cloaths her self in less than an hours time. The poor Creature trembled with Cold, and would willingly have staid by the Fire a little longer; but I thought not convenient to defer any longer such precious moments.

As soon as this Creature was gone, I was lead[1] into another Chamber, where my Gallant, who had almost split his Sides with laughing (considering the good Success of this Enterprise) waited for me with extream Patience, and without amuzing our selves, and losing of time, in making a great number of impertinent Complements, and ridiculous Chatterings: For not only Hours, but Minutes were precious to us at that time: We got upon our Bed, and did our Business at so swinging a Rate, that that day I was no less sprinkled within than without—

After we had spent above half an hour in taking our Pleasures, I took my leave for to withdraw into my little Room; where having found the Woman of the house, who had all the while stood Sentinel, I sate down with her by the Fire, until that my Maid brought me other Cloaths.

Tho' my Husband in his Youth had much frequented the voluptuous Sinks,[2] yet he knew not at this time, that this Affair had been contrived in this manner, by reason that he had never known this Tavern otherwise than a house where the People would not have in any manner suffered such things to be committed: And he was not the only Person herein deceived, but all those too who ever haunted that House. For all was done then with so much Tranquility, that the least thing could never have been perceived; and before they let you know of that Conveniency, they must have found you persons liberal, and such as might be trusted and confided in: But at present the Vintners of the principal Taverns are not so scrupulous; and tho' they know with what Design a Man and Woman comes to their House, yet they will not refuse them a Room: So that we may with Justice say that most of the Taverns in *London* are at present Bawdy-houses; and that there is no difference between them and Bawdy houses, than that there they ask you no Money for the use of the Bed.

A little after this Adventure, as I was going one morning up into our Garret, I found a Letter upon the Stairs, just by my

---

1 Obsolete spelling of "led."
2 Gathering places of vice and corruption (figuratively).

Husband's Study, which without doubt he had by chance let fall out of his Pocket. Curiosity made me open it without thinking however that I should find therein something of Importance; but I was much surprized, and strangely amazed when I saw that it contained what follows in very good and expressive Characters.

Sir,
I was very much grieved when I saw you married to that Woman who is at present your Wife; but I was much more concerned, when I heard she Jilted you all manner of Ways. If you are willing to be perfectly informed as to this Affair, get by one means or other to a certain Widows House, called Mrs. G— in Drury-Lane, and be assured, that by the help of Money you will come to the Knowledge of more than you desire. I do not tell you how you are to comport your self in such Encounters, since you have had sufficient Experience of 'em, not to want Cunning in those Occasions. Neither did I think it convenient to discourse you by word of mouth, fearing it might put you out of Countenance. Believe only, that as I am your Friend, so I love to keep things secret: Provide against this Disorder the soonest you can possibly.

I remained very much troubled when I had read this Letter, and then was out of the Doubt and Suspence I had so long been in: For I had applyed my Thoughts to a thousand things for the endeavouring to discover what it was that could have brought my Husband to the forementioned place: But at the same time I took also the Resolution of being so reveng'd at one time or other, that this Tale-bearer should remember it for a long time: For it was not necessary to see the Name, since I had received several from the same hand, as well before, as since the day of my Marriage, tho' there had been a falling out between us for some time, because he would have enjoyed my Body without being at any Charges, which is a thing I could very rarely be brought to; and undoubtedly Spite and Vexation had inspired him with this Genteel Pranck.

As soon as I was got down again I flung this Letter into the Fire, not being willing to put it up; and besides, I was afraid if I had kept it, it might have been found about me, which would have been taken for a Sign that I was not at all concern'd at it. In the mean while I lost no occasion of playing my part sometimes, tho' all the manner of Stratagems which I put in Practice had not over often a happy Success: Wherefore I wrote a Letter to that Spark who had so swingingly besprinkled me, and for whom I had without Dissimulation a great deal more Affection than for my own Husband; and I gave him to understand, that he should make use of all manner of means to insinuate himself into the Esteem and Friendship of my Husband; For I was in hopes that by so doing, he would furnish me at least with the Satisfaction of seeing him oftner than I had then the Opportunity: To which I was inclined with so much the more Passion, in that I promised my self to find his Visits infallibly followed by some Presents, which he would be obliged to make me for to purchase the more of my Heart and Affection: For it is a certain thing, that Money is the most Powerful means to make a Conquest over a Womans Heart. This Friendship was no very difficult matter to contract, seeing I had acquired this Lover at the time of our Wedding; and by consequence my *Husband* could not be prepossessed with any ill Opinion of him. And indeed I quickly saw him seated at our Table, and afterwards he frequented our house with so much Familiarity as one of the nearest Relations, to which the Wife he had contributed very much, because that she was not ugly; and that he for his part knew how to comport himself with so moderate a Reservedness, as if he had been of the Number of those who keep the Great *Turk's* Concubines. This Friendship augmented to such a Pitch, that he frequently brought his Wife to our House that he might make my Husband so much the less suspect that he came with any Design upon me.

This Acquaintance of ours had lasted about four Months, and during all that space of time he had hardly had so many Opportunities to testifie to me his Love as there had been Months passed. One certain Afternoon, as we were sitting talking in the Parlour after Dinner, some Merchants having a mind to see some Rolls of Tobacco, sent for my Husband out. Immediately my Lover flew and took me about the Neck, and kissed me with so much Fervency and Eagerness, that his whole Body was seized with a Shivering; and not expecting that my Patron would return so soon, we began a Game which had like to have cost us our Lives: For we had hardly half done the Feat, when my Husband, who was not entirely cured of his Jealousie, came in softly behind us, and found us in the Posture of one upon the other. Cursed Whore, said he, as soon as he was got into the Room, I have now at length caught thee at what I so long watched for: But, added he, you two shall not go glory[1] with your having made this

---

1 Possibly a variant of "go to glory," that is, become exalted, a subject for joy, usually employed in a religious context.

Bargain; and then, thrusting his hand into his Pocket, he would infallibly have effected his Word, if my Servant had not taken me off his Knee, and leap'd upon him. Certainly when I think still of that Combat, tho' at that time I was under the saddest Affliction imaginable, I cannot forbear laughing; for that my Lover not having time sufficient to put himself in Order, his Shirt hung out of his Breeches, and what with that, and other thing of greater Consequence that was to be seen, it was the pleasantest Sight that ever my Eyes saw.

The two combating Parties fell at length so violently to work, and struggled so hard, that at last they fell over one another, which gave me room enough to escape out of the Parlour, wherein I had till then expected every moment to have had my Throat Cut. I ran in all haste to the Room where we lay, where I took in all haste a little Trunck, in which was my Jewels: For not being willing to forget them in such a Necessity, I seized on them with all speed, and decamped from the House, and withdrew to the Room which I had always kept, and sent for the Chyrurgion, that he might let me Blood:[1] For I had been in that Emotion, that I did not doubt but to fall into some great Fit of Sickness by reason thereof: But no sooner were some ounces of Blood taken from me, than that I found my self very much at ease, and within a day or two after I was as brisk as I had been before.

There were several reasons which made me think it convenient after three or four days to abandon that Room, and to take a House where I might be something farther distant from the Eyes of my Husband: For when I thought but of him I trembled for Fear: Whereupon I took a House in *York Buildings*,[2] which tho' it were near the Court, and, therefore as the World goes, now one should think not over-charged with; yet as Persons of Quality and Estate flock about that end of the Town; yet as I had the Art of Jilting to Perfection, I was in hopes my Gains would be pretty considerable in those Quarters.

But the Truth is, when I make Reflection upon the Disquiet which attends those who lead a disorderly Life, I cannot suffi-

---

1 Bleed me. Letting blood was viewed as therapeutic in the seventeenth and eighteenth centuries.
2 Located on one part of the site of York House on the Strand. Built for the Bishops of Norwich in 1273 and owned by the second Duke of Buckingham, York House was demolished in the 1670s and rebuilt by the speculator Nicholas Barbon in the 1680s.

ciently admire[1] that there are Persons who commit such Sins, without being obliged thereto by Necessity: For to see a Woman abandon her self to Pleasure, for the maintaining her self in a handsome Estate and Condition; and who has not nevertheless the Conveniencies, is methinks in some manner worthy of being excused, because that Poverty is a very terrible thing; and besides it is very troublesome, nay, almost insupportable for Persons who have been well bred and born, when they are constrain'd to subject themselves to go to Service; but as for those Women who give themselves to those villanous Abominations, when Misery does not force them so to do, Methinks there is nothing in the World that merits more Blame and Chastisement; and tho' I have liv'd my self after the same manner that I now give the Relation of, yet I can declare to you, that I would not counsel others to follow my Example, if they are willing to have their Minds at Peace and Quiet: For when you are once engaged in Marriage, if you violate the Faith you have promised, I assure you that you lose all the Pleasure, thro' Disquiet, in doing a thing which ought to be done without any Fear. Quite on the contrary we all find real Pleasures in the practise of Vertue, it maintains the Mind in an agreeable Tranquility: It fills the Soul with an Interiour Joy. It — But hold! I shall presently fall into a Province that I am not very well acquainted with: For not to lye, it is not long since I have made Profession of being vertuous; and perhaps I should not yet say a word of the Care and trouble, if I had still that Beauty which I was endued with formerly: But I think it convenient to pawse a while upon this Point, not to give the Reader an Occasion to have too good, or too ill an Opinion of my Life.

But as soon as I was got into Possession of my new Quarters, I bethought my self of going to learn what had been the Issue of the Battel between my Lover and my Husband: Whereupon I went one Morning betimes to a Tavern near my Lover's Habitation, and sent him a Letter by the Drawer, that if he could not come conveniently to me there, he should nevertheless not fail of coming to my Lodging that same day, telling him in the Letter where it was.

The Drawer acquitted himself dexterously of his Message; but some Affairs hindering my Spark at that time, he sent me word, that my Commands should be performed in the other place. Whereupon I returned home, not in the least doubting

---

1 Wonder.

but that my Enterprize would be attended with the effect I expected.

Towards the Evening this honest Gentleman came to my Lodging, and after some amorous Embraces, I asked him how he had disingaged himself from the forementioned Disorder? He made me Answer, that he had got the Victory over his Antagonist. But, pursued he, when your Husband knew that you had made your Escape, and that he had not Strength enough to overcome me, he cried out so long for help, that at length I heard some of his Workmen coming down Stairs, which put me into such a Fright, that away got I out of the House, without so much as thinking of taking my Cloak along with me: For the Servants were already almost at the Bottom: the Maid who was in the Shop, thinking she could stop me; but taking her by the Arm, and flinging her into a Corner, I got into the Street, and taking a Coach, I went to the *Half Moon* Tavern in the *Strand*,[1] whither I sent for some of my Friends, and so past away my time till it was late, when coming home to my House, I found that your Husband had been already there; so that my Wife made me the finest Speech that was ever read in any History. I would willingly have disowned the Matter;[2] but having been forced to leave my Cloak in the Hurry, and that your Husband had brought it to our house with weeping Eyes, my Wife would not have given the least Credit to my Discourse; but this Storme is almost already wholly appeas'd: Nevertheless, have a Care on both Sides, continued he, for my Wife has vowed your Ruine, as well as your Husband.

But as I was so far out of their Reach, these Menaces produced so little Effect in my heart, that I was not in the least paler or redder; and far from having any Fear, I desired my Gallant to continue to me his Visits with all manner of Boldness, for which we had, methoughts both of us sufficient Reasons, since we had both been in the same Peril; and indeed he was not negligent in the Execution of this order: For he came to see me almost every day, and paid me so liberally for the Favours he had obtained from me, that during all the time he frequented me, I had not any reason to complain of his Generosity.

As I had already dwelt some time in that place, I began to think on him who had sent that cursed Letter to my Husband. I was considering how I could reward him for his Pains, and I

---

1 A common tavern sign in late seventeenth-century London.
2 Refused to acknowledge it as one's own.

fancied I had at length found the Opportunity, he being married, as were most of my Lovers: I was not long contriving the means to effect this, before that I had managed my Design with so much Cunning, that he came at length to my House: For tho' he had played me that Prank, it was not for want of Love; but only by reason I would not comply with his covetous Humor.

I quickly began to make him believe by all the means imaginable, that I was so far transported with Love for him, that I could hardly live in his Absence; and because it is not handsome to exact money from Men for whom one has so strange an Inclination, I never spoke to him thereof, which was so pleasing to him, that I had him at least three times a Week at my House, insomuch, that he made his Wife several times believe that he was obliged to go out of Town, that so he might come and spend those Nights in my Company: To which I consented as willingly, as if I had had for him the most violent Passion in the World.

This familiar Frequentation had hardly lasted three months, when I perceived by all his Ways and Carriage that he began to be weary of me; which I might easily have prevented, if I had but some times denied him, and shewn some Repugnance to the Business: For it is certain, when we grant all things to men, without making any Resistance, their Inclination will never be of long Continuance. On the contrary, a Refusal done with Cunning and Artifice re-inflames their amorous Passions, and makes 'em lavish all, so as they may but compass their Designs: For a Victory which is obtained without any Fatigue, is not the most pleasant and agreeable; and tho' they often do well enough see, especially if they be sharpers[1] and Cunning Gallants, that these Denyals are only counterfeited, yet they will be a thousand times more desirous of the Embraces of those Women, who knew how to behave themselves with Art in that respect, than they are towards those who like Hackneys,[2] are always ready to let men mount upon them; but my Intention was not always to keep this Spark; and therefore I lived with him after a quite different manner, than I did with those whom I only loved for Profit's sake.

At first I complained very much of his Indifferency towards me; and reproached him, that he must of all necessity have to do with some other to whom he payed his Vows and Incense; and

---

1 Cheats, swindlers, rogues; those who live by their wits and by taking advantage of the simplicity of others.
2 Wordplay on horses for hire, whores.

tho' the Oaths he made gave me sufficiently to understand, that what I said was not true, I could sufficiently comprehend, that he would not be over scrupulous at making his Addresses to another. As soon as I had made this Remarque, I thought it was time to put my Design in Execution: For that Purpose I kept at my house for two days together a very pretty Nymph, upon Condition she would be faithful to me in all things: Whereupon I promised her a handsome Reward besides what she could obtain from him: When then that Alderman B— (so was the Name and Title of him for whom all these Preparations were made) came again to my house: He asked me, strangely smitten, who that pretty Creature was; and if that Damosel was to dwell with me? I told him yes, and that it was one of my Neeces, whom I had taken to keep me Company. To make short, I pretended to have some Business to do abroad; and so pack'd out of the Room, that he might have an opportunity to discourse her, and he was so inflam'd in that Conversation, that when I came back above three hours after, I found him still in her Company. At Night she told me that he had courted her for you know what, but that according to my Order, she had showed her self somewhat disdainful, yet without making him lose all hopes.

The Alderman was much more passionate for this Wench than for me, insomuch that within the space of a Week, he came six times to my Lodging; and during that time he had contracted such a Familiarity with this *Daughter* of *Venus*, according to the opportunities that I had given them, that methought the time was come to accomplish what I had projected to do: whereupon I one day told him, that three days afterwards I was to be at *Windsor*,[1] and that I should stay there a day or two. But that there might be the more probability in the Design of this Journey, I told him a Story which would really have required my Presence of an absolute Necessity. In the mean while I pretended to have some other Affairs in the Chamber where I lay, insomuch that the two Parties had the Leisure to conclude their Bargain, as I had ordered the matter, for the passing those two Nights together that I was to be absent. He protested, that she should meet with such an Acknowledgment as should be much more considerable than she imagined; and that his words might find the better Credit, he had already let a Guiney slip down her Breast, because the poor Innocent did really believe she was a Virgin, or at least that she

---

1   A town in Berkshire on the south bank of the Thames.

had been but very little used, tho' she had maintained her self for four years only by the labour of that Calling; and if we may believe the Testimonies of some brave Persons, she understood her self better in those Affairs than can be expected from a Maiden as was but newly come out of her Parents Kitchin.

When that the day appointed was come, I told my pretended Neece, that she should neither lock nor bolt the Door: For that I hoped to return home at twelve a Clock at Night, and that then I would teach her a way how to appropriate to our selves the Alderman's golden Purse. Thereupon I departed; but not for *Windsor*: But went directly to an Officer in the Spiritual Court, and told him, that if he would give me a fourth part, as I was informed the Custom was, I would deliver to him that Night a married Man, and a considerable Citizen, from whom there would be a swinging Sum of Money to be got. This Officer was presently ready, and having given me his hand, he promised me that I should have the half exactly. After which I told him who the Person was upon whom we were to execute our Designs, as also his whole Estate, the Trade he drove, and all that was necessary, that so when he came to make the Agreement, he might not be too hasty to conclude the Bargain. Moreover, I told him, that about Midnight I would return to his house, to go afterwards both together to mine, and surprize the Bird there in his Nest.

It had hardly struck twelve when I got again to his House which this Officer, who was a great Lover of Money, was no sooner informed of than that we began to set forwards on our way, and came at about half an hour past Twelve at my House; where in we went so gently, that it was impossible for us to be heard: Then I lighted a Candle, and went up Stairs with the Officer, while that one of his Serjeants staid in the Kitchin, and the other at the Door. We found our Lovers lying folded in one anothers Arms, and reposing so peaceably, that it seem'd almost Pity to interrupt their Sleep. But as I have never been subject to a silly Compassion for men, I advanced towards the Bed-side; and having pull'd him by the Arm so long as that he awaked. Mr. Alderman, said I to him, if I had known you would have kept my house so well, I should not have returned so soon. The Alderman rubbed his Eyes to dissipate the Sleep, and seem'd very much amazed to hear my Voice; but he was much more surprized when the Officer told him, that he should be his Prisoner for that time, if he pleased, since that having a Wife in Marriage, he proceeded to have to do with another Woman. *Jane*, who in the mean while awaked upon this Noise, trembled for Amazement when she saw this Officer before her: For she knew not that I had done this Business with a set Design; and I had not declared it to her, for that I was not well enough assured, that she would be contented to go through with it; and besides that, tho' she had consented to it, she might have suffered her self to be corrupted, and have discovered all to her Lover for a reasonable Sum of Money: For there is no great Stress to be laid upon the Words and Oaths of Wenches or Wives, who get their Living by their Bums. The Alderman not being ignorant that such Affairs may be terminated by a Sum of Money, leap'd out of Bed as soon as he was somewhat recollected from his first Amazement, and desired the Officer that he would allow him to speak a word in private with him: Whereupon I went below Stairs with *Jane*, and within a quarter of an hour, after there had been some Contest between them, I was called above with a Pen and Ink; and I saw the poor Devil, who signed a Bond of an hundred Pound, which he was to pay in a Fortnights time. Thereupon the Officer was thinking of being gone, when that the Alderman, whose Fury sparkled in his Eyes, would infallibly have broke my Neck; wherefore I desired this honest Gentleman to take the Alderman along with him; and this last was forced to go along, tho' he would willingly have done somewhat else. When they were out of the Door, I put a Letter into this unhappy Lover's Hands, wherein I related to him amply with the most bitter words imaginable, for what reason I had served him this Trick. I would couch that Letter here; but that I am afraid by reason of its Length, it would not give overmuch Satisfaction to those should read it. I shall desist there from, and fill the Sheets I have still left with some matter of more importance.

Tho' poor *Jenny* had practiced this Trade, as long as is before mentioned, she was so concerned at the Officers unforeseen Presence, and so much the more, as that she had been found in Bed with a man, which is commonly rewarded with a *Bridewell*, the Purgatory of Whores,[1] that the day following she was taken with a violent Fever, which moved me so to Compassion, by reason I could not deny but that I was the Cause thereof, that fifteen days after, having received my Part or Portion of the Booty, I gave her the half thereof, which was so powerful a Cordial and Remedy to that fair Damosel in her

---

1 Located on the west side of Fleet Ditch abutting the Thames, Bridewell was the site of a prison for women until the middle of the nineteenth century.

Sickness, that in a short time she recovered her former Health and Beauty.

Tho' this Action of Revenge had been very much to my Advantage, yet afterwards I would have given more than I got by it, that I had managed the Affairs in such a manner, as that he might have been seized on in another House: For this Officer, who could gladly have wish'd, that I would from time to time have put a Gallant of this kind into his hand began to be very troublesome to me, insomuch that he threatned me, that in case I did not do him other Services, he would make the Town too little for me. Wherefore for this Reason, and two others more, for I had heard my Husband was informed of the place of my Abode; and that he only sought for an Occasion to have me catch'd by one or other. In the third place I was very much afraid the Alderman would set one or other to spie me by Night: Whereupon I found my self obliged to decamp from the City, and to seek for my Abode out of its Jurisdiction: And in a few Days after I took a House near *Fulham*,[1] hard by the High Way that goes to *Windsor*; and went to dwell there with a Maid, making *Jane* believe that I was going for *Norfolk*:[2] For as she was young and beautiful, her Presence would have caused too much Prejudice to my Commerce; and moreover I had also taken notice, that there were two more of my *Gallants* whom she had supplanted me of. The Desire of Revenge must without doubt have darkened my Eyes at that time: For I believe there is nothing more miserable to see, than an Officer of Justice before our Eyes, upon whose Account we are oblig'd to trouble and disturb honest People, when at the same time we would willingly keep our Friends; and indeed I ought to have had then the same thoughts; but as no body is always wise and prudent, I imagined that the Business would be done, but found quite the contrary: For those Gentlemen resemble Horse-Leeches, and never leave sucking their Prey, as long as they find the least Humidity.

But when I was entred with my Maid into my new Quarters, and had set all things in due Order, which kept me several days employed: For as I was a Damosel of such a Quality, I became something coy and haughty. I compleated my Affairs so well, that I got to speak with three or four of my best Gallants, to whom I

---

1 A village in Middlesex about six miles west of St. Paul's on the north bank of the Thames, opposite to Putney.
2 A county on the east coast of England.

made known in what place I had set up my Standing: these did not in the least fail to be there upon occasion, which they might do without any Apprehension: For indeed they had no reason to fear the Neighbours should spie them: For I was in somewhat a solitary place, and for many days together I saw no body but my Maid and my Dog, which did not ill resemble that *Cerberus*[1] the Poets so much talk of; the only difference was, that my Dog had not three Heads like him.

Amongst these Blades there was one who, after I had dwelt there for some time, brought with him a certain Spark of about thirty seven, or thirty eight years old, that he might be made Partaker of my Favors. At the first I pretended to be somewhat shy and scrupulous, neither more nor less than if I was not over desirous that others should come to see me; whereas, on the contrary, I could very well allow of all those who made no difficulty to spend their Money: I grumbled at him who had brought this Stranger to my House; but as this pettish Humor was only a Fiction, it did not last long; and within a few days this new comer was as welcome to me as the rest: For the kindness he obtained from me was pretty dearly paid for: But after some weeks were past over, I perceived I had made a wrong Judgment, when I imagin'd, that in regard of Liberality, he was a man that did not yield in the least to his Companions: For when he fancied, by reason I caressed him so extreamly, that I was as much smitten with him as he was with me: He began to flatter himself that he was no longer bound to give me Money, and would willingly have obliged me to have discarded all the rest, that he alone might have had the Enjoyment of my Person. I was extreamly displeased at this Carriage of his, yet let him not know it by the least word; but I took a firm Resolution, that upon the first opportunity I would play him a Pranck, which should be sufficient to furnish my Maintenance for the space of a Month.

Do but, I beseech you, take notice of the ingratitude that all these Men are guilty of: This fine Gallant had obtained of another the Favour of being brought to my House; and as soon as his Crotchets[2] had made him fancy, that he was pretty deeply rooted in my Heart, he would willingly have recompensed him to whom he had this Obligation, by having him banished from a house that

---

1 In Greek and Roman mythology, the proper name of the three-headed watchdog who guarded the infernal regions.
2 Whimsical fancies, perverse conceits.

he had frequented for so long a time. When I consider well on all these things, I find my self wholly amazed at the Disorder wherein Men have been for so many Ages, when they have described the Vices under the Figure of Women,[1] seeing the Men are therewith every where infected, I will say no more; but at least as much as we, poor innocent Creatures as we are: For who would not be of my Opinion, that we ought to represent Pride as a young wanton Youth, since we see a number of those Sparks swarm at present about *London*, whose Bodies are strait laced, that they may acquire a long and handsome Shape. And they not only amuse themselves in such villainous Trifles; but I know some also, who like women, make use of *Spanish* Paper to give a red Colour to their Cheeks: And thus beribbon'd, painted and curl'd, do these 'Squires strut it about the Streets.

I had a Design for at least three Months together to make a Cully of *Florian* (for so was the name of this Gallant; or at least so shall he here be called), before that I could ever find the Opportunity for so doing; and perhaps I might still have waited a pretty while if he had not given it me himself; and behold after what manner: Coming one morning to my House very early, he related to me, that he had some Affairs which obliged him to be at *Kingstone*[2] for a day or two, having some Merchandise to dispose of there. He desired me at the same time I would keep him Company in Quality of his Wife, without one moments Delay. I chuck'd him under the Chin, and embrac'd this poor man after a very amorous manner. You know very well my dear Angel, said I to him, that I can refuse you nothing, so strong is the Love I bear you: These words were followed with some Kisses, which insinuated me so far into his good Opinion, that he did not in any wise doubt but that I was mortally smitten with Love for him.

When we had attained to the day appointed for our Journey, *Florian* came with a Hackney Coach to my Door, from whence we departed for *Putney*,[3] and so to *Kingstone*, where we took up our Inn near the Market Place: After we had refreshed our selves with a Bit and a Glass, the Landlady asked if she should make

1 The generic term "Vice" was frequently personified as a Woman: "I hate when Vice can bolt her Arguments" (John Milton, *Comus* [1637], 760).
2 Kingstone or Kingston Bottom was a small village on the old London to Portsmouth road.
3 A village in Surrey on the south bank of the Thames opposite to Fulham.

ready one or two Beds for us? We are very well contented with one when we are at *London*, Landlady, answered my Servant; and by consequence there needs no more here. Thus the poor Woman, thinking we were married together, garnished but one Bed, which we made so hard that night with our petulant[1] Members, that it less resembled a Feather-Bed than a Seaman's Quilt. The Day after *Florian* went out to dispatch his Business, and received about fifty or threescore Pounds. While we were upon the way, he had informed me of all his Affairs as amply as was requisite for the bringing about my Enterprize. Thus he came about Noon to our Inn, and having given his money to the Landlord to keep, we went to Dinner, and spent the rest of the day in seeing the Town; But my good or malicious Reader, for I know not which I have to doe with, not to importune you any longer with a great number of Circumstances, know that after my Lover was gone out the next morning, I sent for a Silk-Mercer[2] that was there in Town, and having bought of his goods, as much as came to ten pounds, I desired the Landlord to give me my Husband's bag of money; he imagining that it was the same thing whether he gave it to me or to *Florion*, made not the least difficulty in the business. Whereupon I made use of the money to pay that Mercer, and delivered the rest to the Landlord to lock up again, for my Intention was not to deprive him of all the sum, tho' I might have done it very easily if I had not been afraid of some ill consequence; but I only designed to be paid for the use of my Body, and as he had not had the Civility to do it, I thought I should have been a very great fool if I had not made use of the power I had in hand. Poor *Florion* was no sooner returned to the Inn than that he asked me with a meen full of astonishment to whom that Silk belonged, or I was so busie with it that he could easily perceive I had some concern therein. It belongs to us, my dear heart, answered I him in the presence of the Inkeeper and his Wife; you know you promised me a new Gown a long while ago: *Florion* became as pale as Death, and having asked me with what I had payed for it, I told him the truth, insomuch that he could hardly forbear unravelling the whole Mystery, so vexed was he at this loss which he had not in the least expected. He called me aside, told me that it was not handsomely done to make use

---

1 Impudent, insolent, rude (obsolete).
2 A shopkeeper who dealt in textiles and fabrics, especially silks, velvets, and other fine materials.

of his money as if it had been my own without first knowing if it was his will and pleasure so to have it, and I ought first to have inquired if he should not have stood in need of it himself at *Kingstone*. How, Sir, said I to him, as soon as he had done speaking you shall not need to be much concerned for your money, since as soon as we are got back to *London*, I will repay it you every farthing. And that you may not think that these are only vain words I will give you a Bond immediately for the performance of what I say. I should never as long as I live have any good luck in a Gown, said I still, that was given me so unwillingly.

Thereupon I called for a Pen and Ink. But *Florion* in his turn would needs act the Generous Man, because he fancyed that I had taken his procedure[1] in very ill part, and was by consequence afraid he should be put out of my favour. Whereupon he seized me by the Arm, saying, that for the money that was no great matter, but that he had thought to have had made use of it himself, and that it had fallen out very unluckily, that I had taken so great a quantity of it, but nevertheless he knew how to provide against that Inconveniency; thus perceiving that this piece of cunning had succeeded well with me, I put my self into a much more haughty posture, and would needs by all means give him a Bond, tho' I had not the least thought of restoring to him one farthing of his money, but it became me to carry high as if it was to show that I had an honorable Education, and that I stood in no need of money, insomuch that *Florion* seeing me, so out of humour, made use of all manner of flatteries to regain my Affection; imagining without doubt that for this money he should take his pleasures with me for a pretty while; but the poor man did not think that I made quite an other account; for it came into my Head that we were then but two at play, and that if he meant to receive new favours, it was easie for him to judge that it was necessary for him to show new money, which presently after I gave him so well to understand by new tricks and Artifices, that at length my Amorous Caresses seem'd too dear to him; Insomuch that he began to wean himself from me by little and little, for then he could easily see that it was not his Person but his money that I loved, and that I had only let him be free-cost[2] sometimes that I might make him pay the dearer for my Merchandise.

---

1 Act of proceeding or going on to something (obsolete).
2 Cost-free, gratis (obsolete).

Without lying I cannot forbear laughing when I think on those poor innocent Cullies, who seeing themselves flattered and caressed by such a Nymph as I was at that time, imagine, when we do not speak to them of money every Bout, that they are the only Men who enjoy our Favour and Affection: Whereas on the contrary it is certain they may haunt Misses at a much cheaper Rate, when they know how they must pay every time, than those who have the Fancy, that they are the well-beloved, by reason they never hear 'em speak of reward or recompence: For these Misses always stand in need of something; and if one would have the enjoyment of their Bodies, you cannot be so uncivil, unless you have a mind to lose that counterfeited kindness, to refuse them the Favours they demand; so much the more, as that these demands are accompanied with so many Kisses and Caresses, that it is hardly possible to refuse them; and those things are commonly so dearly sold, that the same Price would often buy Diamonds and Jewels; Here perhaps might an Objection be started, that these Misses are as sensible to love as others; and that by Consequence I do not establish my Opinion strong enough, and perhaps some examples might be alledged to the Contrary; but these Sparks who are of this sentiment, may be pleased to know, that we seldome see those things done with sincerity, besides as that it is impossible to sound the Heart of a Woman so as to lay any Foundation thereupon, and that there are those of that nature that when they seem to bear you the greatest love in the World, they hate you more than the Plague at the bottom of their Hearts, and they only give you Testimonies of their good will to fleece you of your Wool, which you have no sooner lost, than that you will find, that you will be treated after the same rate as a Prodigal Child.[1] However I can easily perswade my self that a Miss who gets her livelyhood with her back Cheeks may grow enamoured, but yet I cannot believe that she will place her Inclination upon one man who is of an Honourable breeding, and of a reasonable Conversation, and especially at this time, when those who seek their maintenance in this commerce are Daughters of Orange Women[2] and the *Billingsgate*-crew, and by consequence of a vile and base Education; these having bought a Gown or a Manteau which they find here and there in the Shops pass

---

1 An allusion to the parable of the Prodigal Son. See Luke 15:11-32.
2 Women, especially young girls, employed in selling oranges. The celebrated actress, Nell Gwyn (1650-87), began her career selling oranges in the theatre.

for Misses, and are imployed in that quality by one or other; but as their sorry Education had used them to all manner of ill carriage and behaviour, and as by getting on a Gown and by sprucing themselves up fine they do not shake off those effects which are rooted in their Hearts, you must never expect that they will come to cast their Eyes upon a man of extraction,[1] but upon some Clown or Bumpkin whose Inside manners suit better with theirs; for it is a truth beyond all contest that the conformity of passions and courses of living do engender the greatest love, whereas I could here urge several examples if I had a mind to't, but since that those Brutal passions do not deserve the Name of love, I shall advance into other matters, and leave every one the freedome to have the opinion and belief he thinks best.

By this way of dealing, I mean by scraping up money from Sparks by all imaginable means, I now and then lost one of those whose Means were not sufficient nor rich enough to resist the insatiable avidity of my love towards money. Perhaps you will here think, my Reader, that I could not lose many Gallants, since I had already said that their number did but consist in three or four; but be pleased to know that this number did so wonderfully encrease in a year or two, that I could well spare some without remaining so destitute of Servants as Misses often do at present. What contributed very much to my happyness was, that then I did not shew my self so coy, so nice and scrupulous, for as I perceived that my Beauty and Youth began to perish by little and little, and that by consequence I foresaw that in the sequel of time I should not be so passionately nor so frequently sought after, I made use of all manner of diligence to provide for my self against Old Age that I might not be obliged to beg Alms.

Amongst those whom my Charms captivated under my Laws, there was an *Italian* of about thirty years of Age, and in whose Person I had had a very good Gallant; for I never asked of him any thing but what he immediately gave me. But if I had known the *Italians* could have practised so great a dissimulation as they are used to do, I should have been much more cautious of him, tho' however I ought not to take the thing so very ill; for as it was my custome to deceive others, and as I should not have taken delight in seeing that men had been wanting to treat me with all manner of respect and civility, methinks it is but just, likewise, that I forget what has been done to me, to which I find my self

---

1 A man of noble or distinguished origin, lineage, or descent.

obliged with so much the more reason, as that I cannot say, that he stole from me more than I had got from him before. Yet it might well be that I should not speak so much of forgetting that pranck, if I had only the opportunity to pay him in the same Coyn, but by reason he returned to his own Country, he deprived me of the means of satisfying my desire of Revenge, otherwise it should have been a wonderful Prodigy if I had been of so sedate a temper to be served such a trick; or I must at least have lost the whole nature of the Female Sex; for this passion, namely the desire of revenge, takes its Birth jointly with the Females, and remains with them until that they have given up the last Gasp. But not to amaze our selves too long, I am going to tell you the whole matter.

He had frequented me for about half a year when that we took a journey together to *Gravesend*[1] whither he said he was to go by reason a Ship was arrived there from *Holland* wherein he expected some Cloaths; on the morrow morning after we had lain together and enjoyed to our full the delights of love, he took my Pendants[2] into his hand, for which my Husband had given forty pounds, and having considered them with great speculation, they are something too plain said he to me with a smiling Countenance, for a fair Creature to whom I bear so much affection, and thereupon calling the Landlord up into our Room, he asked him if he had not any acquaintance with some Jeweller who could fit up a pair of fine Pendants, the man made answer he had, and added that there was a Jeweller who frequented his House from whom he might buy what he desired for as reasonable a price as of any other Merchant about *London*.

Jukomo (so was the *Italians* name) desired him, immediately that he might be sent for, which was accordingly instantly performed; in the mean while I was so overjoyed that my joy was apparent in my Eyes; for I expected no less then the value of sixty or seventy pounds, and I had still more hopes when I heard this deceitful *Italian* tell the Jeweller, that none of the Pendants he had brought along with him pleased him, tho' there were some perhaps worth fourscore pounds. Sir, answered the other, I have of all prizes,[3] and if you please to take the pains to go along with

---

1 A port in Kent on the south bank of the Thames, thirty miles from London.

2 Ornaments of some precious metal or stone attached to a bracelet, necklace, or ear-ring.

3 Obsolete spelling of prices. A word, perhaps pendants, may be omitted before "of all."

me to my House, I do not doubt but that we shall agree upon the matter. I would willingly have gone along with them, but *Jakomo* would not consent to that, which made me fancy that he designed to make me a better Present than I expected. I had had this in my imagination for about half an hour, when that the Jeweller came back to our Inn to ask me for the Pendants which the *Italian* had undoubtedly left me only so long that I might so much the less perceive the design he had. I asked him what he intended to do with them, and if they should have concluded the Bargain. It is only Madam, to see the bigness of them, who took me without doubt for a Woman of great Quality, and as for what concerns the Bargain, persued he, your Husband has offered me money for a pair, but he must still raise the Sum he offers. Yes, said I, but I hope you'l use him kindly. And thereupon I took off my Pendants, and wrapped them in a piece of Paper, and delivered them to him without any ill suspicion, since he came himself in Person to receive them, for to have confided them to any other, I should have made some scruple.

In the mean while, I expected some joyful Tydings, but my Husband came not back to our Lodging. Yet I durst not at first seem to be uneasy, though my heart misgave me strangely; but when it was past twelve, and that I saw no Body yet come back, I desired my Landlord that he would lead me to the Jewellers House; where I was no sooner come, than that he told me they could not agree upon the matter, for that my Husband, said the Jeweller to me, had only offered for a pair of Pendants, sixty pounds, which had cost him above Eighty.

I presently asked him what were become of mine; and having had for answer, that my Husband had taken them along with him, my Heart was as much troubled as if I had been seized with a violent Fever: Yet I durst not let any Sign thereof appear, both for that the Inkeeper was with me, and that we had lain together in his House, as if we had been Man and Wife: So that it would have been very improper to have made a hurry for my Jewels, since that they had been put into my Husband's hands, or at least in his who was taken to be so; and on the other side, I had no reason since I had not forbid the Jeweller to give them to any other than my self. Thus we returned to the Inn, and though I ought to have been well assured, that I should never see the Pendants or the *Italian* again, yet I continued to flatter my self a long time with such hopes, that he was perhaps, gone to some other Jewellers House: But at length seeing he came not home again at Night, I lost all Courage, my Tears gusht out in Torrents accompanied with Sobs, while that my Landlady kept me Company, which she would undoubtedly have spared her self the trouble of, if she had known for what reason I afflicted my self in that manner; but the Poor Woman imagined, that if I so abandoned my self to Sadness, it was for no other reason than for the absence of my Husband, to whom she fancied some Mischance had happened. I stayed some days still at *Gravesend*, as a Person void of Comfort, as you may well think, and I ran through all parts of the Town inquiring after my Husband, in all the Inns and Taverns, where I thought that he might be gone, but the Bird was already flown, so that I was at length constrained to return to my own Home. Being in the Boat, I imagined that I might easily come to the knowledge of the place of his Abode, by the means of the Person who brought him first of all to our House, and so get again what I had lost. I did not delay in the least to make use of this Way; but afterwards I wish'd heartily that this Thought had never come into my head; for as soon as I had found out his Lodging, and had conceived some good hopes, I saw my self forced to renew my affliction, because his Landlord told me, that he had taken his leave of him four or five days before, to go to *Gravesend* and so into *Holland*, where he said, he had some business, and that from thence he intended to return into *Italy*. I plainly conjectured from this Answer, that I was to entertain no more hopes of ever recovering my Pendants again; wherefore from that very Moment I used all my Endeavours to banish them from my Memory, tho' that it was not without a great deal of trouble; but time which makes all things forgotten, brought some Moderation to my Sadness; and perhaps, I should have almost lost all remembrance thereof, if it did not spight me to this very day, that I accompanied him so far.

How great soever my grief and trouble was, I durst not complain to any Body of the loss I had had, fearing I should be laught at, and the remembrance thereof was still very fresh, when I drew into my Snares an Old Seignior, of whom I got in a little time as much as was necessary to repair the dammage I had received, for it is an incontestable truth, that those who have passed the Age of Fifty Years, are much more easy to disburse Money than those who are between twenty and forty, for these imagine, because they rarely want Strength and Vigour, that they are not obliged to give money, or at least that they ought not to give much, whereas on the contrary, the others willingly recompence for their Impotence with Cash, and are ordinarily so careful of their Reputation, that there is no fear of their Visits causing Scandalous Reports;

but because Accidents equally rare, do not happen to all manner of Persons, though I could easily fill this Piece with Adventures and Rencounters,[1] altogether wonderful, if I would in the least pass the bounds of truth, I shall only say this of that good Man, that I prospered very well by his frequenting my Company; and that I hardly ever demanded any thing of him but what he gave me immediately; insomuch, that during ten or eleven Months, that he haunted me, I heaped up as much Money as was necessary to defend me against the Injuries of a sharp and severe Winter.

About two or three Months after the Death of this Honest Gentleman, I was one day sitting upon a little Seat before my Garden, and from thence I heard a most sad and doleful Cry at some distance. I turned immediately my eyes towards the place from whence that voice came, and I saw a Middle-Aged Woman dressed like a Citizen's Wife, who came running towards me with all her Strength, being persued by two Furious Men, who had each of them a naked Sword in his hand. I got up, and entred into the Garden, that I might not receive any offence from those *Furioso's*;[2] but I had hardly set my foot over the Threshold when the Woman, who it seems was lighter of foot than those who persued her, came flying to me, and shutting the Door with a trembling hand, for the *Love of God*, Madam, said she, *save my Life*, for those two Men.—She would still have said more, but her weariness and weakness would not allow of it.

In the mean while, those two Men must either have been gone back, or must have hid themselves somewhere: For as soon as the Woman was got into the Garden I heard no more Noise. I call'd my Maid, and having made her fetch a Bottle of Wine, I gave this damnable Creature to drink, considering her as a good and honest Woman, and so I comforted her heart. Then we went into our House, where I ask'd her for what cause those two Rogues had pursued her with so much Fury? Madam, if I was assured, said she to me, that we could talk here, without any Body hearing us, I should undertake to relate to you a Story which you will be extreamly surprized at; and tho' I have been in such Danger as you know, I would never open my Mouth of it; but by reason of the seasonable help which I have received from you, I will under-

---

1 Encounters or engagements between two opposing forces.
2 Furious persons, probably suggested by the title of Ariosto's *Orlando Furioso* (1516).

take to relate to you a Story which will extreamly surprize you; and tho' I have been in the danger you saw, will never open my Mouth thereof; but upon the account of the seasonable help which I have received from you, the duty of Acknowledgment obliges me not to refuse you any thing: For those Men whose Bloody Hands pursued me, and from whom your Goodness has delivered me, are so nearly related to me, that I cannot make any Complaints against 'em, without drawing upon my self the hatred of all my Race. I told her thereupon, by reason that this Introduction did very much augment my Curiosity, that she might speak with all manner of Safety; that there were but we three in the House; and that my Maid was too wise and secret to go cackle abroad what she ought to keep in Silence. As soon as I had utter'd these Words, she fell to telling a Story, which seem'd as if it would never have been at an end, insomuch that I began to conceive some Suspicion, that this was only the Pretext to some concealed Design. I had so much the more reason to be jealous, that tho' this Story was told after a pertinent manner enough, yet there was such prodigious, and such Romantick Circumstances, that it could not be taken to be made up altogether of pure Truths; and particularly amongst persons who have somewhat more Understanding than what's common in the World. Whereupon I told her, that her entertaining Story had lasted for above three quarters of an hour, and that it was time to make an end, by reason, that it being near Eight a Clock, it would be late before she could get to Town. But, Madam, said she, I hope you will not be so pitiless as to refuse me a Lodging this night; for I am sure, pursued this Bitch, that my Enemies will wait for me hereabouts. You must not take it ill tho' I do, Good Woman, replied I, my Husband is not at home, and for that reason I cannot allow any other person to lie at my House. I added several other reasons more of the like Nature (for I began to dread some ill Event of this Enterprize) so that at length she told me, since that you make so much difficulty in this Matter, I will abridge my Discourse, and shew you a Letter, wherein you may learn all things you stand in need of for the Abridgement of my Business. Thereupon feeling in her Pocket, she took out a Letter which I quickly knew again, and which set me a trembling and shivering after so terrible a manner, as if I had fallen into a Convulsion Fit: For it was the same I had put into the Rope-Dancer's Hands when I sent him to *Thistleworth* in such an Equipage as was described in the First Part of this Book.

While I was reading this Letter, and that I seem'd to dwell

upon it with the highest Attention, I considered so well this counterfeited Woman, that at length, tho' it was a long time since, and
that his Cloaths were very different from those he was used to
wear, I knew again the Countenance of that abominable Thief,
who had caused his Face to be shaved very smooth. Hereupon
some one might tell me that there needed no more than to hear
his Voice to perceive that it was a Cheat; but that of this Rogue
was none of the deepest, insomuch that lisping and affecting a
little of the Tone of the Female Sex, he might pass for a Woman
of a middle Age. After that I had held this Letter for a pretty
while, with trembling hands I delivered it to him without having
almost the Power to utter word but in Stuttering. Well, my dear
Angel, said the Rogue, with a smiling Countenance, have not I
spoke the Truth, and can you not easily perceive by this Letter,
all that my Business requires to have the perfect Understanding
thereof? I made him Answer with a stuttering Tongue, that I knew
not what he meant by that Letter, by reason that it was not at all
conformable to the Story he had related; and that by Consequence he must have taken one Letter for another. However I am
very well assured, replied he after a hasty manner, that you know
well enough the Person to whom that Letter was written; and not
to trouble our Heads with impertinent discourses, added he,
know that I am the Man whom you sent in a Boat to *Thistleworth*;
and that there was no other reason that made me keep this Letter
so long than to convict you of that cursed Pranck by your own
hand writing. Do not believe, pursued he, that I have forgot your
Face: For Spite and Vexation have so deeply imprinted it in my
Heart, that it would be eternally ineffaceable. My Maid, to whom
I had related this Story, look'd upon me fixedly, with Eyes full of
Sadness: For she certainly foresaw that this would not pass thus
without some hurry and mischief: nevertheless I still pretended
to be ignorant of the matter; and told him, that I knew not what
he meant by all his Discourse, and that I could not imagine what
he pretended to do, in shaping himself sometimes in the Posture
of a Woman, and sometimes in that of a Man. I will then make
use of other means, and taking at the same time out of his Pocket
a Knife prodigiously long, Come, you Whore, said he to me,
produce me immediately that Money thou tookest from me at
that time, and my Cloaths also, with the Interest of so many years
that have passed since; or immediately prepare thy self for Death.
I started up as soon as ever I saw the naked Knife, and thought
to have got out at the Garden Door, to have Recourse to crying
and bawling out for Help; but seizing on me, he put the Knife to

my Throat, swearing he would run it in, if I made the least Noise. Thus knew not I what to do in this Extremity: For tho' I did my best to perswade him that he was mistaken, my words found no Credit; and having no Design to rid my self of so much Money, I imagin'd that there was no better means to rid my self of this Misfortune, than to confess the thing, and endeavour to make him believe, that all I had done had only been through my Mothers Counsels, and afterwards to Caress him to such a degree, that his Coller[1] might be at length appeased; but these means were all to no purpose, insomuch that I should then have been obliged to have given him as much and perhaps more Money, if I intended to preserve my life, which however would not have been the less in danger, when that of a sudden I heard a noise that was made by beating uppon a Brass Kettle from the Top of our Garret, and such a terrible crying out of Murder, that all the House rung again. This Rural Alarum[2] was given by my Maid, who, while the Rope-Dancer was holding his Knife at my Throat, had stole up Stairs. God damn you, you execrable Whore you, said this Bloody Villain, as soon as he had heard this Sound and this Voice, thou shalt not come off however so cheaply; and thereupon shutting the Door, that I might not make my Escape, he ran up above; but the Maid had had the Prudence to pull up the Ladder after her, so that he could not do her any Mischief.

In the mean while, having opened one of our Windows, and being got out there I set our Dog at Liberty, flattering my self, that I was then sufficiently secur'd against all Misfortune: For that Animal was prodigiously big and would easily have torn to pieces two or three men; and by Consequence this Devil of a Murderer, if he had not been too cunning for him: for he no sooner perceiv'd that the Dog came in all haste towards him, than that he stretched forth his left Arm, and the dog planted his Teeth therein immediately. Now as my *Cerberus* stood upright, and had his Fore-Feet against his Arm, he cut open all his Belly at one Slash with the Knife he had in the other, insomuch that the poor Creature fell upon the Ground, having still life enough to see his own Entrails drop out; and tho' several People came to my help from the Houses thereabouts, as we could sufficiently perceive by the Noise they made, yet he pursued me so fast, and came so near me, that striking at me, he cut me over the Head, by which I

---

1 Obsolete spelling of "choler"; anger, heat of temper.
2 A variant of "alarm," now confined to poetical usage.

could pass no other Judgment than that he intended to cut my Throat: And to make him believe that he had done my Business already, and to prevent any farther Mischief from his (for I had already perceived that my running away was all to no purpose), I fell topsy turvy upon the Ground, without uttering one word. As soon as he had committed this abominable Action, he let fall his Robes, under which was his Nuns Cloaths; and having got in a Moment to the Pails,[1] which he mounted over, and so skudded away like a Hare, with such Swiftness, that he made a shift to escape before People could come in. By these means he made me lose the Pleasure I should have had in seeing him upon a Gallows. As soon as People saw the Condition I was in, they carried me to *Fulham*, where I had my Wound bound up for the first time.

The day following a Justice of the Peace came to inquire into the business, I gave him a very pertinent account, except that I did not declare to him the cause for which that fatal accident had happened to me. But not to trouble the Reader with circumstances of small importance, I will only say that this fact was taken for a piece of robbery, and by consequence all manner of diligence was used to find out the Authors thereof, but all in vain.

For my part, tho' I was so bravely marked yet I thought my self happy in my misfortune, for if I had kept him a night at my House, he would infallibly have robbed me of all that I had in the night, and perhaps he would have marked me ten times as much, if he had not broke my Neck. It is not to be doubted but that the Devil himself inspired him with this design, and had made him find out the place of my abode, for I cannot imagine how he could have discovered it, for I was very rarely to be seen abroad, by reason I was very much afraid of my Husband and the Alderman, tho' it seemed as if by the length of time those Sparks had forgotten the mischief I had done them; for as for my Husband I had nothing to fear from him, by reason that I would not in any wise own that I had been his Wife; and touching the Alderman, that unlucky adventure had rendred him so Virtuous, that he no longer thought of me nor such like Persons; from whence I draw a sure consequence that he was obliged to me, and that therefore he would have done very ill, had he done me any mischief, because he might look upon me as the occasion of his Virtuous Life. Here it might be objected, that we must never do any mis-

---

1   Containers for food, kitchen vessels (obsolete).

chief that good may come thereof, but my Maximes[1] were wholy different from this, and I was very little concerned whether they were conformable or not with the Prophane or holy Philosophy.

But being half cured of this wound which I should not perhaps have received, if after having let loose the Dog in the Garden, I had immediately made use of my Heeles; but I was willing to have the pleasure of seeing that Battail, wherein I did not doubt but that my *Cerberus* would remain the Conquerour, I went to take my Habitation again in the Town, by reason I was in fear that such like misfortunes might again happen to me; but tho' there Chirurgeons had me in cure, it was not however so well cured but that my Forehead remain'd scarrified[2] and spoiled, because the scarrs continued so visible, that they might have been perceived a Muskets-shot distance, Insomuch that since that time, I have been always obliged to wear Cornets, and my Forehead-wear of very thick Laces, that this imperfection might not be seen through the holes. At first by reason I had a very fine Fore-head, I have shed many a tear upon that account, but afterwards custome became nature, with so much the more reason that I came to consider that there are many others, who for that they have an ill shaped Forehead, are obliged to dress themselves in this manner, for certainly it is not allways to follow the Mode that Women wear Cornets; but it is most commonly to hide the imperfections of the Forehead; neverthless I should yet have been happy if I had been quit for that;[3] but I had not dwelt full a year in the City, then that my Face, my Hands and all my Body became so yellow, by having been too often at the sport, that one would have said I had dwelt five or six years under the Equinoctial Line, so that I was constrained to make use not only of *Spanish* Paper, but also of Paint, unless I intended to lose my Commerce I would make here the description, after what manner it is used, as I have done in the former part touching the Red Colour that is given to the Cheeks; but because there are so many several sorts of paint, and that this artifice is become very common in our time, perhaps the pains I should take would be very little to the purpose; besides, I have another reason for which I am not willing to engage in this matter, which is, that I should stand in need of ten times as much Paper as is fitting for the bulk

---

1 Variant spelling of "maxims."
2 Covered with scratches or scars.
3 Had gotten off with that, had suffered nothing more than that.

of this Book to be, if I would relate here all the practises which the Female Sex makes use of to help nature, and tho' I should say nothing but what is conformable to truth, yet perhaps I should not always be allowed of as an infallible Author; for they practise so many strange things in this matter, that they seem at first absolutely incredible. By example. Who would believe if experience did not banish all Contradiction,[1] that there are young Women who fasten Ropes to the top of their Beds, or some other thing, where lying on their Backs, they thrust their Hands therein? And this is done only that the Blood may retire, and they seem the whiter: And for that purpose they must endure the Pennance of continuing lying in that manner for a whole night together without being able to turn on the one side or other: But I shall add here to something more surprizing, which is, that as there have been some who having Warts, Freckles, or some such other like Deformities in their Faces, have taken off the Skin with biting Waters[2] and such other like means, for the recovering a new Skin which might not be subject to be disfigured like the former. I am willing to believe that there are many Maidens to whom this will seem incredible, and particularly to those who have yet but very little experience, and who have always been kept under the lash of their Parents, yet it is as true as that we may with our Eyes discern the light and darkness: But this point has been sufficiently talked of, and methinks I hear some of those proud Creatures saying, that I ought to be burnt alive, because I so clearly reveal their secrets; but I am so little concerned at all their murmurings, that if I was resolved to spoil more Paper, I would tell a thousand things more which I now pass under silence. There is no other reason which witholds me from so doing, but that I find my self weary of writing of Books. Yet people must not however imagine, that I am too great an Enemy of the Female Sex, on the contrary I know very well that my duty engages me to bear it affection: But at present I hate all manner of dissimulation, and am in love with nothing so much as plain dealing.

Thus when I had dwelt about a year and half in the City, I had the adventure of making acquaintance with a certain Spark who was newly come from the *East-Indies* in the quality of a Merchant, and who, as is the custome of those Gentlemen, had brought along with him so much riches, that he might well

---

1 If experience did not teach otherwise.
2 Stinging, caustic waters (obsolete).

enough spend the rest of his Life without putting himself to the Peril of going [on] such an other Voyage.

As soon as I was informed hereof by him who had had the goodness to bring him to my House, I put all manner of tricks and stratagems in practice to get part of his riches. The truth is, I succeeded reasonably well in this design; but I was forced to do and suffer more for him, than I had ever done for any other; for he had the Imperfection common to all those who come from that Countrey, which is, that he was of a very Brutish humour, and very subject to jealousy, that I could hardly pass an hour in peace with him, tho' for his money I show'd him ten times more kindness than I should have done in my tender Youth.

But it was now quite another thing; for since my age was encreased, and that my Beauty was diminished, I had lost from time to time some or other of my Gallants, Insomuch that I found my self constrained, if I meant to satisfie my insatiable desire of heaping up money, to endure much more than I was used to do before. And indeed I became at length so audacious that he often threatned me to make me feel the heavyness of his Cane, and if I would have played the Beast, his threatnings would undoubtedly have been followed with Execution, as I found afterwards by experience that he was no Man that lyed of his word: Tho' I then gained great profit by my commerce with him, yet I took this in terrible Dudgeon,[1] and moreover took a firm Resolution to hinder his ever coming to those extremities, or at least to do on my side all that was possible for me, to which purpose, in a little time a very fair opportunity was offered.

One evening he came to my House where he found a Gentleman sitting by me, with whom I had had Frequentation[2] a long while before his coming. He told me after a surly manner that he did not intend I should render my self so familiar with others, and that he had connived at it for a considerable time; but that henceforward he would prevent it, since he furnished me with sufficient to live upon. Very well, Cavalier, said I to him, perhaps you fancy you are still in the *Indies*, and that you have one of your slavish Wives. How long is it since you bought me, added I, since you arrogate so much Authority over me? Since I kissed you the first time, reparteed *Maximus* (so was his name) with a dreadful look, and since I have given you your livelyhood. Well you

---

1 Feeling of anger or resentment.
2 Act or habit of frequenting a place or person.

scoundrel, said I to him (for I could no longer dissemble seeing he affronted me so villainously in the presence of an other), I never let my self be kiss'd yet by such Asses as you are, and I hope I shall never have the thought of having acquaintance with such a Beast.

I had hardly uttered these words than that he applyed to me two very fine Boxes of the Ear, which were followed with three or four swinging Strapadoes of the Cane, with a Garnish of about a dozen injurious words. I ran immediately to the Bed, where there was a Chamber-Pot, wherein I had cacked[1] seven or eight times, for I had taken Pills that morning to purge my Body a little; and having run in both my Hands, I cast it upon *Maximus's* Breast with all the Strength and Fury of an enraged Woman, insomuch that the Pieces which were none of the thickest, flew so abundantly about his Ears, that his Eyes were quite blinded; and not being satisfied with this Revenge, I flew at his Hair and Face as if I had been some infernal Fury, while he was endeavouring to clear his Eyes that were all be meared with T—d, and I imprinted my Nails so deeply in him, that *Don Quixot* was never more hideous to see when he had that famous Battel with the Cats in the *Dukes* House.[2] I was also transported with such a Rage (for, as they say, a woman in Anger is worse than the Devil)[3] that I should have render'd him incapable of ever having the use of his Sight, if the honest Gentleman, who, without opening his Mouth, unless it were to laugh, had all this while been Spectator of this Bustle, had not pull'd me from him.

Maximus had no sooner got loose from me, than that he was thinking to get Satisfaction for this Affront: But his Eyes not being well enough open, he ran so blindly against a Chair that stood near the Chimney, that he fell head-long into the Fire, wherein he burnt the Curles I had left him; and if the honest Gentleman, who had already freed him once out of the Peril, had not come again to his Relief, he had had his Face in the most miserable Condition imaginable. Ha, Heavens! said he, as soon as he was got on Foot again, shall it then be said that I must endure so many Mischiefs for a Cursed Whore? And then flouncing again upon me, he intended to have renewed the Battery, but he was repulsed by the other, who, after having twice freed him out of

---

1 Voided excrement.
2 See *Don Quixote*, Part II, Chapter 46.
3 A proverbial expression akin to "Hell hath no Fury like a Woman scorned."

the Danger, that not only he would not give him more Relief, but that he would himself become his Adversary.

Maximus thus perceiving there was no Revenge to be had at that time, went out of the House, his Cloaths all covered with a Sirreverence,[1] and his Head without Hair; but it was not without giving himself a thousand times to the Devil, that he would make me pay dearly for the Pranck I had play'd him.

In the mean while the Devil had an absolute Protection over him: For before ten days were at an end, he sent to beseech me, like a perfect Fool and mad man, that he might have the happiness of Drinking with me for the terminating our Quarrel. It seems he could not live without my Presence; and that Love and Jealousie were the Cause that he was always quarrelling with me.

I told the Person who had received the Commission to come and make me this Compliment, that it was a Proposition that I could not at all comply with, unless I might have absolute Assurance of his good Will: For I had a Fancy that all this was done only to seek an Occasion to do me a Mischief. To make short, we became afterwards good Friends, by the Mediation of this Embassador, and our Intrigue lasted for a Year, during which, *Maximus* was very careful to frequent me: But at the end of that time marrying with a Widow our Familiarity was lost by little and little. I say by little and little: For tho' he was married, he could not so well forget my Caresses, but that he still came to visit me from time to time; but because his Hands did not scatter Money with the same Liberality they did before; and that there were no more *Indian* Rarities[2] for me to expect (for his Wife look'd after them too narrowly) my counterfeit Inclination did cool so much with time, that at length he stayed at home without returning any more to my House.

Now must I laugh at the foolishness of some men, whose unbounded Petulancy carries them sometimes so far, that they will forget the most horrible Affronts, only that they may not be banish'd from the Favor of a Woman, whose Caresses, they must purchase, while that another may as well as them enjoy her Affections for his Money. Without lying, those men shew that their Bodies have an Empire over their Minds, and that they are only Men, because they have the Figure of them: For is it not the greatest Sillyness; and the highest Madness that can be commit-

---

1 Variant spelling of Sir-reverance, a lump of excrement.
2 Rare and exotic imports from the East Indies.

ted, that to satisfie the desire of a little Bit of Flesh, they proceed to the losing their Estates, their Reputations, and all they have dearest in the World, and undergo, and forget all manner of Affronts; neither more nor less than if you were obliged to endure them. Nevertheless, it would be in some manner excusable: For the Wisest that have ever been upon Earth, suffer themselves to be seduced by Women; if these Sparks were assured of the Inclination of those who cost them so much Money, and who make them suffer so much without their growing impatient.

But to act in that manner with those Nymphs, who, like Hackney Horses are ready to serve every one, methinks, that since men have received so much Prudence,[1] that it is a Shame for them to be led away to such Extravagancies. True it is, that *Maximus* had no great reason to treat me in that manner: But however I fancy, that he was still more to blame to court my Amity after I had used him so scurvily in the presence of another. Methinks that Shame alone ought to have forbidden him to have ever any Thoughts of me, unless he had a desire to shew that he had a Resentment for those Affronts. But there are those who are yet more silly: For I have seen those, who without having given any Occasion, suffered themselves to be ashamed and affronted a thousand times a day, without however thinking of drawing the Foot out of the Snare, wherein their lascivious Passion has made them fall. But I will engage no farther in this matter, that I may not deviate any farther from my Subject.

For two years time after that I had rid my self of my *Indian* Merchant, I had so few Adventures of any Importance, that they do not deserve I should take the trouble to describe them; and to speak the Truth, I had, during that time, so little Commerce in Gallantry, that I did not gain so much as I had done before: for by reason that I still became more and more ugly, I received no Benefit from any body, unless it were from those whom I knew how to please by my Wit; but considering that's no great harm in Gallantry, especially to the Citizens, where they expresly desire Corporal Beauty; and on the contrary side what was worst, my Tricks began to become something too well known, that I lost one day one, and the next day another, which made me begin to think of the means of getting my Livelyhood after another manner, namely by some Merchandise, for which I had Opportunity enough, being provided with a good Sum of Money. And I

---

1 Here, innate wisdom or foresight.

had also the less reason to be uneasie, in that I had Annuities to live on, as I have said in the first part; and that by Consequence I might live conveniently without troubling my Head with any Trade. True it is, that I must have taken Delight in a solitary sort of Life, and must have retrenched my Expences which I had no great Inclination to do: On the contrary, I was so accustomed to a Libertine way of Living, and Pride had took such deep Root in my Heart, that it was a hard matter for me resolve to go after the Rate[1] of a Shop Keeper's Wife.

While I was thus contriving what would be most convenient and most useful to undertake, I began to imagine, that I should not do ill in setting up a Lace-shop, because that it is a Trade that requires no great trouble, and which brings a great deal of Profit; and particularly if you have the convenience of buying your Lace at the best hand.[2] This design having been firmly concluded on, I left my House to the keeping of a Marryed Woman, and having taken with me a good Sum of Money, I went into *Flanders* and so to *Bruxels*,[3] to furnish my self with all things necessary for the garnishing a handsome Shop.

Amongst other Passengers there was a *German* Lord, attended with two Footmen in rich Liveries. He had no sooner cast his eyes upon me, than that he imagined, perhaps, that my Face was as Beautiful, as Paint and *Spanish* Paper made it seem; and presently began to show his inclination, and upon the first occasion, he came and sat on the side of me, and as he had made good Provision for eating and drinking, he would not suffer in the least that I should meddle with my own Victuals; for really though the *Germans* do not for the most part contain a huge deal of Wit in their great Noddles, yet we must however give them this Commendation, that they show themselves much more Civil and Courteous towards Women, than many other Nations. His Civility made me immediately imagine, that some advantage might accrew[4] to me from him; wherefore I us'd the Spark as amourously as was possible.

To make short, before that we came to *Newport*,[5] we agreed to spend a Night or two together at *Antwerp*,[6] and to bring this to

---

1 Total estimated value, amount, or sum of anything (figuratively).
2 Most profitably or cheaply (obsolete).
3 Variant spelling of "Brussels," capital of modern Belgium.
4 Variant spelling of "accrue."
5 Seaport in southeast Wales.
6 Capital of a province in north Belgium on the Scheldt River.

pass, he had gently slipt into my Breast three or four Broad-pieces of Gold.

As soon as we were come to *Antwerp* we went to one of the most Considerable Ordinaries,[1] where we Dined, and then we asked if we might lie there for two or three Nights, and that we had occasion for three Chambers at the least; namely, one for us, another for the *German's* Foot-men, and a third for my Maid. The Landlord expecting to gain a considerable Sum of Money upon this Occasion, quickly caused all to be prepared we stood in need of, after which the Count and I took a turn to see the fine City of *Antwerp*, towards Evening we returned to our Inn, where my *German* who was a Brave Drinker, as are most of his Countreymen, fell to drinking Bumpers so hard with some Sparks who were also lodged there, that he became as drunk as a Beast, and in that condition came he to Bed to me. Certainly if I had then been something more given to Carnal Pleasures, I should have been something vexed and disappointed, for with Drunken Men there may be a great deal of Wind, but it seldom Rains; but as the principal Question was that of Money, I made no great Ceremony upon the point; yet since I make Profession of having a sincere heart in all things, I am willing to confess, that the Amorous Sport was not so unpleasant to me, yet you must also know that I was not over-well pleased with all those I had to do with, and that by Consequence I could not find my Divertisement with all manner of Gallants, for assure your self when Misses endeavour to make Sparks believe, by their Counterfeit Motion, that they receive an unspeakable Pleasure; this is not out of a good intention, but to oblige the Cavalier to do his Work the sooner; and indeed, without being of a Nature insatiable in Lasciviousness, a Woman cannot find satisfaction in the Embraces of a Man she had never seen before.

After we had been a pretty while in undressing him, wherein I was also assisted by his Men, we went to Bed, and I expected to have enjoyed a very peaceable Repose. But things do not always go according as we promise our selves. Which you may see by my *German*, for though he was so beastly drunk, yet he had not forgotten for what reason he had desired to have me his Bedfellow, and tho' I used all imaginable means to make him defer that business until the Morning, for I was never willing to have to do with drunken Men, he would not be prevailed with, insomuch, that I

---

1   Inns or public houses.

was forced to prepare my self for it, unless that I had a mind to lose all I promised my self to gain by the Bargain.

Whereupon I put my self into such a Posture as I thought most suitable to undergo the management a long time, for I foresaw he would be a long while doing his Work. But while we were thus busily taken up in our Affair, for I did also my best to be so much the sooner disengaged from him; the jogling[1] did so raise the Wine, the Meat, and all the *German* had eaten that Evening, that in a moment he Vomited upon my Face a pot full of Filth, and this Evacuation being followed by three or four more of the same nature, I began to fear that Night would have been the last of my Life; for being so weary that I could hardly draw my Breath, which perhaps made me open my Mouth something too wide, there entred into my Throat such a great quantity of that villainous stuff, that I thought I had been stifled, and if I had not forced my Knight to quit the Saddle, I should have been but in a miserable Condition. Besides, that villainous stuff stunk so horribly, that having been put altogether in a *Granado*,[2] they would have obliged a Man of War[3] to have yielded, though it had been mounted with four and twenty pieces of Cannon.

An other Inconvenience followed upon the Heels of this, for as I was busy in cleaning my Mouth, my Stomach received the Air of this insupportable stink, so that I vomitted all I had therein, with such a Violence, that I began to bleed at the Nose.

In the mean while as I could not cry out I made such a noise with my Hands against the Beds teaster,[4] that at length one of the Maids came up with a light, and seeing us in that posture, she set the Candle upon the Table and ran to tell her Mistress that we had spoiled one of her best Beds; for which reason she did not fail to make a terrible Noise; but this storm was appeased in a moment because the *German* who was very much ashamed at this accident, and who was then become something more sober, payed according to the Tax she set upon that he had spoyled.

In the mean time while they were preparing another Bed, and I put on one of my Landladyes Smocks, and my Spark of a *German* who was something better furnished with fine Linnen

---

1 Variant of joggling: shaking to and fro, as by repeated jerks.
2 Obsolete spelling of grenade.
3 An armed sailing ship.
4 Variant spelling of "tester," which is a canopy over a bed supported on the posts of the bedstead or suspended from the ceiling, or the wooden or metal framework that supports such a canopy.

than my self, had clean Linnen took out of his Port-Mantle, for those we had on could not be more Dirty nor more wet, tho' it had rain'd T—rds and Surreverences upon them with full Palefuls, and we had marched naked in our shifts quite through it all.

In the mean while the honest Gentleman drank a good quantity of Pump-water, and by this means the Fumes of the Wine which were already half evaporated by the vomiting, dissipated themselves so well by his vomiting, that it could hardly any longer be observed that he had been drunk, to which also his shame did much contribute he had of so Beastly an action. As for my part I remain'd peacebly sitting, and was studying of the means to make him pay for this disorder, for tho' he asked me a thousand pardons which I willingly granted him in appearance, I was loath to let him come off at so cheap a rate as to let him go scot-free.

A thousand sort of thoughts roll'd in my Head; but amongst all, there was not one wherein I did not find either impossibility or a too visible affectation,[1] wherefore none of those means seem'd to me more proper than the first which came into my fancy, whereof I will give you an immediate account.

When that our second Bed was made ready, and that the Count imagined that the peace was entirely concluded, we went to sleep; which I could do with so much the more tranquility for that I saw there would be nothing to do until the depth of the night. However I, as I never knew what profoundly sleeping was, I heard the *German* several times make water, for tho' he had so swingingly skinned the Fox[2] there was still in his Body humidity enough remaining, to fill the Chamber pot. It was about break of day when he was again awaked out of his sleep, and he almost filled the Pot quite full, as I could easily perceive by the noise he made.

Methoughts it was then time to put my design in execution: Wherefore I pretended to start out as a Dream; ah my dear little Angel, said I to him, I desire you would give me the Pot a little, my dear heart, said he to me, it is so full I know not if you can make use of it. Yes well enough, replyed I, my Bladder is not so great, and besides I know not if I can make water. Then the poor Ninnyhammer took the Pot in both his Hands and gave it me, and stood till I had done, for by reason the Pot stood upon a Chair by the Bedside, and that he lay on the same, expecting to set it in its

---

1 A too visible striving after, aiming at, earnest pursuit (obsolete).
2 Slang expression for come to a sexual climax.

place again, and indeed I was for above a quarter of an hour without letting fall a drop, tho' I still made Faces as if I strained hard; but when I perceived he was fallen again asleep, I got me up and fell plump upon his Body, neither more nor less than if I had been intangled in the Bed-Cloaths, I overturned the Pot and so let all the Urine fall upon his Face. S'Blood[1] and Death, said the *German*, as soon as he felt he weight of my Body and that innundation of unexpected rain, I believe that the Devil reigns in this House, otherwise how should one receive so many misfortunes in one night alone? Thereupon leaping with his naked Breech out of the Bed, he blasphemed and made such a noise as if the Man had been possessed with a Devil. He call'd out for light. At the same time I jump'd also out of Bed, for in a moment he was so wet, that you could hardly find a dry place the bigness of a Pin's-head, and tho' I had the greatest pain imaginable to contain my self from laughing, I beseech'd him in terms of Lamentation, that he would not attribute to me the fault thereof; that it was a mischance; and that I was ready to do all that he pleased to give him Contentment. Done upon that Condition, said the *German*, and moreover I cannot take it in ill part, tho' it had been done on purpose, but yet I am willing to have a better Opinion of you.

In the mean while the Landlady came up with a light grunting all the way, because she was not suffered to sleep at rest, and seeing this second Bed was as well spoiled as the other. By my soul, said she, I cannot but believe that you are resolved to make me mad to night: Ah my dear Landlady, I conjure you to be silent, said the *German*, who could hardly open his Eyes by reason of the sharp humour of the Piss, reckon only what is due for this dammage, and give us another Bed; I am resolved to see if the Devil will come and play his part too there.

All this while I bit my Lips so hard that the blood was ready to gush out, for as I saw the Piss still trickling from his Hair into this poor Wretches Eyes, I was taken with so great a desire to laugh, for I would willingly have given a Guinney or two to have eas'd and given that satisfaction to my Breast. Thus were we led again into another Chamber by the Woman, grumbling and scolding, after which the *German* put on another clean Shirt; thus did he shift himself[2] three times that Night, which undoubtedly he never did before since he was Born.

---

1 Abbreviation of Christ's or God's blood.
2 Bestirred himself (obsolete).

After this disastrous Night, we sojourned two days longer in this Inn; but it was with more good luck, for afterwards there happened no Mischances to us.

After which, my Honest *German* departed for *Nechelen*,[1] where he said he had some Affairs, and would very willingly have took me along to have accompanied him thither; but because I was willing to think on my Concern, I gave him many thanks for his offer, and went my way to *Bruxelles* with my Maid, though perhaps, I had not done ill, if I had gone along with him, for he was a Debonnaire Spark, and as Amiable and Courteous, as a Woman could desire.

We staid about a Week at *Bruxelles*, as well to see the Town and Court, as to buy the things for which we came thither; I do not question but that I might have made some Gains there, for New Flesh is commonly desired, and sought after; but the fear I was in that the poor *Spanish* Courtiers would not pay me according to my Merit, I thought I should do better in sparing my Glances, and bestow them upon others who had wherewith to recompence me well, in case that Fortune[2] was still so favourable to me, that she would address some more of those Sparks to me again. But whereas during my Youth, she had been as a Mother in such Encounters, she began to become a Mother-in-Law towards me; for since this Voyage into *Brabant*,[3] I have had so few Occupations, that one would have believed by seeing the closing of my *Tuzzy-Muzzy*,[4] that I had recovered a new Maiden-head in my old days. Nevertheless, I might have found some few to whom I should not have been so unacceptable, if I would have suffered them to have made use of me for nothing; but that I could never be brought to, because by that means I might have come to be despised; with so much the more reason as that I stood not in so much need of Money as to run the danger of losing my health for a Crown or an Angel.[5]

As soon as I was returned from *Flanders*, with a sufficient quantity of Laces, I caus'd the entrance of my House to be pre-

---

1 A mispelling of Mechelen, a city lying halfway between Brussels and Antwerp in the Spanish Netherlands.
2 Chance, hap, or luck regarded as a cause of events. Often personified as a goddess whose emblem is a wheel betokening vicissitude.
3 A territory, located between the modern Netherlands and Belgium, ruled by a duke.
4 Vagina (slang); literally, a garland of flowers.
5 A gold coin.

pared for the making a shop thereof, and not to live on that trade alone, for I knew not if I should gain by it, and I was used to keep a good Table, I took a Miss to lodge with me, who according to appearances, should serve me in the Quality of a Shop Maid, though this was only to exercise with her the same Trade I had done before with my own Flesh; and for that cause, for the drawing the more profit from thence, I instructed her with all those things which a Lady of Pleasure ought to know, for the heaping up a Sum of Money wherewith she may maintain her self during her Old Age. I acquainted her after what manner she was to show Affection to Men in Years; how she was to comport her self with the younger; what she was to observe in the first Visits; by what marks she might judge if a Man was liberal or stingy.

In short, I imparted to her all those Instructions that experience had taught me, and if my Lessons were set down in Writing, I am sure, that those Women who could make due use of 'em would receive no small profit by 'em; but because I have no design to spur on others to do ill, I will rather bury them in an Eternal Silence, that I may not be accused of having led into a wrong way the Children of Persons of Honour.

My design succeeded as well as I could have desired, for my Shop served for a pretext to Gentlemens coming into my House, and all was so peaceably governed there, that my nearest Neighbours hardly knew that I committed the least thing that was not honest, becoming and Civil.

This Commerce had lasted about four years without my receiving the least Cross or Traverse, when I was taken with a fit of Sickness, which in a few days brought me to the brink of Death. As then in such rencounters people become something wiser than they used to be, and as the thoughts of Death makes us often make promises to him, whom one does not think of in ones Health, I also made Vows that if ever I recovered again, I would lead a better Life, and that I would abandon all the Means which I had thitherto made use of: I know not if my Prayers were heard, or if my Sickness was come to its terme, yet by degrees I returned to my former Condition; the truth is, I put the Miss out of the House as I had made a Vow to doe, and that after this time I have never had any other of the same Condition; but yet I must confess by reason I will not have the reputation of having ever been a Dissembler, that the Flesh has been some times stronger than the Spirit; nevertheless I have at last gain'd the Victory over that Enemy, or if you will have it so, Years have rendred me so ugly, that no Body now comes to torment me any more for such like things. However I do not speak after this manner, but that infallibly I shall not be believed if I would pass for a Vertuous Person, which might be contradicted by a certaine place of this second part, as also by my way of writing which is something bold and libertine; but I content my self with the testimony that my Conscience gives me, and it is the same thing to me whether I am thought discreet, vertuous or debaucht; because that I have Experience enough in the World to know that it often blames Wise and Sober Persons, and often praises and extols such as are lewd and vicious. Nevertheless I am not of the rank of those who after having led a vicious Life during their Youth, and then becoming Converts, pretend to bygottism,[1] and walk holding their right-Hand upon their Heart as the truly Devout do, or, if you please, seem as modest and as plain as poor *Susanna* is commonly painted between those two old Ruffions.[2] On the contrary I am like to those old Coachmen who can willingly hear the sound of the Whip, with so much the more reason, as that it seems rather a folly than a probity to forbid Men Joy and Mirth, by sad and Melancholly Grimaces. It is a priviledge that we have preferably to all other Creatures, and for that reason I have done it as often as things required, and I do not believe that I can desist from it tho' a number of curious Fools should tax me with being a Person of ill Conduct, until that Death has clos'd up my Mouth.

FINIS.

---

1   A neologism, probably related to "bygones," the notion that past offences are past and hence best forgotten: "let bygones be bygones."

2   See Daniel and Susanna in the Apocrypha. A popular subject in seventeenth-century religious paintings, Susanna and the Elders were represented by Rembrandt van Rijn (1636), Anthony Van Dyck (1621-22), and Artemisa Gentileschi (1610) among many others.

Appendix A: Some Versions of the Picaresque

1. From Cervantes, *Don Quixote, Part I* (1604, 1620)

[The term "picaresque" is used in comparative literature studies to designate those narratives that feature low-life characters in a series of relatively discrete adventures. Introduced by the anonymous *Lazarillo de Tormes* (1554), Mateo Aleman's *Guzman d'Alfarache* (1599), and Miguel de Cervantes's *Don Quixote* in late sixteenth-century Spain, this genre provides realistic alternatives to the lofty, noble heroes and heroines of chivalric romance. Appearing in an interpolated tale in Cervantes's *Don Quixote, Part I* (1604), Dorotea is an early example of a female protagonist who, by virtue of her experience as the manager of her parents' estate, acquires the habit of evaluating human interaction in terms of its practical consequences. The specific passage in which Dorotea describes her managerial duties must have been disturbing to some seventeenth-century readers, for it was omitted from the decorous Peter Motteux translation of 1700. The extract is taken from the first English translation, by Thomas Shelton.]

I WAS the mirrour wherein they beheld themselves, the staffe of their old age, and subject to which they addresst all their desires. From which because they were most virtuous, mine did not stray an inch, and even in the same manner that I was Ladie of their mindes, so was I also of their goods. By mee were Servants admitted or dismissed, the notice and account of what was sowed or reaped, past thorow[1] my hands, of the Oyle-mills, the Wine-presses, the number of great and little Cattell, the Bee-hives: In fine, of all that which so rich a Farmer as my father was, had or could have, I kept the account, and was the Steward thereof and Mistrisse, with such care of my side, and pleasure of theirs, as I cannot possibly indeere[2] it enough. The times of leisure that I had in the day, after I had given what was necessary to the head Servants, and other labourers, I did entertaine in those exercises

---

1 Obsolete spelling of "through."
2 Variant spelling of endear: here, endear means "praise."

which were both commendable and requisite for Maydens, to wit, In Sowing, making of Bone lace, and many times handling the Distaffe:[1] and if sometimes I left those exercises to recreate my mind a little, I would then take some goodly booke in hand, or play on the Harpe, for experience had taught me that Musick ordereth disordered mindes, and doth lighten the passions that afflict the Spirit.

[In the following moment of self-reflection, Dorotea rationalizes her acquiescence to the sexual desire of a wealthy and titled seducer, Don Fernando, and in so doing justifies to herself the hard bargain that she subsequently makes with him: the surrender of her virginity in exchange for his promise to marry her.]

I at this season made a briefe discourse, and said thus to my selfe, I may doe this, for I am not the first which by Matrimony hath ascended from a low degree to a high estate: nor shall *Don Fernando* bee the first whom beautie or blind affection (for that is the most certaine) hath induced to make choice of a Consort equall to his Greatness. Then since herein I create no new world, nor custome, what error can be committed by embracing the honour wherewithall fortune crownes mee: Although it so befell, that his affection to mee endured no longer then till he accomplisht his will: for before God I certes[2] shall still remaine his wife. And if I should disdainfully give him the repulse, I see him now in such termes, as perhaps forgetting the dutie of a Nobleman, hee may use violence, and then shall I remaine for ever dishonoured, and also without excuse of the imputations[3] of the ignorant, which knew not how much without any fault I have faln into this inevitable danger. For, what reasons may bee sufficiently forcible to perswade my father and other, that this Nobleman did enter into my Chamber without my consent? All these demands and Answeres did in an instant revolve in my imagination, and found my selfe chiefly forced (how I cannot tell) to assent to his Petition, by the witnesses he invoked, the teares hee shed, and finally by his sweete disposition and comely feature, which accompanied with so many arguments of unvairied affection, were able to conquer and enthrall any other heart, though it were as free and wary as mine own.

---

1 Cleft staff about three feet long on which wool or flax was wound.
2 Certainly (archaic).
3 Accusations.

2. From Lòpez de Ubeda, *La Picara Justina* (1605, 1707)

[In the following passage from Captain John Steven's English adaptation of Lòpez de Ubeda's *La Picara Justina* (*The Spanish Jilt*, 1707), the heroine displays the wit and hard-headed realism typical of the *picara* in evaluating male suitors. In a sense, her comments are delivered in opposition to the conventions of chivalric romance and are intended as an antidote to them. Her overriding message is that a woman of consequence, in considering suitors, should be cognizant of their true motives for courting her and not be taken in by their posturing gestures.]

IT would be endless to give an Account of all the Pretenders to me, they were so Numerous. Some finding me *Haughty*, endeavour'd to look *Big*, and walk'd as stiff as if Stakes had been drove thro' them: Others imagin'd that *Gay Cloaths* would carry me, and Dress'd themselves like *Merry-Andrews*,[1] or *Monkeys* at a *Bear-Baiting*. Some thought to try to win me by dint of *Love*, and these spent their time in gazing at my Windows, *Sighing*, and making *Dismal Faces*, and Expressing *Wonderful Transports* if ever I happen'd to cast a *Careless Glance* towards them. Others concluded none could take me but a downright *Bully-Ruffian*, and therefore walk'd my Street with long *Swords* by Day, and made the Stones strike Fire with them by Night, as if they had been engag'd in *Quarrels*. I remember one of these spying me at the Door, turn'd up his *Whiskers*, cock'd his *Hat*, and laying his Hand on his *Sword*, said to me, *My Sovereign Lady, has any one Offended you? If he has, by the Lord he shall not live till to Morrow*. I answer'd, If you were to kill him that Offends me, you ought to make your Will this Moment, but I had rather you should live to make Sport for the Ladies. Observe here the Folly of Men to make themselves a *Merit* of their *Absurdities*, believing that looking *Big*, *Tawdry Drest*, *Whining*, or *Ranting*, are Ingredients to win a Womans Heart; but this is the Fault of the Women who encourage them, for want of distinguishing between *Worth* and *Grimace*. Thus you see one Fool is gain'd by a *Formal Starch'd Countenance*, another by a *Gaudy Dress* and *Flittering Wig*, a third by *Sighing* and *Weeping*, and a fourth by *Ranting* and *Swearing*. But enough of these Fops, for I am ask'd to mention a parcel of *Numskulls*, who came with a full Resolution to Enamour[2] me with fine *Speeches*,

---

1   Persons who entertain others with antics and buffoonery.
2   Seduce or arouse (sexually).

and when we met had not a Word to say for themselves; or to speak of the Numberless *Billets Doux*,[1] which for a long time furnish'd the *Pastry-Cook* and *Grocer* of our Town; or mention the many *Songs* Sung under my Window; or reckon up the *Bumpkin* Pretenders that flock'd from all the Country about. None of these mov'd me for now a-days *Love* is Bought and Sold, and fairest Bidder carries the Prize; *It is Money makes the Mare to go*, and an *Ass* loaded with *Gold* is more acceptable than the Noblest Creature without that Ornament.

3. From Richard Head, *The English Rogue, Volume I* (1666)

[In the following scene from the last chapter of Richard Head's *The English Rogue, Volume I* (1666), Meriton Latroon, the picaresque hero, represents himself as having undergone a spiritual reformation. For the modern reader, the account not only raises a question concerning the genuineness of his change of heart but also contrasts with Cornelia's ostentatious refusal to embrace the comforts of a religious conversion. The juxtaposition of the two suggests that the spiritually redeemed protagonist is as much of a stereotype of picaresque narratives as the unregenerate figure he or she replaces.]

I NOW again considered how he must live, that intends to live well; and upon that consideration, concluded upon this resolution, Not to neglect my duty to Heaven, my Self, or Neighbours: for he that fails in any of these, falls short in making his life commendable. For our Selves, we need Order; for our Neighbour, Charity; and for the Deity, Reverence and Humility. These three duties are so concatenated, that he which liveth orderly, cannot but be acceptable to his Maker and the World. Nothing jars the Worlds harmony more, than men that break their ranks; and nothing renders Man more contemned and hated, than he whose actions only tend to irregularity. One turbulent spirit will even dissentiate[2] the calmest Kingdom: so did my past unruly and disordered life ruine my self, as well as many families. I have seen an Orthodox Minister in his Pulpit with his congregation about him; and since revolving in my minde the comeliness of that well-order'd sight, I have thought within my self how mad he would

---

1 Love notes.
2 Sow dissention or discord (rare).

appear, that should wildly dance out of his room. Such is man when he spurns at the Law he liveth under; and such was I, that could not be contain'd within due limits, living like the Drone on others labours; taking no pains, but onely making a humming noise in the world, till Justice seiz'd me for a wandring, idle, and hurtful vagabond, (an *ignavum pecus*)[1] and so had like to have thrust me out of the world, the Hive of industrious Bees.

Ill company at first misled me, and it is to be feared by my example others have been misled. For he that giveth himself leave to transgress, he must needs put others out of the way. Experience giveth us to understand, that he which first disorders himself, troubles all the company. Would every man keep his own life, what a concord in Musick would every family be: It shall be my own endeavour to do this, and my cordial advice to others to do the like.

Doubtless he that performeth his duty to Heaven, shall finde such a peace within, that shall fit him for whatsoever falls. He shall not fear himself, because he knoweth his course is order: he shall not fear the World, because he knoweth he hath done nothing that hath anger'd it: he shall not be afraid of Heaven; for he knoweth he shall there finde the favour of a servant, nay more, a Son, and be protected against the malice of Hell.

I know I shall be lookt on no otherwise than an Hypocrite; neither will the world believe my reformation real, since I have lived so notoriously and loosly. Let a man do well an hundred times, it may be he shall for a short time be remembred and applauded; whereas if he doth evilly but once, he shall be ever condemned, and never forgot. However, let me live well, and I care not though the world should flout my innocence, and call me dissembler: it is no matter if I suffer the worst of censorious reproaches, so that I get to Heaven at last: to the attaining of which, the best counsel I can give my self and others is, *Bene vive, ordinabiliter tibi, sociabiliter Proximo, & humiliter Deo:* Live well, orderly to thy self, sociably to thy Neighbour, and humbly to thy Maker.

4. From Francis Kirkman, *The English Rogue, Volume III* (1665)

[In Francis Kirkman's continuation of *The English Rogue* (1665), Mrs. Dorothy relates how she murdered her maid without compunction after the maid had secretly served as a virginal stand-in

---

1 A lazy drone. See Virgil's *Georgics* (37-29 BCE), 4, 165, 168.

for her on her wedding night. In so doing, Mrs. Dorothy displays a chilling treachery that sets her apart from the heroine of *The London Jilt*.]

THERE was a Servant Maid in the House, whom I usually had for my Bed-fellow, and with her I was very free in all my discourse, acquainting her with all passages between me and my Sweet-hearts; and many pleasing discourses we had upon those occasions, and commonly we spent some hours every night when we were in Bed, in these Conferences: I asking her which of my Sweet-hearts was the best, and likeliest to prove a good Husband; she and I both jumped in one mind, and she seemed to rejoyce at the good Fortune I was likely to enjoy, in having so handsome, and so accomplish'd a Person, as he was with whom I was to be Married; saying, that of all men breathing, she never saw one whom, she thought, she could love better; and adding, that she would give all the money in her Pocket to have my place on the Wedding Night. Well, thought I, are you there? I'le be with you anon.[1] Truly, said she, I am a perfect Maid, not having yet had to do with any Man; and for deed, nay, for thought and word, untill this time, was a pure Virgin; but methinks, since I saw your Sweet-heart, I have such pleasing imaginations, that I could willingly experiment[2] the effects; but, continued she, I hope you will take all this in good part, and not be jealous of me for I shall not in the least injure you, no, though your Sweet-heart should desire it; besides, my Quality and condition is so much beneath yours, that it would be but a folly to expect it; but shall wish you all happiness with your beloved Bridegroom. She having opened her mind thus freely to me, it was the thing I only aimed at, and above all things wish'd for; and therefore, that I might now strike while the Iron was hot, I thus replyed; come, come, do not counterfeit more Modesty than needs, but tell me truly, and sincerely, if I can find a way to compass your desires, and be therewith content, and willing, will you obey me in what I shall desire of you? This is a strange proposition, said she, and I believe, far from your heart to do, and only to try me farther; but I pray let us talk no more of this matter.

I quickly answered, that I was now in earnest, and would (if she would swear to me to be secret) discover a secret that was of the

---

1 Immediately, at once.
2 Establish the effects by trial.

highest importance, and that then all things would be as she had wished; she wondring what I meant, and being desirous (as all Women are inquisitive after secrets) to discover mine, soon made many protestations and vows, to be secret in what ever I should impart to her; and thereupon I told her, that indeed about twelve moneths since, being in my fathers house, a Gentleman of quality lodging there, and having divers times courted me, and I alwayes refusing to hear him, and being very obstinate, notwithstanding all his endeavours by Presents, and otherwise; he, I said, being wholly impatient, and resolved to venture all for my enjoyment, took his opportunity, and came to bed to me; I feeling him near me, cry'd out, but in vain, for my Lodging was at too great a distance from any bodyes hearing; and so in the end, notwithstanding my strive-ing, and strugling, he had his will of me; and indeed, to tell you the truth, the danger of the brunt[1] being over, and I well knowing that what was past could not be recalled, was, in the end, willing a second, or third time, to permit him the same enjoyment; and so he went away in the Morning well satisfied, and I better pleas'd than when he came to me. I was resolved to keep this from the knowledge of my Parents, and did so, though he offered me Mar-riage, which would have been advantagious enough for me, he being, as I said, a Person of Quality; but however, he continued his practice with me all the time of his stay at my Fathers, which was two Months; and then he departing, promised a sudden return, and that he would then discover himself to my Father, and request me in Marriage; I trusted to his fair words, and permitted his departure; but he had not been long absent ere I perceived my self to be with Child: I kept this from the knowledge of all, so long as I could; but in the end, my Mother suspecting me, charged me so roundly, that I confessed the Fact; she thereupon took the best remedy she could, and, unknown to my Father, sent me away to a Friend of hers, where I lay in of a Child, which soon after dying, and I recovered, I again removed hither, where what hath befaln me you already know as well as I; and now, my dear Friend, said I, the case being thus, you may do me a great kindness, and please your self, as you say, by taking my place on the Wedding-night; and he lying with you in my stead may be deceived, and take me for a pure Virgin; whereas otherwise I am in much doubt to be dis-covered, in regard, that not only I have lost my Maiden-head, but have also so lately had a Child.

---

1 Sharp blow, assault.

My Bed-fellow gave diligent attendance to what I had related, and after I had satisfied her how she should behave her self in every respect, she consented to take my turn. My business being in this forwardness, I quickly consented to clap up[1] the bargain with my Sweet-heart; and the Wedding-day being come, we were accordingly Married; and at Bed-time I went to Bed with my Bride-groom, but feigning Modesty, commanded all to depart the Room; which they did, leaving one Candle burning; I seeing the Company gone, leap'd out of the Bed to put the Candle out; the which I did, and then, according to appointment, the Maid, who was ready in her smock behind the Hangings, quickly got into the Bed, and enjoyed my place; I staid in the Chamber, and could well enough discover all passages between them, and how she made some faint resistance; but not long it was ere they fell asleep, and slept so long, that I was at a very great stand what to do, lest day-light should come ere she should awake, and then be seen by my Husband, and I disgraced and lost for ever: I ruminated in my mind many wayes; at last I was resolved to proceed to violence, and hazard all, rather than lose my credit; and therefore seeing they still slept on, I went out of the Chamber into the next; where, with the help of a Tinder-box, I struck a light; and getting a Torch, and lighting it, set-fire on some part of the House, which soon encreased to a great flame; I then made no great difficulty to make a noise, and cry out, fire, fire; this was soon seen, smelt, and heard by my drousie bed-fellows, who both arose; and I being there, caught hold of him, as if I had lain with him; and his Bed-fellow being now a little come to her self, and seeing me, began to consider what she was to do; and ran where her cloaths were, put them on, and then came to help me to mine.

My Husband, and all the rest of the Family being thus raised, ran about for Water to quench the fire; I being left alone with my Husbands Bed-fellow, could have found in my heart to have kill'd her with a Sword there in the Chamber: because she had been the occasion of all this mischief; and the thoughts of that, and remembring what hurt she might do me hereafter, in discovering my secrets, or, at least, in being my Corrival; these considerations made me resolve to dispatch her into the other world; and therefore desiring her to go down with me into the Yard to fetch water at the Well, she did so; where I spying my opportunity, in the

---

1 Shake hands, in token of a bargain.

absence of the rest of the Family, as she was stooping to draw Water, I turned her head forwards into the Well; where, before any came to help her, she was dead. I pretended to bewail her misfortunes; but the fire, by the assistance of some Neighbours, being now quench'd, we all retired into that part of the House that was unburn'd; where every one lamented, not only the misfortune of the fire, but that of the Maids death; in which I alone was principally concerned.

5. From Daniel Defoe, *Moll Flanders* (1722)

[In the following scene from *Moll Flanders* (1722), Daniel Defoe preserves the motive of revenge that is so prominent a feature of *The London Jilt* and other picaresque narratives but relegates it to a single, minor episode in which Moll is merely an advisor to a female friend. In the process, Defoe sanitizes the conduct of the two women, transforming the episode into a relatively benign and humorous event.]

BESIDES this, I observ'd that the Men made no scruple to set themselves out, and to go a Fortune Hunting, *as they call it*, when they had really no Fortune themselves to Demand it, or Merit to deserve it; and that they carry'd it so high, that a Woman was scarce allow'd to enquire after the Character or Estate of the Person that pretended to her. This, I had an Example of, in a young Lady at the next House to me, and with whom I had contracted an intimacy; she was Courted by a young Captain, and tho' she had near 2000*l.* to her Fortune, she did but enquire of some of his Neighbours about his Character, his Morals, or Substance; and he took Occasion at the next Visit to let her know, truly, that he took it very ill, and that he should not give her the Trouble of his Visits any more: I heard of it, and as I had begun my Acquaintance with her, I went to see her upon it: She enter'd into a close Conversation with me about it, and unbosom'd herself very freely; I perceiv'd presently that tho' she thought herself very ill us'd, yet she had no power to resent it; that she was exceedingly Piqu'd she had lost him, and particularly that another of less Fortune had gain'd him.

I fortify'd her Mind against such a Meanness, *as I call'd it*; I told her, that as low as I was in the World, I would have despis'd a Man that should think I ought to take him upon his own Recommendation only, also *I told her*, that as she had a good Fortune, she had no need to stoop to the Dissaster of the Times; that it was enough that the Men could insult us that had but little Money to recommend us, but if she suffer'd such an Affront to pass upon her without Resenting it, she would be render'd low-priz'd upon all Occasions, that a Woman can never want an Opportunity to be reveng'd of a Man that has us'd her ill, and that there were ways enough to humble such a Fellow as that, or else certainly Women were the most unhappy Creatures in the World.

I found she was very well pleas'd with the Discourse, and she told me seriously that she would be very glad to make him sensible of her just Resentment, and either to bring him on again, or have the Satisfaction of her Revenge being as publick as possible.

I told her, that if she would take my Advice, I would tell her how she should obtain her Wishes in both those things; and that I would engage I would bring the Man to her Door again, and make him beg to be let in: *She smil'd at that*, and soon let me see, that if he came to her Door, her resentment was not so great, to let him stand long there.

However, she listened very willingly to my offer of Advice; so *I told her*, that the first thing she ought to do, was a piece of Justice to herself; namely, that whereas he had reported among the Ladies, that he had left her, and pretended to give the Advantage of the Negative to himself; she should take care to have it well spread among the Women, which she could not fail of an Opportunity to do in a Neighbourhood, so addicted to Family News, as that she liv'd in was, that she had enquired into his Circumstances, and found he was not the Man as to Estate he pretended to be: Let them be told too Madam, said I, that you have been well inform'd that he was not the Man you that expected, and that you thought it was not safe to meddle with him, that you heard he was of an ill Temper, and that he boasted how he had us'd the Women ill upon many Occasions, and that particularly he was Debauch'd in his Morals, *&c.* The last of which indeed had some Truth in it; but at the same time I did not find that she seem'd to like him much the worse for that part.

As I had put this into her Head, she came most readily into it, and immediately she went to Work to find Instruments, she had very little difficulty in the Search; for telling her Story in general to a Couple of Gossips in the Neighbourhood, it was the Chat of the Tea Table all over that part of the Town, and I met with it where ever I visited: Also, as it was known that I was acquainted with the young Lady herself, my Opinion was ask'd very often, and I confirm'd it with all the necessary Aggravations, and set out his Character in the blackest Colours; and as a piece of secret

Intelligence, I added, what the Gossips knew nothing of (*viz.*) That I had heard he was in very bad Circumstances; that he was under a necessity of a Fortune to support his Interest with the Owners of the Ship he Commanded: That his own Part was not paid for, and if it was not paid quickly his Owners would put him out of the Ship, and his Chief Mate was likely to Command it, who offer'd to buy that Part which the Captain had promis'd to take.

I added, for I was heartily piqu'd at the Rogue, *as I call'd him*, that I had heard a Rumour too, that he had a Wife alive at *Plymouth*,[1] and another in the *West Indies*, a thing which they all knew was not very uncommon for such kind of Gentlemen.

This work'd as we both desir'd it, for presently the young Lady at the next Door, *who had a Father and Mother that Govern'd both her, and her Fortune*, was shut up, and her Father forbid him the House: Also in one Place more where he went the Woman had the Courage, *however strange it was*, to say No; and he could try no where but he was Reproached with his Pride, and that he pretended not to give the Women leave to enquire into his Character, *and the like*.

Well by this time he began to be sensible of his mistake; and seeing all the Women on that side the Water alarm'd, he went over to *Ratcliff*, and got access to some of the Ladies there; but tho' the young Women there too, were according to the Fate of the Day, pretty willing to be ask'd, yet such was his ill luck, that his Character follow'd him over the Water and his good Name was much the same there, as it was on our side; so that tho' he might have had Wives enough, yet it did not happen among the Women that had good Fortunes, which was what he wanted.

But this was not all, she very ingeniously manag'd another thing her self, for she got a young Gentleman, who was a Relation and indeed was a marry'd Man, to come and visit her Two or Three times a Week in a very fine Chariot and good Liveries, and her two Agents and I also, presently spread a Report all over, that this Gentleman came to Court her; that he was a Gentleman of a Thousand Pounds a Year, and that he was fallen in Love with her, and that she was going to her Aunt's in the City, because it was inconvenient for the Gentleman to come to her with his Coach in *Redriff*,[2] the Streets being so narrow and difficult.

---

1 Town 240 miles southwest of London.
2 Street running along the south bank of the Thames.

This took immediately, the Captain was laugh'd at in all Companies, and was ready to hang himself; he tried all the ways possible to come at her again, and wrote the most passionate Letters to her in the World excusing his former Rashness, and in short, by great Application, obtained leave to wait on her again, as he said, only to clear his Reputation.

At this meeting she had her full Revenge of him; for *she told him*, she wonder'd what he took her to be, that she should admit any Man to a Treaty of so much Consequence, as that of Marriage, without enquiring into his Circumstances; that if he thought she was to be huff'd[1] into Wedlock, and that she was in the same Circumstances which her Neighbours might be in (*viz.*) to take up with the first good Christian that came, he was mistaken; that in a word his Character was really bad, or he was very ill beholden to his Neighbours; and that unless he could clear up some Points, in which she had justly been prejudiced, she had no more to say to him, but to do herself justice and give him the Satisfaction of knowing, that she was not afraid to say NO, either to him, or any Man else.

With that she told him what she had heard, *or rather rais'd herself by my Means, of his Character*; his not having paid for the Part he pretended to Own of the Ship he Commanded; of the Resolution of his Owners to put him out of the Command, and to put his Mate in his stead; and of the Scandal rais'd on his Morals; his having been reproach'd with such and such Women, and his having a Wife at *Plymouth*, and another in the *West-Indies*, and the like; and she ask'd him whether she had not good Reason, if these things were not clear'd up, to refuse him, and to insist upon having Satisfaction in Points so significant as they were?

He was so confounded at her Discourse that he could not answer a Word, and she almost began to believe that all was true, by his disorder, tho' she knew that she had been the raiser of these Reports herself.

After some time he recovered a little, and from that time was the most humble, modest, and importunate Man alive in his Courtship.

She carried her jest on a great way, she ask'd him, if he thought she was so at her last shift, that she could or ought to bear such Treatment, and if he did not see that she did not want those who

---

1 Blustered, bluffed.

thought it worth their while to come farther to her than he did, meaning the Gentleman who she had brought to visit her by way of sham.

She brought him by these Tricks to submit to all possible Measures to satisfie her, as well of his Circumstances, as of his Behaviour. He brought her undeniable Evidence of his having paid for his part of the Ship; he brought her Certificates from his Owners, that the Report of their intending to remove him from the Command of the Ship, was false and groundless; in short, he was quite the reverse of what he was before.

Thus I convinced her, that if the Men made their Advantage of our Sex in the Affair of Marriage, upon the supposition of there being such a Choice to be had, and of the Women being so easy, it was only owing to this, that the Women wanted Courage to maintain their Ground, and that according to my Lord *Rochester*

> *A Woman's ne'er so ruin'd but she can*
> *Revenge herself on her Undoer, Man.*[1]

After these things this young Lady plaid her part so well, that tho' she resolv'd to have him, and that indeed having him was the main bent of her Design, yet she made his obtaining her be TO HIM the most difficult thing in the World; and this she did, not by a haughty Reserv'd Carriage, but by a just Policy, turning the Tables upon him, and playing back upon him his own Game; for as he pretended by a kind of lofty Carriage, to place himself above the occasion of a Character and to make enquiry into Character a kind of affront to him, she broke with him upon that Subject, and at the same time that she made him submit to all possible enquiry after his Affairs, she apparently shut the Door against his looking into her own.

It was enough to him to obtain her for a Wife, as to what she had, she told him plainly, that as he knew her Circumstances, it was but just she should know his; and tho' at the same time he had only known her Circumstances by common Fame, yet he had made so many Protestations of his Passion for her, that he could ask no more but her Hand to his grand Request, *and the*

---

1 John Wilmot, 2nd Earl of Rochester (1647-1680), *A Letter from Artemiza in the Town to Chloe in the Country* (1675?), 11, 185-86. Defoe has substituted "ruin'd" for "wretch'd."

like ramble according to the Custom of Lovers: In short, he left himself no room to ask any more Questions about her Estate, and she took the Advantage of it like a prudent Woman; for she plac'd part of her Fortune so in Trustees, without letting him know any thing of it, that it was quite out of his Reach, and made him be very well contented with the rest.

Appendix B: The Virgin and the Whore

1. The Whore's Tricks: from *The Whore's Rhetorick* (1683)

[The specialized knowledge acquired by a lady of pleasure during the course of her career was assumed to be a body of professional "secrets," the artifices and ruses she employed to ensnare men. In *The Whore's Rhetorick* (1683), an anonymous adaptation of Ferrante Pallavicino's *La Retorica delle puttane* (1642), a famous London bawd, Mother Creswell, teaches the impoverished daughter of a ruined Royalist, Dorothea, how to convert her body into a commodity while concealing her real mercenary motives and maintaining an outward façade of respectability. Wittily but pointedly, Mother Creswell teaches many of the same tricks that are embedded in *The London Jilt*'s narrative. In the following passages, Mother Creswell insists on the whore's need to investigate the character and condition of her suitors.]

[THE Whore] will find it much to her advantage, to enquire particularly into the state and quality of all her Suitors affairs, to hinder any disappointment or surprize: for if she has well informed her self of their busy hours, and when the necessities of their vocation, or the impulse of pleasure, do oblige their attendance; it will be easy to appoint times of meeting, as may give general satisfaction, and enable her to observe her particular engagements. This enquiry into the condition of her Lovers may be in another respect of no mean use. It is hard to know a mans temper from the lines of his Face, or any other extrinsick mark; and it is no less difficult to give a Judgment of his fortune or estate, by his spending, or the figure he makes in the World. Some Men are for this day, and let to morrow provide for it self; others look on futurities; remember the precedent of the Ant, in providing against a wet day.[1] Some imitate the Snail, I do not mean in their gate, but in carrying their Houses on their backs; others are solicitous to satiate their Bellies, and third to replenish his Purse. A Whore then ought to understand Men in all these circumstances, to avoid contracting a familiarity, or making any strict alliances with such as live beyond their bounds, and promise in a short time to become Bankrupts.

---

1   Alludes to the proverb of the ant who stores up food in order to prepare for winter while the grasshopper is content to play.

[...]

A Whore indeed ought to have skill in Physiognomies. Reading Men is the great work of her life.

[In the following passage, Mother Creswell describes the whore's skill in altering her identity and moving from one part of town to another in order to preserve her reputation as an honest woman.]

Whores are all knowing in that maxim of changing Names and Quarters, from one part of the Town to another; when they become crackt in their reputation. This is no ill project, to enable them to treat Lords and Grandees, with that flesh, which Porters would not have tasted at their former station.... Thus then it is plain, a Whores work is no more than to be well skilled in leger-demains, to know how to raise a Fog, and artificially to throw it before the Fops Eyes: then all her Cheats, Slights and Juggles pass for Honesty, Sincerity, and Plain-dealing. Let her Fren-chisie[1] her Commodities, or, (to avoid ribaldry) her Merchan-dize, not with that Country Pox, but with hard names, and *Je ne sçaiquois*.[2]

[Here Mother Creswell insists on the superiority of merchants and citizens to gentlemen as suitors.]

Let my Pupil rest full assured that the most profitable, easy and secure Traffick is to deal with honest wealthy Citizens. A rich Mercer can with more ease rig out a Whore, than a score of ranting blades: and an Apprentice that is Cash-keeper to a sub-stantial Citizen can oblige a young Lady, with larger supplies than a Regiment of modish Gentlemen. These are the golden Lovers, you must by all possible arts endeavour to make your own: a small proportion of Flattery, and a spice of counterfeit Affection will be sufficient baits to captivate these mute Fish; when once they are fast in the Net, there is but little danger of their making escape; a frown, a contracted Brow, or a harsh word will quiet them at any time, and make them willing to gratifie their most exorbitant demands.

---

1 Possible variation on Frechify: to render French in fashion, manners, etc.
2 French: I don't know what.

2. Exchanging Roles

a. From *Advice to the Women and Maidens of London* (1678)

[In prescriptive writings of the seventeenth-century, women were granted but one of two acceptable identities—that of submissive virginal daughter or exemplary wife and mother. At the same time, the splitting of women into two opposing categories might conceal the extent to which they might be called upon to perform enactments of each other's roles. In *Advice to the Women and Maidens of London*, the anonymous female speaker exhorts the women of London to cultivate the practical intelligence associated with bookkeeping rather than take up their usual "Needle-work, Lace, and Point-making." By acquiring "the method of keeping books of account," women, "either single, or married, ... may know their Estates, carry on their Trades, and avoid the Danger of a helpless and forlorn Condition, incident to Widows." The strong and self-reliant woman to be produced by this kind of education bears a strong resemblance to the independent-minded lady of pleasure.]

METHINKS now the objection may be that this art is too high and mysterious for the weaker *sex* it will make them proud: Women had better keep to their Needle-work, point laces, &c. and if they come to poverty, these small Crafts may give them some mean relief.

To which I answer, That having in some measure practiced both Needle-work and Accounts I can aver, that I never found this Masculine Art harder or more difficult then the effeminate achievements of Lace-making, gum-work or the like, the attainment whereof need not make us proud: And God forbid the practise of an useful Virtue should prompt us to a contrary Vice.

[Like Dorotea in *Don Quixote*, the speaker attributes her skill in bookkeeping to the education she received from her parents.]

Know then that my Parents were very careful to cause me to learn writing and *Arithmetick*, and in that I proceeded as far as Reduction, the Rule of Three and Practice, with other Rules, for without the knowledge of these I was told I should not be capable of Trade and Book-keeping and in these I found no discouragement for though *Arithmetick* set my brains at work, Yet there was much delight in the end, and how each question produced a fair answer and informed me of things I knew not.

Afterwards I was put to keep an exact account of the expence of *House-keeping*, and other petty *Charges*, my Father made it my office to call all persons to an account every night what they had laid out, and to reimburse it them, and set all down in a book, and this is the way to make one a Cashier as they are termed, and one that can keep a fair account of receipts and payments of Money or Cash-book, is in good way towards the understanding of Book-keeping: *Shee* that is so well versed in this as to keep the accounts of her Cash right and dayly entred in a book fair without blotting, will soon be fit for greater undertakings.

b. From *The Whore's Rhetorick* (1683)

[In *The Whore's Rhetorick*, by contrast, Mother Cresswell urges Dorothea to be ready to present herself to her suitors, when necessary, in the guise of a romance heroine. In this role, the whore is to feign the cruel misfortune, credulity, recklessness, or failure to reckon consequences that distinguishes the heroine of romance and the later novel of sensibility from the worldly woman who has learned how to choose between competing options and best pursue her own self-interest.]

THE pretence of having been lately snatched from under her Parents Wings, or deserted the imbraces of a cruel Husband, may serve sometimes to gain her a reputation, of being sound fresh Food, and sufficient likewise to excuse a weak and slender beginning. When this sham will not fix (do not interrupt me by finding fault with the word) let her feign some unlucky disaster, almost unavoidable, and which may be apt to move compassion: as that some barbarous *Debauchée* had lately seduced her out of her Virginity and Fortune, with the promise of Marriage, or Maintaining her as his Mistress with a plentiful Annuity for life.

3. The Term "Jilt"

a. From Aphra Behn, *The Younger Brother; or, The Amorous Jilt* (1696)

[Like other loaded terms, the word "jilt" appears frequently in the poetry, fiction, and drama of the late seventeenth century, often in a variety of different contexts. A dictionary definition might contain the following usages: to jilt. v. To successfully deceive, betray or cast off someone, usually a previously accepted lover or fiancé].

George. 'Sdeath, you have made these Pauses and Alarms to give her time to Jilt you.

Prince. Pray heaven she do—I'd not be undeceiv'd for all the Sun surveys.

b. From Aphra Behn, *The Younger Brother; or, The Amorous Jilt* (1696)

[jilt. n. (1) Faithless. A dissembler. Often a term of bitter expostulation, usually referring to a woman but occasionally to a man.]

Mirtilla. All Things in Nature Cheat, or else are Cheated.

George. Well said; take off thy Veil, and shew the Jilt.

Mirtilla. You never knew a Woman thrive so well by real Love, as by Dissimulation: This has a Thousand Arts and Tricks to conquer; appears in any Shape, in any Humour; can laugh or weep, be coy or play, by turns as suits the Lover best, while simple Love has only one Road of Sighs and Softness.

c. From *The German Princess Revived; or, The London Jilt* (1684)

[jilt n. (2) A whore, a common prostitute, a thief, a notorious female criminal.]

AMONGST the many Instances of Persons Infamously Remarkable for their Predatory and ill Lives, none certainly ever Surrendred their Breath at the *Fatal Tree*, leaving behind them a Name more generally known for all sorts of Crimes, than the Subject we are now treating of; Insomuch, that but to mention *Jenny Voss*, is sufficient proof thereof; she having even from her Youth followed the Thieving Trade, and grown so famous therein, that few who live in London, are Strangers to her Name and Reputation.

4. Two Conflicting Images of the Jilt

a. From Aphra Behn, *The Younger Brother; or, The Amorous Jilt* (1696)

[Two conflicting images govern the representation of the jilt during the Restoration: on the one hand, she is presented as participating in a libertine fantasy of free love outside the constraints of custom and society.]

> Mirtilla. Think not the mighty present of your Jewels, enough to purchase Provinces, has bought one single Sigh, or Wish: No, my dear Prince, you owe 'em all to Love, and your own Charms.

> George. Oh damn'd dissembling Jilt!   *Aside*

b. From *A Catalogue of Jilts* (1691)

[On the other hand, the jilt is often represented as a mercenary jade who represses her own desires in order to maximize her powers of accumulation.]

> MRS. *Mary* H—n, a tall, graceful, comely Woman, indebted for two thirds of her beauty to Washes and the Patch-box; she mightily frequents the Raffling-shops, very shy of allowing her Favours; but the present of Silver Furniture for her Chamber may mollifie her, which will cost you but—20 lbs.

c. From Aphra Behn, *The Rover* (1677)

[Anything that brings about the collapse of the wall separating one image from the other is likely to produce scandal. While most jilts were portrayed as calculating, rational agents, female desire is far from being contained in a few representations. Her repressed sexuality may return, as in Aphra Behn's *The Rover*, where the Spanish courtesan, Angellica Bianca, is depicted as succumbing to the charms of the English rake, Willmore, in a way that leads her to contemplate violent revenge.]

> Angellica. Love that has robbed [my heart] of its unconcern,
> Of all that pride has taught me how to value it.
> And in its room

A mean submissive passion was conveyed,
That made me humbly bow, which I ne'er did
To any thing but Heaven.

d. From Eliza Haywood, *The City Jilt* (1726)

[Or the reverse may occur: the abandonment of a woman by her lover may lead to her metamorphosis into a steely-minded dissembler, willing to resort to almost any means in order to wreak vengeance on her seducer. In Eliza Haywood's *The City Jilt*, Glicera, the daughter of an eminent tradesman, is abandoned by her lover, Melledore. Intent upon securing payback, Glicera displays no scruples in jilting with false promises of sexual favors the amorous dotard, Alderman Grubgard, so that she can secure the means to purchase the mortgage of the improvident Melledore's estate.]

IF I encouraged thy Addresses, or accepted thy Gifts, 'twas but to punish thy impudent Presumption.—I raised thy hopes to make thy Fall from them at once more shocking, and receiv'd thy Presents by way of Payment, for the pains I have taken to reform thee, which sure, if not incorrigible, this Treatment will.

[Glicera's plot succeeds and she later responds without feeling to the news of the ruined and penitent Melledore's death in combat abroad.]

Glicera being in a State of happy Indifference, heard the News of his Death without any Emotions either of Joy or Grief: And having now a sufficient Competency to maintain her for her Life, gave over all Designs on the Men, publickly avowing her Aversions to that Sex; and admitting no Visits from any of them, but such as she was very certain had not Inclination to make an amorous Declaration to her, either on honourable or dishonourable Terms.

Appendix C: First- versus Third-Person Narrative

1. First-Person Narrative: from Mary Carleton, *The Case of Mary Carleton* (1663)

[The choice of narrative mode can dictate the way a morally compromising situation is interpreted. A first-person narrative, like *The London Jilt*, can be a means by which readers are encouraged to identify imaginatively with a character whose actions they are likely to regard as blameworthy. In her brief memoir, *The Case of Mary Carleton*, Mary Carleton, the "German Princess," uses this narrative technique to evoke sympathy for her plight even as she admits culpability in a scheme in which she lured John Carleton into marriage by pretending to be titled and wealthy.]

WHAT harme have I done in pretending to great Titles? Ambition and Affection of Greatness to good and just purposes was always esteemed and accounted laudable and praiseworthy, and the sign and character of a vertuous mind, nor do I think it an unjust purpose in me to contrive my own advancement by such illustrious pretences as they say I made use of.

[...]

I come now to the matter of fact, the first place I touched at was *Gravesend*,[1] where I arrived towards the end of *March*, and without any stay took a Tide-boat [and] came to *London* in company with a Parson or Minister, who officiously, but I suppose out of design, gave me the trouble of his service and attendance to the *Exchange-Tavern* right against the *Stocke*,[2] betwixt the *Poultry*[3] and *Cornhil*,[4] the house of one Mr. *King*, not having any knowledge of the Master or his acquaintance, and free, God knows from any design, for I would have entred any other house if I had found the doors open, or could have raised

---

1 Kentish borough on the Thames that was a favourite resort for Londoners.
2 The pillory.
3 A continuation of Cheapside, named for the poulterers.
4 The highest hill inside the city.

the folks nearer to my landing, for I was distempered with the nights passage; but it was so early in the morning, five a clock, that there was no body stirring elsewhere, onely here by mishap *Mr. King* himself was up and standing at the Bar, telling of brass farthings, whom the Parson desired to fill a pint of wine, which he readily performed, and brought to a room behinde the Bar. While the wine was a drinking, (which was Rhenish wine, the complement being put upon me by the Parson as the fruit of my own happy Country) Sir *John* [Carleton, Senior] very rudely began to accost me, and to offer some incivilities to me, which I found no other way to avoid, then by pretending want of rest to the Master of the house, and acquainting him with my charge of Jewels, and that I was as I do justifie my self to be a person of Quality. Hereupon a room was provided for me to repose myself in, and the Clergyman took his leave with a troublesome promise of waiting upon me another day to give me a visit, which I was forced to admit, & to tell him, I would leave word where-ever I went; but he considering as I suppose of the unfeasibleness of his desires, and the publiqueness of the place, neglected his promise and troubled me no more.

He being gone, *Mr. King* began to question me, what Country woman I was, and of what Religion, I frankly told him; and acquainted him with all what charge I had about me, which to secure from the danger of the Town, that was full of cozenage and villany, he advised me to stay with him till I could better provide for my self.

I rested my self here till eleven a clock at noon: when I arose, and was very civilly treated by *Mr. King*, who well knowing I was a stranger and well furnished with money, omitted no manner of respect to me, nor did I spend parcimoniously, and at an ordinary rate, but answerable to the quality and account, at their fetching and itching questions, I gave of my self.

This invited him earnestly, with all submissive address to request my staying with them till I had dispatched, and had provided all things for my publique appearance, for the better furnishing and equipping whereof, I acquainted Him I would send by Post to my Steward, for the return of some moneys to defray the expences thereof, which Letters he viewed, and conceived such imaginations in his Head thereupon, that it never left working till it had wrought the effect of his finely begun, and hopefully continued Enterprise.

These Letters he himself delivered at my desire, to have them carefully put into the Male [sic], to the Post-House; and thereafter observed me with most manifest respects. In the *Interim* of the return of these moneys, I was slightly, and as it were by the by, upon discourse of my Country (wherein they took occasion to be liberally copious) engaged into some discovery of my self, my estate and quality, and the nature of both, the causes of my coming hither, &c. but I did it so unconcernedly, and negligently, as a matter of no moment or disturbance to me, though I had hinted at the discontent of my match, that this did assure them that all was real, and therefore it was time to secure my estate to them by a speedy and secret marriage.

Let the World now judge, whither being prompted by such plain and publique signes of a design upon me, to counterplot them, I have done any more then what the Rule, and a received principle of Justice directs: *to deceive the deceiver, is no deceit.*

I knew not nevertheless, which way their Artifices tended, till Master *King*, brought into my acquaintance old Mr. *Carleton* his Father in Law, and soon after Mr. *John Carleton* his Son: it seems it had been consulted, to have preferred *George* the Elder Brother: He troubled with a simple modesty, and a mind no way competent to so much greatness, was laid aside, and the younger flusht and encouraged to set upon me. By this time they had obtained my Name from me, *viz. Maria de Wolway*, which passage also hath suffered by another leuder Imposture, and allusory sound of *De Vulva*: in the language of which I am better versed, then to pick out no civiller and eleganter impress.[1]

To the Addresses of Mr. *John Carleton*, I carried my self with so much indifference, not superciliously refusing his visits, or readily admitting his suit, not disheartening him with a severe retiredness, or challenges of his imparity,[2] nor encouraging him with afreedom or openness of Heart, or arrogance of my own condition, that he and his friends were upon the spur to consummate the match, which yet I delayed and dissembled with convenient pretences, but herein I will be more particular in the ensuing Pages.

In the mean while, to prevent all notice of me, and the disturbance of their proceedings, that might be occasioned thereby, they kept me close in the nature of a Prisoner, which though I perceived, yet I made no semblance thereof at all, but colluded with them in their own arts, and pretended some aversness to all

---

1 Imprint, expression (obscure).
2 Inequality.

company, but onely my enamourate,[1] Mr. *Carleton*: nor was any body else suffered to come near me, or to speak with me; Insomuch, as I have bin informed, that they promised 209 *l.* to one *Sackvil*, whom for his advice, they had too forwardly, as they thought imparted the business, the sum of 200 *l.* to be silent, lest that it should be heard at Court, and so the Estate and Honour which they had already swallowed, would be lost from their Son, and seized by some Courtier, who should next come to hear of this great Lady.

After many visits passed betwixt Mr. *Carleton* and my self, Old Mr. *Carleton* and Mr. *King* came to me, and very earnestly pressed the dispatch of the Marriage, and that I would be pleased to give my Assent, setting forth with all the qualities and great sufficiencies of that Noble person, as they pleased to stile him. I knew what made them so urgent, for they had now seen the answers I had received by the Post, by which I was certified of the receipt of mine, and that accordingly some thousands of Crowns should be remitted instantly to *London*, and Coach and Horses sent by the next Shipping, with other things I had sent for, and to reinforce this their *commendamus*[2] the more effectually, they acquainted me, that if I did not presently grant the suit, and their request, Mr. *Carleton* was so far in love with me, that he would make away with himself, or presently travail[3] beyond Sea, and see *England* no more.

I cannot deny, but that I could hardly forbear smiling, to see how serious these *Elders* and *Brokers* were in this *Love-killing* story, but keeping to my business, after some demurs and demands, I seemed not to consent, and then they began passionately, urging me with other stories, some of which long repetition I will now insert:

Wednesday the first of *April*, Mrs. *King* made a great Feast, where were divers persons of quality, as she said, amongst the rest, her Brother Mr. *John Carleton*. At which entertainment Mrs. *King* did advise me to call her Cozen, the which I did. *Thursday* the second of *April*, Mr. *John Carleton* came in his Coach, with two Footmen attending on him, calling him my *Lord*, and Mrs. *King* did also call him my *Lord*. With that I asked Mrs. *King*, if it was not the same person that dined with us yesterday; she said,

---

1 Lover (obscure).
2 Commendation (legal term).
3 Travel.

True, it was so, but he was in a Disguise then, and withal, that in a humour he would often do so: *But*, saith she, *I do assure you he is a Lord*. Upon that I replied, *Then his father must be an Earl, if living*. She affirmed, that he was a person of great honour. The same time my Lord presented me with a rich box of Sweetmeats: I could do no less then thankfully accept thereof.

[...]

I was altogether ignorant of what estate my Husband was, and therefore made no nicety to take those places his friends gave me, and if I be taxed for incivility herein, it was his fault that he instructed me no better in my quality, for I conceited[1] still that he was some landed, honorable and wealthy man.

Things yet went fairly on, the same observances, and distances continued, and lodgings befitting a person of Quality taken for me in *Durham Yard*,[2] at one Mr. *Greens*, where my husband and I enjoyed one another with mutual complacency, till the return of the moneys out of *Germany* failing the day and their rich hopes, old Mr. *Carleton* began to suspect he was deceived in his expectation, and that all was not gold that glistered: but to remove such a prejudice from himself, as if he were the Authour of those scandals that were now prepared against my innocence, a Letter is produced, and sent from some then unknown hand, which reflected much upon my Honour and Reputation; and thereupon on the fifth or sixth of *May* ensuing, I was by a Warrant dragged forth of my new Lodgings, with all the disgrace and contumely that could be cast upon the vilest offender in the World, at the instigation of old Mr. *Carleton*, who was the Prosecutor, and by him and his Agents devested and stript of all my cloaths, and plundred of all my jewels, and my money, my very bodyes, and a payr of silk Stockings, being also pulled from me, and in a strange array carried before a Justice.

2. Third-Person Narrative: from Francis Kirkman, *The Counterfeit Lady Unveiled* (1673)

[If a first-person narrative tends to provide a dynamic and apparently sympathetic representation of motives and actions, the

---

1 Conceived, apprehended (obsolete).
2 On the north side of the Strand, formerly the residence of the bishops of Durham.

third-person narrative can be used to deflect our attention from the agent to the act and to encourage us to pass judgment on the erring wrongdoer. In *The Counterfeit Lady Unveiled*, a criminal biography of Mary Carleton, Francis Kirkman inserts a lengthy extract from the narrative quoted above and then follows it with a third-person account and burlesque romantic ballad intended to supplant Mary Carleton's voice. Kirkman acknowledges the cupidity and gullibility of the Carleton family but also seeks to affirm Mary Carleton's guilt as well. To encourage the reader to become both judge and jury, Kirkman supplements his third-person prose narrative with a satirical ballad.]

THUS have you read her Case, as she her self relates it, and by this you may see how this Cheat was managed on both sides *Carleton*, and his Friends were as Covetous as she was Cunning, how she contrived to have answer of her Letters from the Forreign Post, which coming to their hands blinded them, and caused them to imagine her no less then a Princess; I know not but these Letters were her Master-peice; It was this that was the best Card in the whole Pack. They had seen her Jewels before as her Landlady told her Brother *Carleton*.

Jewels she hath as sanguine Ruby,
Onix and Saphyr with a blew dye
Diamond and Topas with the Opal
Emerald and Agate Turquex: take all
What shall I say she hath Gems in plenty
Pray enter on her Rome is empty.

The sight of these Jewels were enough to perswade an easie Soul to great matters, but when the Letters come that mentioned thousands of Crowns, and a Coach and Horses, they were all then Cock a hoop,[1] and stark[2] nothing then but clapping up[3] of a Marriage was discoursed of; but her Landlord was mistaken in his opinion of this *German* Princess, for no less did he take her to be, and therefore being very desirous to advance his Brother *John Carleton*, the Father, Mother, and all the Friends sat in close Consultation.

Their Daddy, Mammy, Friend and Knight,
In Judgement one did all Unite

---

1 Drunk, reckless, as in having abandoned all inhibition.
2 Inflexible, stern.
3 Imprisoning, with little formality, or delay.

And did agree without long tarry
That Knight should Lady Princesse Marry.
But as the Counsel was adjourning,
The Lady Sister entered Mourning,
Acquainting them that Forreigne Knight
With Cole black hair and eyes like spright,
Had at the house enquiry made
For German Princess, and like Blade
Or Gallant, A la Mode did Swear
That Heart from Body he would Tear
Of him that durst Crack Princess Nut,
Or dare with her to go to Rut,
And wheresoere he found the Man
Should dare to Usher Princess hand,
Withal head give two hundred pound
Princess to see on English ground,
That he might Carry her to Cullen[1]
With greater Joy then Anne *from Bullen.[2]*

This Message, if it were true, must needs amaze and terrifie them all much more when it was seconded by another Alarum: Letters sent to enquire of her.
They finding fresh pursuit by Letters
To find out Princess though in Fetters,
With promise fresh to give more mony
To him should tell where lay dear hony.

All these passages how contrived I know not, but it put them all upon the Spur to finish the Marriage, which as you have read, was Celebrated at Great St. *Bartholomews,*[3] And then
They drove away to place called Barnet,[4]
And with them took a friend called Garnet,
Where being come they fell a eating, And hungry, All threw Wine and
*   Meat in*
Like Misers at a City Feast
That eat ten Meals, nine at least;

---

1 Cologne.
2 An allusion to Anne Boleyn (1504-36), who was married to Henry VIII (1491-1547) and subsequently beheaded for adultery.
3 Chapel of St. Bartholomew's Hospital in West Smithfield.
4 Village in Hertfordshire, subsequently incorporated into greater London.

At length their Guts being stuff'd with food,
And all being set on merry Mood,
They did begin to Dance and Caper,
Like Poppet [1] *made up with brown paper.*
Princess began a German *Dance,*
And Friend to Buff [2] *like Mars did Prance.*
The Lord did Dance in order meet,
And Elder Brother on's bare feet,
An Ancient Custome where young Cit,
Before his Elder—doth hit.
At length the Couple went to Bed
And Cap was put on young Lords head
The Posset [3] *too of Sack was eaten,*
And Stocking thrown too (all besweaten)
Which Ceremonies being ended,
And that days work by all Commended,
The Elder Brother and his Friend,
Bid him Ride soft to's Journys end,
Wishing them sport at very heart,
They left the Lord at Princess Mart.

Our young Lord being thus assured of his Princely Bride, was
very well pleased, but so was not his Father, who like a grave Pol-
litician, thought fit first to secure her Person better by a second
Marriage, for the first being done on haste, was without a
Licence, and secondly he intended to secure her Estate by a
Writing drawn to that purpose, which was offered her to Seal, as
thus you have it.

When house was cleared of all but Friends,
On Princess there was further ends
Intended to be done in instance,
Married to be again with Licence
For to prevent the Lawyers bawl;
In Court Ecclesiastical,
The which was done, and then Old Sir,
With Instrument well drawn Suns blur.
Reciting Princess Earth in hand,
And personal goods about to land,

---

1 Doll, puppet.
2 Puff out.
3 A drink composed of hot milk curdled with ale, wine, or other liquor.

Desiring the sum might be made over,
To Lord his Son and her great Lover,
To this he hoped sheed not be shie
Being to prevent Mortalitie,
Sir Quoth the Princess, I'le consult
My Pillow and give you result,
But till I die, I think not fit,
To part with State, or wealth one bit,
Besides your Son's to me but light wood,
And hant received Honor of Knighthood,
Though in regard of my high Birth,
He's called Lord with Cap to the earth,
And Judge pray Sir when Friends Arrive,
And see their Princess Scriveners Wife.
Wilt not disparage high Discent,
As Garters in Rump Parliament. [1]
Like Child rebuk'd crying for knife,
Stood Father without Soul or Life,
Or without Fodder Cow in pound,
Or Ape in Chain with Whip scourged round,
At length he spake to Princess face
With homespun Language Coblers grace;
May it please your Highness Daughter I
No harm did think most verily,
Quoth she, pray Sir, no more of this,
We do forgive what is a misse,
And for to satisfie your Will,
Time and his Love shall it fulfil.

Ah witty Baggage, she had her answer as ready as they their question, and still she carried her self in all actions with such bravery,
that they had not the least suspicion, for the old man being fully
satisfied, let loose some of his old angels, furnished her with
Cloaths, as she her self hath related, and her Husband *Carleton*
told me within these few days, that the whole expense upon this
account did cost 160*l.* and this was all spent in one Months time,
for no longer did they live together, the occasion she hath already
told you, was by a Letter, and so saith her Husband, and I believe
it so to be, but some say it was by a Shoemaker that coming to

---

1   Name given to the Long Parliament of 1648, after the House of Lords
    was abolished in Pride's Purge.

make her Shoes, knew her when she had lived with her Husband
Stedman; that she knew him, and took no notice but sent him
away angry, wherefore he
Contrived in his Horny Pate,
Malice against the Lords Bed-Mate.
And hereupon one day waiting for our Lord and his Princess
   return from *Hide Park*,
where they were gone to aire themselves;
At coming home unto their Court,
St. Hugh to Lord did strait resort,
Told him he could relate sad Story
Would make him weep in all his glory,
And curse the time that ever be,
His Hawk at Hobby[1] did set flee,[2]
Enough to put him into lax,
Not to be staid by Coblers wax.[3]
The Knight did wonder what he meant,
And pray'd him to declare intent.
Of his address, for he did make
His teeth to Chatter, knees to shake,
Why then quoth he, your Lady Gay
Is Kentish *breed, and Crowders spray,[4]*
And Married is to a Shoemaker,
That is no Cobler nor Translator,
And hath to boot (tak't not in dudgeon)[5]
Another Husband called a Surgeon,
And you in order make the third,
And Princess is not worth a —

This must needs be heavy news to our young Lord, but whither
the discovery was made by this Shoemaker or the aforesaid
Letter, matters not much, but her husband tells me, that she her
self attempted it several times her self to him, for she would be
melancholy, and say she neither desired nor deserved that attendance, and great expence, and that she was undone unless he
would pitty her; and many broken speeches out of which he
might, but at present did not, pick out her meaning, for although
he did not believe her to be a Princess, yet he was very confident

---

1 A species of falcon.
2 Flight. No hawk dares fly as high as the hobby.
3 Thick resinous compound used by shoemakers.
4 One who plays a crowd.
5 Anger, resentment.

that she was a Lady of that Name and quallity which she had named her self to be; as for her Estate he never enquired what and where it was, but did not question but some she had, and that considerable; but however he does protest to me that he loved her not so much out of respect of that, as her good parts, with which she was plentifully stored, and knowing how in all Companies to demean her self so, that it was clearly her person and parts that he esteemed her for, neither could it be expected he should look for much, for he was very young, not full 19. years old, he followed his own inclinations as to her person, and the advice of his Friends as to her Estate, they had examined that as much as they durst, or indeed could. But in conclusion, thus they found themselves outwitted, she not what they expected, and then their anger and revenge caused their carriage to her to be very coarse, and indeed scurvy, as she hath already, and I shall once again relate it.

The Lackey-Boy was sent away
To Father and to Mother; Nay,
His Sister too, the good Match-maker,
Of Story true must be Partaker:
Who being come, the Lord did tell
His sad mischance, which made 'em yell,
And to exclaim 'gainst German *Lady*
That had abus'd poor little Baby.
At last they went into Bed-Chamber,
Where Princess lay like Dog in Manger,
Till aged Sir did her importune
The truth to tell, if such a Fortune,
Or where she was a German Princesse,
Or who had taken her by th' Inches
'Fore Son did enter Lower Quarters,
Or who wore Senior Coblers *Garters*
When he did Marry her in Church,
And who she lam'd and brought to Crutch;[1]
And who it was besides did scrub her,
And what the Surgeon was did probe her.
This fierce assault did make the Lady
To stand as mute as Joynted Baby,
And was surpriz'd to hear the Gabble
Of this connext and joyned Rabble,

---

1 Staff for an infirm person.

By which the Women thought her guilty,
With hand and knee they hilty tilty[1]
Most shamefully did her assault,
Which made her Royal Back to halt,
Whilst antedated Lord stood by,
And like Boy whipt did sob and cry:
At last Old Man as fierce as Hector,
Having more of Henbane then of Nectar
Lay'd hands upon the Ladies Garments,
Jewels and Rings, and her Attirements,
And Gouty Shank was held aloff:
And new Silk-Stocking, plucked off:
In fine, they stript her to her Smock,
So fine, you might have seen her Nock.[2]
Then much despis'd by bawling Litter,
Which made before their Chops to twitter.
When all Indignities were over,
In German Vest *they did her cover,*
With Justacore[3] *and a Night-Rayle,*
And Petticoat all black to th' tayle,
The same reserved by Ships Master,
When she escaped from forraign Cloyster,
Thence brought 'fore Godfrey not of Bullion,[4]
For this did use her like a Scullion;[5]
And so by Beadle fell and Hostile,
He sent her to the Gate-house Bastille:
Where being come, the Gates flew open
For to receive Dutch Fro Van Slopen,[6]
As great Companion come to dwell
In Prison close much like to Hell.
The noise of Princes close restraint,
Sent Persons great to hear her Plaint
But when they heard her to discourse,
They netled were like Pamper'd Horse;
And did applaud her high-bred Parts,

---

1 The phrase is unknown.
2 Cleft in the buttocks.
3 A loose wrap or jacket worn by a woman, usually after dressing.
4 Probably alluding to Geoffrey of Vinsauf (fl. 1200), author of the *Poetria Nova* (circa 1210).
5 Domestic servant of the lowest rank.
6 The allusion is obscure.

Not to be equaliz'd at Marts,
Or Ladies some with face like Maple,
That spend their time in tittle-tattle,
With great respect they did her treat,
And sent in Money, Wine and Meat,
And Bribes to Keeper to be civil,
As he that Candle holds to Devil:
Where I will leave her to her Fate,
Still great, though in confin'd estate:
And for her high-conceited Lord,
When Reputation he had scor'd
On Tick and borrow, then he went
To Chamber where he Body pent,
Believing German *Knight would call*
His Lordship to account for all
His base abusing Princely Dame,
And using her with so much shame:
And Parents full with shame and ire,
Did mope and dote like Cats by Fire.

Appendix D: Attribution

1. From Alexander Oldys, *The Female Gallant* (1692)

[In his *List of English Tales and Prose Romances* (1912), Arundell Esdaile attributed *The London Jilt* to Alexander Oldys, confusing it with Oldys's *The Female Gallant* (1692), which had as its subtitle, *The London Jilt: or, the Female Cuckold*. In spite of Esdaile's obvious mistake, however, the ascription of *The London Jilt* to Oldys has been preserved in library catalogues to this day. The vastly different style and substance of the opening section of *The Female Gallant* suggests, however, that Oldys is unlikely to have been the author of the 1683 *London Jilt*.]

SIR *Beetlehead Gripely* liv'd in a great, ugly, old-fashioned House, somewhere in the City; in a Place almost as Obscure as That of his Birth, and *as dark as his Deeds*; and was a Money Scrivener,[1] which (as I am told) is a *devillish good Occupation*. In this he got, within the Space of Seven Years, an Estate of near 12000 *l.* and purchased him a Wife of his own Houshold, worth twice as much for her incomparable Qualities, had she been expos'd to Sale at a more convenient Market. Her Unmarried Names (I won't say her *Maiden Names*, though she was his Chamber-maid) were *Winny Wagtail*, of the Great and Notorious Family of the *Wagtails* in *Castle-street*, near *Long Acre*, not far from the Square, where, at present, I have an Apartment: But, upon her Marriage to Sir Beetlehead, she was Dignify'd and Distinguish'd by the Name and Quality of The Lady *Gripely*; by whom the Knight had Issue only *Philandra*; a Lady of most Prodigious and Various Qualifications.

When she was about Eight Years old she went twice a Week, besides *Sundays*, to hear either the Painful Mr. *B*..... Mr. *D*...... or Mr. *F*.... where she would Sigh and Weep as heartily, as if she were already in Love and Despair; and would sing Psalms till she was e'en Black in the Face again for want of Breath.—(Is not that better than to say she sung like a Nightingale? for I never heard a Nightingale sing Psalms.) These Acquisitions (doubtless) she had from her Observation of the Pious Lady her Mother, who (possibly) had been one of the *Sweet Singers of*

---

1 One who receives or lends money at interest.

Israel.[1] At least, we cannot doubt that she was *always one of the Family of Love.*[2] At Twelve Years of Age, the Beautiful and Zealous *Philandra* could tell who was the Fairest, who the Strongest, and who the Wisest Man, which I hope she has not yet forgot; since they were all for her Turn, especially the last; for he had most Love, most Money, and most Honour. At Thirteen she could say all *Perkin's* Catechism[3] by Rote, both Questions and Answers; and could give as good an Account of all the Sermons she heard, as any of those that preached 'em. Besides, she had a most Rapacious Apprehension, and Tenacious Memory of all the newest Jests and Songs about Town and Court; could quote you any part of the Academy of Complements, as readily as her Teachers did the Scripture, and apply it more properly, and with less Abuse. At Fourteen she was sent to the Boarding-School at *Hackney,*[4] not without the Tutelage of an Old Aunt by her Father's side, who died in less than a Twelve Month's Time of a Surfeit of those Vanities she daily saw there. After which, the Niece improv'd to a Miracle in all the Arts of Gallantry: Though, to give her her due, she was at *First* a very good Proficient in either of 'em; but now, all on a suddain, she became most perfect in all, in each, and singular of 'em. When she sung, the Angels would stand listening to her with their Fingers in their Mouths: What then d'you think poor Men would do? Why (Faith) nothing but hold their peace, that they might the better hear her; and silently wish, that they had the spoiling of so good a Voice. When she Danc'd, the Sparks have sworn that she was Begotten by *Mercury:*[5] And I am apt to believe it; for, Men say her Father was a Thief by his Vocation,—But their Reason was, because she mov'd, as if she had Wings at her Feet. When she Writ a *Billette doux,*[6] she did it with more Elegancy and Tenderness than

---

1 Sect demanding strict adherence to Hebrew in English translations of Holy Scripture. Its members sought for abolition of chapter and line numbers from the books of the Bible and meter from the Psalms.
2 Sect founded in 1540, advocating a belief in the inner light. However, as it is used here, the phrase also suggests lewd women, whores (slang).
3 Catechism formulated in the late sixteenth century by the Puritan theologian William Perkins (1558-1602).
4 Village east of London that acquired a reputation for gaiety and pleasurable activities.
5 A person having attributes ascribed to Mercury; here, the attributes of a dexterous thief.
6 French: love letter or note. The phrase is usually spelt "billet doux."

Madam *Scaron* [or *Maintenon*].[1] When she Dictated to Madam *Montespan*,[2] the Letters she writ to *Louis Le Grand*. In short, she had an abundance of Grace in all her Words and Actions, but the Devil a bit in all her Thoughts. Yet this I am oblig'd to say for her, that, notwithstanding all these Egregious Acquisitions, and Extraordinary Imbellishments, she was not *Spiritually* Proud though the World may believe, by the Sequel, that she was *Carnally* Proud; witness the several Intrigues she had at the Chaste Boarding-School, before she came to Converse in this Leud Town and Court: Not that she ever *finish'd* one, till about the Eighteenth Year of her Tyranny. As to her Person, she was really very Beautiful, being extreamly like our late Famous Dutchess now in *France*,[3] as nearly resembling her as the Knight of *Tunbridge*,[4] or my self, resemble the Figure of the late Incomparable *Scaron*;[5] and she was as Cunning as t'other for the Heart of her.

2. From *The London Bully* (1683)

[A more plausible candidate for the authorship of *The London Jilt* is the anonymous author of *The London Bully*, a first-person picaresque narrative also published in 1683, albeit by a different bookseller. Even though it lacks the authorial reflections that are a distinctive feature of the jilt's narrative, the following episode in which the youthful narrator agrees to serve for one night as a secret substitute in bed with his master's wife is similar in tone and style to *The London Jilt*.]

DURING the time of my leading this pleasant life, there happened to me a very strange Accident; for my Master having made an Intrigue with a Woollen Drapers Wife, which I had discovered some time before, though I did not seem to take notice of it; in

---

1 Françoise d'Aubigné (1635-1719) first married the French poet and novelist, Paul Scarron (1610-1660). After his death, she became the governess of the children of Louis XIV (1638-1715) and later married him in secret.

2 Françoise-Athenéc, marquise de Montespan (1641-1707), a mistress of Louis XIV.

3 Barbara Villiers, Duchess of Cleveland, formerly mistress of Charles II.

4 Turnbridge Wells located in west Kent, just north of the border with east Sussex.

5 Paul Scarron, author of plays, poems, and novels, especially *Le Roman comique* (1651).

the mean while it happened that that honest Cuckold was obliged to go into the Countrey upon some Business he had there, my Master having notice of it immediately, and not being willing to let slip so fair an occasion to enjoy the Delights which he was in hopes of from his Mistress, he was contriving all the Means imaginable to bring this Affair to pass, for his Wife was too jealous, and would quickly have smelt out the business, if he had absented himself for a whole night from his house and home: Thus one Afternoon he commanded me to accompany him to go dress a Patient; in the way he began to speak to me of such things as put me in a maze; he told me he had a thing to request of me, which *I must not refuse him, and that I must take an Oath to comply with, and obey his Desires and Order.* I made him Answer, *That I was ready to do all for him, provided no ill might come thereof, and that I would most willingly confirm to him my fidelity by the greatest Oaths imaginable.*

Whereupon he spake thus to me; *Dear* Will. *You know how much Affection I have always bore you, and what freedom I have always allowed you; wherefore, methinks, you ought to acknowledge my kindness by some good piece of Service which I demand of you. Know then, that I am obliged to go lie this Evening in a certain place, and that my Wife may not take notice of it, you shall lie by her side in my place; to the doing of which, I will furnish you with an opportunity, but upon condition of observing punctually these three Articles; First of all, You shall not speak to her one word: As for the Second, you shall not touch her in any manner: And Thirdly, You shall rise before day, that I may get in as soon as you open the Shop.* I was so amazed at this Proposition, that I had hardly the power to give him an Answer; but seeing at length that he was absolutely resolved on it, and that he demanded it as it were by force, I granted him his Request, swearing to him to perform all that he commanded me.

Hereupon we returned together to our House; when, as soon as my Master came in, he began to quarrel with his Wife, and to chide her more than I had ever heard him do before; which he did, that he might have a pretence not to speak to her the Night following, and quash all her desires of hugging him.

After this, he commanded me in a surly manner to rise betimes on the morrow Morning; adding, that he would rise early himself, upon some extraordinary Affairs he had: Then he continued to grumble and to play the Mad-man all the Afternoon, and as soon as his Wife would have spoke a word, he bid her hold her peace and get her gone to bed. In short, he made use of all such things as he judged necessary for the executing his Design.

The poor Woman went away to bed all bathed in tears, and the Maid was constrained to do the like. In the mean while he called for me to undress him, for form sake; and pulling off his Coat, he hit one Sleeve of it against the Candle, which went out, and fell upon the floor with the Candlestick: I asked him if I should go light it? But he took me up crabbedly; that I easily perceived he had done it on purpose.

Being thus in the dark, he stole away softly, and left me trembling by the Bedside; however, I took courage, and after I had undress'd my self, I went to Bed, lying as far off from the Woman as was possible; but I fell again to trembling every moment, for fear she should discover the Trick. In the mean while, the Woman crept nigh me by little and little, and every time she stirr'd, I was like to die for fear. But do but think of the extremity I was in when she began to handle my Arms; Ile assure you I was possessed with a mortal terror; I took her hand away, but she imagining this was only some remnants of her Husbands Anger, fell again to handling and taking it by the Head: Said she, *How, my little Rogue, is it not better to live in good intelligence and repose, than to quarrel and be always in an anger against one another?*

When I perceiv'd she found no alteration in that part, I took heart of Oak, and did the Feat without saying a word, notwithstanding all the Caresses this woman made me.

This first Course was performed with so much satisfaction on my side, that I renewed it four or five times, until that she was desirous to take her rest, as she did accordingly. I got up early on the morrow Morning, and after having dressed my self, I opened the Door, and saw my Master coming just in the Nick; he asking me immediately *if all were well, and if I had kept my word?* I answered him, that *I had*; swearing once more, *that I had not spoke a word to his Wife*; for the poor Cuckold was very far from believing that I had fitted him with a pair of Brow-Anclets in so great a Silence.

My Mistress being got up, went immediately to embrace her Husband, and coax'd him the best she was able; the Husband too shewed himself more tractable after having spent the Night so pleasantly; insomuch that all things were very well reconciled. About Noon the Mistress went to the Market, and bought the best she could find; for she had a mind to treat her Husband for so many Caresses she had received from him the Night past. My Master and I were in the Shop when his wife return'd home laden with a great many Delicacies; which my Master not being at all satisfied with, ask'd her after a surly manner, *Why she was at so much Costs?* and if she had invited any Friends to Dinner? *No, my Dear,* said the Woman to him, *I do it for the love of you, and to repair your strength, which is undoubtedly very much lessened by the last Nights work, and wholly to confirm the Peace we have made this Night. Do you believe then,* reparti'd my Master, *that I kissed you to night; But my dear Puggie,* reply'd the Woman, *to what purpose is all this dissimulation? you know very well you did it to Night five or six Bouts, though indeed without speaking a word; wherefore prithee Chuckie, let me desire thee to lay aside thy Anger, and let us make merry and chear our selves together: If we are at peace, all will go well, and there will be nothing but Love and Peace in the House.* My good Cuckold was wholly in a Maze, and did easily guess at the truth of the Matter; but what remedy? he himself was the cause thereof: Nevertheless he fail'd not to shew by his looks that he was sorry, and that he would reward me to some purpose; but I was too cunning, for I had no mind to stay there any longer.

Select Bibliography

Anon. *Advice to the Women and Maidens of London*. London: Benjamin Billingsley, 1678.

Anon. *A Catalogue of Jilts*. London: Printed for R.W., 1691.

Anon. *The German Princess Revived or The London Jilt: Being a True Account of the Life and Death of Jenny Voss*. London: George Croom, 1684.

Anon. *The London Bully*. London: Printed by Henry Clark for Thomas Malthus, 1683.

Apperson, George Latimer. *English Proverbs and Proverbial Phrases: A Historical Dictionary*. London: Dent, 1929.

Behn, Aphra. *The Rover*. London: John Amery, 1677.

——. *The Younger Brother; or, The Amorous Jilt*. London: J. Harris, 1696.

Brett-James, Norman G. *The Growth of Stuart London*. London: Allen and Unwin, 1935.

Carleton, Mary. *The Case of Mary Carleton, lately stiled the German Princess*. London: Sam Speed, 1663.

Cervantes Saavedra, Miguel de. *The history of Don-Quichote; the first parte*. Trans. Thomas Shelton. London: Ed. Blounte, 1620.

——. *The history of the renown'd Don Quixote de la Mancha*. Trans by several hands and published by Peter Motteux. London: Sam Buckley, 1700.

Chalfant, Fran C. *Ben Jonson's London: A Jacobean Placename Dictionary*. Athens: U of Georgia P, 1978.

Davenport, Millia. *The Book of Costume*. New York: Crown, 1948.

Defoe, Daniel. *Moll Flanders*. Ed. Albert Rivero. New York: Norton, 2004.

——. *Roxana: The Fortunate Mistress*. Ed. John Mullan. Oxford: Oxford UP, 1996.

Esdaile, Arundell. *A List of English Tales and Prose Romances Printed before 1740*. London: Bibliographical Society, 1912.

Faubion, James, ed. *Aesthetics, Method and Epistemology*. New York: The New Press, 1998. Vol. 2 of *The Essential Works of Michel Foucault, 1954-1984*. 3 vols. to date. 1997-.

Friedman, Edward H. *The Antiheroine's Voice: Narrative Discourse and Transformations of the Picaresque*. Columbia: U of Missouri P, 1987.

Grose, Francis. *A Classical Dictionary of the Vulgar Tongue*. Ed. Eric Partridge. New York: Freeport, 1963.

Harben, Henry A. *A Dictionary of London*. London: Herbert Jenkins, 1918.

Haywood, Eliza. *The City Jilt; or the Alderman Turn'd Beau: A Secret History*. London: J. Roberts, 1726.

Head, Richard. *The English Rogue. Volume 1*. London: Francis Kirkman, 1666.

Henke, James T. *Courtesans and Cuckolds: A Glossary of Renaissance Bawdy (exclusive of Shakespeare)*. New York: Garland, 1979.

———. *Gutter Life and Language in the Early 'Street' Literature of England: A Glossary of Terms and Topics Chiefly of the Sixteenth and Seventeenth Centuries*. West Cornwall: Locust, 1988.

Hinnant, Charles H. "*Moll Flanders*, *Roxana* and First-Person Female Narratives: Models and Prototypes." *The Eighteenth-Century Novel*, 4 (2004): 39-72.

Kirkman, Francis. *The Counterfeit Lady Unveiled*. London: Peter Parker, 1673.

———. *The English Rogue. Volume 3*. London: Francis Kirkman, 1665.

Kittredge, Katherine. *Lewd and Notorious: Female Transgression in the Eighteenth Century*. Ann Arbor: U of Michigan P, 2003.

Lessing, Gotthold Ephraim. *Laocoon: An Essay Upon the Limits of Painting and Poetry*. Trans. Ellen Frothingham. New York: Noonday, 1961.

Maurer, A., and F.M. Stenton. *The Place Names of Sussex*. Cambridge: Cambridge UP, 1929-30.

Mowry, Melissa M. *The Bawdy Politic in Stuart England, 1660-1714: Political Pornography and Prostitution*. London: Ashgate, 2004.

Oldys, Alexander. *The Female Gallant*. London: Printed for Samuel Briscoe, 1692.

Oxford English Dictionary Online. Oxford: Oxford UP, 2005 (http://www.oed.com).

Pallavicino, Ferrante. *The Whore's Rhetoric*. Trans. and adapted anonymously. London: George Shell, 1683. Trans. of *Rhetorica della Putane*, 1642.

Picard, Liza. *Restoration London*. New York: St. Martin's, 1997.

Smith, William George. *The Oxford Dictionary of English Proverbs*. Revised by Sir Paul Harvey. 2nd ed. Oxford: Clarendon, 1948.

Solorzano, Alonso de Castillo. *The Spanish Pole-cat; or the Adventures of Senior Rusina in Four Books*. Trans. Roger L'Estrange and J. Ozell. London: E. Curll, 1717. Trans. of *La garduña de Sevilla*, 1642.

Starr, G.A. *Defoe and Casuistry*. Princeton: Princeton UP, 1971.

Sugden, Edward H. *A Topographical Dictionary to the Works of Shakespeare and his Fellow Dramatists*. Manchester: Manchester UP, 1925.

Thompson, Roger. "The London Jilt." *Harvard Library Bulletin* 23 (1975): 289-94.

——. *Unfit for Modest Ears: A Study of the Pornographic, Obscene, and Bawdy Works Written and Published in England in the Second Half of the Seventeenth Century*. Totowa, NJ: Rowman and Littlefield, 1979.

Tilley, Maurice Palmer. *A Dictionary of the Proverbs in England in the Sixteenth and Seventeenth Centuries*. Ann Arbor: U of Michigan P, 1950.

Treadwell, Michael. "London Trade Publishers 1675-1750." *The Library*, 6th Ser. 4.2 (June 1982): 99-134.

Turner, James Grantham. *Schooling Sex: Libertine Literature and Erotic Education in Italy, France, and England, 1534-1685*. Oxford: Oxford UP, 2003.

——. "*The Whore's Rhetorick*: Narrative, Pornography, and the Origins of the Novel." *Studies in Eighteenth-Century Culture* 24 (1995): 297-306.

Ubeda, Lòpez de. *Justina, The Country Jilt*, in *The Spanish Libertines*. Trans. and adapted by Captain John Stevens. London: J. How, 1707. Trans. of *La Picara Justina*, 1605.

Wall, Cynthia. *The Literary and Cultural Spaces of Restoration London*. Cambridge: Cambridge UP, 1998.

Wheatley, Henry. *London Past and Present: A Dictionary of its History, Associations, and Traditions*. 3 vols. London: John Murray, 1891.

Williams, Gordon. *A Glossary of Shakespeare's Sexual Language*. London: Athlone, 1997.